C.M.N. ROGERS

Witchmarked

Book Two of The Bellarose Legacy

House of Nine
PRESS

First published by House of Nine Press 2026

Copyright © 2026 by C.M.N. Rogers

This is a work of fiction. Names, characters, places, and incidents are the product of the author's imagination or are used fictitiously. Any resemblance to actual persons, living or dead, events, or localities is purely coincidental.

C.M.N. Rogers asserts the moral right to be identified as the author of this work.

Stories drawn from shadow, written in light, and stained with truth.

First edition

ISBN: 978-1-7641620-5-0

This book was professionally typeset on Reedsy.
Find out more at reedsy.com

Contents

Acknowledgments

To the readers who returned to The Crescent Enclave—thank you for walking further into the blood, shadow, and soul of this world. Stories have a way of finding us when we're ready for them. I'm honoured you came back.

To my son, still my greatest teacher and the fiercest reminder of what courage and unconditional love truly look like—you remain my heart outside my body and the reason I keep building worlds. And to my grandsons, the newest keepers of my heart—you have expanded it in ways I didn't know were possible. This legacy belongs to you, too.

To my friends, who continue to tolerate writing disappearances, delayed replies, and dramatic updates about fictional people as if they live next door—your patience, humour, and steady belief in me mean more than you know.

And to the story—thank you for growing louder, darker, and braver. I'm still listening.

One

"They call it falling through time.
But it wasn't a fall. It was a tearing. A choosing.
And maybe... a beginning that already knew how it would end."
— Zinnia Hart, inconvenient oracle, reluctant weapon, temporal accident

Zinnia Hart didn't fall.

She was ripped—violently, unforgivably—from one reality into another.

She didn't scream.

There hadn't been time. Just the flash of light and the certainty that something fundamental had gone wrong.

This was a full-body teardown. Something had reached in, grabbed her spine, and yanked.

A heartbeat ago, gravity had rules. The next, it didn't.

The moment stretched, warped, as though her atoms couldn't quite agree on the direction of time.

She dropped through somewhere deeper than space.

Past history. Past cause. Past logic.

The portal didn't open. It cracked wide—teeth first—and bit down. Hard.

She spun. Tumbled.

No up. No down.

Only relentless momentum and the sensation that her insides were being unpacked and rearranged without anaesthetic.

Blackness folded around her ribs, alive and searching, trying her on for size.

A single thread held. The mark.

Born with it, branded by it—a silver, fire-lined tether that had never meant anything until now.

It was molten steel inside her skin. A fuse that hadn't gone off yet. And it wouldn't break.

Not for this. Not for them.

Because she wasn't alone in here.

It slid fingers—slick, invasive—up her vertebrae, searching.

For a seam. A crack. A weakness.

And when it couldn't find one, it spoke.

You belong to us.

A chill went through Zinnia.

The air inside her lungs soured. Her gut curled.

The idea that she was something to be used. Possessed. Handled.

The mark had its own opinion about that. It snapped back.

Her blood ignited—silver current surging, born in bone, sealed in vow, fuelled by rage that never burned out.

The thing trying to take her flinched.

And she ripped free.

Zinnia landed hard. Not like falling—more like being discarded by something that didn't care what broke first.

Stone slammed into her ribs. Air fled her lungs. Her skull caught the echo.

The hit knocked the concept of motion clean out of her.

She lay there, face down, as her nervous system took inventory.

Was she alive? Dead? Somewhere in between?

Her heart wasn't just pounding. It was a riot in her chest, ready to punch its way out.

The sound of it filled her ears, demanding to be louder than whatever had happened.

She tried to lift her head. The ground wasn't having it.

She waited. Let the weight of herself catch up to the rest of her.

Tried again.

Everything hurt—but not in a way that meant broken. No red-flash agony. No wet, sucking puncture sounds.

Just a full-body chorus of fuck this.

A single leg cooperated. The other filed a formal complaint. Her left shoulder felt as though it had fought a meat grinder and lost.

Her brain lagged behind it all—still buffering, stuck somewhere between now and whatever the hell that was.

She rolled onto her back, riding a wave of nausea.

A second passed. Then another.

She cracked an eye open.

The sky was bare. No satellites. No planes. No city glow bleeding from the bones of civilisation.

Stars hung overhead—pure judgment with a front-row seat.

Fear clamped around her ribcage, squeezing the air thin.

This wasn't home.

She turned her head.

And the trees stared back.

Haggard yew and rowan, bark knotted into scar tissue, branches curled into claws.

She sucked in a breath. The air hit her throat dry and sharp, steeped in the heavy musk of a world she didn't know.

She coughed and spat a string of green.

The taste stayed.

The forest floor was a leech, draining warmth from her body.

Her palms pressed into the ground; it took two attempts to push herself to her elbows.

She looked down at herself, taking stock.

Her T-shirt was toast—Shrek's face twisted across her chest. Even he'd noped out of this reality.

Smart Ogre.

She didn't feel dead. But she didn't feel claimed by life, either.

Currently covered in mud, blood and suffering from a catastrophic case of what the fuck.

But it was her magic that really had the attitude.

Testing the edges of her skin, like a wolf pressing against a cage it had no intention of staying in.

She yearned for the simplicity of her former life. Of toothpaste caps and grocery lists and daylight that didn't come with multiple strings attached.

The kind of problems that stayed solved once you crossed them off.

Destiny? Could suck it.

Gateborn? Les Revenantes? Veil-ripping prophecies?

They could all line up and kiss her arse.

She was so not that girl.

She didn't want to be that girl.

She didn't want to be anyone's anything.

Someone show her the nearest Starbucks—she had questions, complaints, and zero interest in being anyone's magical heir apparent.

She licked her lips and tasted copper.

The magic flexed. Measured the perimeter.

It was awake—and she was at the top of its goddamn to-do list.

Two

"The world does not burn witches for being witches.
It burns them for surviving the fire."
— Les Revenantes, forbidden scripture

A twig broke.

Zinnia's hand twitched, reaching for magic she didn't know how to use—then curled into a fist instead, the kind she'd learned to throw in darker alleys than this.

Her muscles braced, waiting for whatever—or whoever—was about to step from the dark.

Fear flared. She took a deep breath, pushing it down as far as it would go.

Light sliced through the trees, and a man stepped into view.

Tall. Broad-shouldered. Early thirties. Jaw like a cliff. Weather-worn coat, mud-caked boots. No sword, no rifle—only a lantern.

He studied her as if she was cursed or contagious.

"Ye wear strange armour, lass." His voice was low and clipped.

"What?" Zinnia eyed him, trying to read the terrain—friend or foe? Hopefully friend, because her tank was running on empty and she didn't like her odds against a guy built like a freak'n linebacker.

His eyes swept her—bare legs, ripped shirt, tattoos spiralling down her arms.

His jaw slackened. "God's wounds."

Zinnia arched a brow. "You say that like you've seen them personally."

"I… what are ye?"

A chill slid under her skin at the tone.

Was he measuring her for a noose?

"Depends who's asking."

"Those markings… be thy painted? Or some punishment?"

"They're tattoos."

Blank look.

"Ink," she added. "Art. You pay someone to stab you with needles over and over 'til it looks pretty."

He recoiled slightly. "Voluntarily?"

"Yeah."

He squinted, probably filing that under dangerous sorcery and worse judgment.

"An' what's that ye're wearin'?"

Zinnia looked down at her shirt. Shrek, grinning because he obviously knew exactly how screwed she was.

"I'm not from around here."

He looked at her. The kind of look that made her want to cross her arms without knowing why. She shifted uneasily. Still not sure what kind of ground she was standing on with him.

"Thy tongue's all twisted. Thy cadence—"

"You mean my accent?"

"Aye—like a drunk crow tryin' to speak French through a sock."

"And you're way too judgy for someone dressed in head-to-toe livestock."

"You're not from any shire I know of."

"Try New Orleans."

"That be French?"

"Sugar." She drawled slow, with a syrup-and-knives kind of smile. "It's American."

His shoulders squared, like she'd named the Devil outright.

"Ye're from the colonies, then?"

"Something like that." She gestured to the woods—crooked and black as gallows. "Where am I exactly?"

He tilted the lantern slightly. Shadows stretched.

"Hedgemoor Wood. Ashwick Vale. Lancashire."

"England?"

She cracked her neck. The popping sound rang loud in the quiet.

"What year?"

The pause said it all. He was clearly evaluating her sanity—hell, so was she.

"Sixteen ninety-five."

Her stomach dropped.

Her mouth went dry.

She knew the history. Pendle. Salem. Women punished for breathing in the wrong direction.

And here she was. Inked, half-naked, and glowing with the kind of magic that made mobs hungry.

"You're shitting me."

"Beg pardon?"

Zinnia couldn't respond. Internally, she was in freefall.

This wasn't TikTok magic or bathtub spells with rose petals and moonlight.

This was real.

This was dangerous.

This time period had a high mortality rate for her kind—especially if you glowed in the dark.

Her skin prickled.

"Shit. I've landed in the goddamn witch trials."

"What's that ye said?"

"Nothing."

He stepped back and raised his lantern to light up the path he had come in from.

"I've a place not far. A fire, a roof. I'll not touch a hair on ye head. Ye've my word." He met her eye. "These woods ain't safe at night, what with hunters and such. They'd name ye witch just lookin at ye."

Zinnia studied him. She knew he was right.

He didn't spook easy. That much was clear.

But beyond that? Closed book. Locked cover.

And every page could be a trap.

Her thoughts slipped to her grandmother, Pauline—the woman who'd raised her.

Don't judge a book by its cover, chère, Mémère always said.

And never go home with a strange man.

Her grandmother was never wrong.

She would've smelled a lie on this man before he finished speaking.

Zinnia couldn't even finish a thought.

She was so damn tired.

The cold was eating her, and her legs were starting to shake.

Pride wasn't going to keep her warm.

And it sure as hell wouldn't keep her alive.

She apologised to Mémère in her head for what she was about to do—then offered up a quick prayer to whoever might be listening that she wouldn't end up barbecued.

She sighed. "Okay. Lead the way."

They walked in silence at first—Zinnia trailing behind, feet slipping over frost-hard roots. Her tee flapped, torn and absurd.

"You're not a serial killer, right?"

He turned his head towards her, one brow lifted. "A what?"

"You know… someone who murders people. On purpose.

Repeatedly."

"That common where ye're from?"

"Very."

He gave her a long look but said nothing.

She held out a scraped hand. "Zinnia."

He hesitated, then took it. Rough-palmed. Warm. Strong grip.

Definitely a man who hauled more than herbs from the dirt.

"Matthew Thorne. Of Ashwick Vale."

"Pleased to make your acquaintance, Matthew Thorne of Ashwick Vale." She laid the drawl on thick just to see what it did to his face. Not much—but his mouth twitched.

The woods murmured. Leaves whispering in a tongue she didn't know but somehow understood.

Matthew kept the lantern low, guiding her with the ease of someone used to leading lost things out of the dark.

Her body continued to throb. The air here was fresh—far fresher than she was used to.

"Why do they hunt witches?"

Zinnia didn't ask out of politeness. It was one of history's worst screw-ups, and she was walking through the middle of it. She needed to know what made a whole society turn against its own women.

"They hunt what they fear lass. But lately? It's worse."

"How bad's worse?"

"The fires in Essex haven't cooled. Lancaster's trials still haunt the pews. Anything strange—anything with power—gets named afore it can speak for itself."

"So, they condemn it?"

"Folk fear what they don't understand. And these days, there's plenty they can't."

"Like what?"

He glanced her way. Shadows deepening the tired under his eyes.

"Children gone missing. Stillborn beasts. Lights in the hills come dusk. Milk turning. Crops rotting from the inside."

"Sounds like bad farming."

"Be omen to them."

The forest was eerily quiet.

"Some say it's the Devil, walkin' again. Others reckon it's old gods come to collect. Most just blame the women."

"Why the women?"

They walked a few steps in silence before he answered.

"Because they mend what men can't. Because they bleed, and birth, and still rise with the sun. Because they see what's comin' afore it shows its face."

Her throat tightened. She wanted to laugh—say something snarky—but that kind of truth didn't leave room for sarcasm.

"Fear needs a shape, and the Church gave it one. Said witches fly by night. Sign the Devil's book in blood. Poison wells. Lie with shadows. Birth storms. It's rot, but belief makes it true."

"So, they burn them?"

"Aye. Or hang. Or drown. Whatever quiets the mob."

This wasn't a textbook. Not some sanitised version of horror, neat and footnoted.

The magic inside her? A loaded gun playing Russian roulette—with her skull as the jackpot.

Double shit.

Zinnia didn't feel like a witch.

She didn't have the rules. The tools. The ten-step spellbook.

Just a name passed down, which quite frankly felt like nothing more than a curse.

And now?

She was stranded in a century where women with bad vibes got dragged to the river or were used as kindling.

The path narrowed. Briars closed in, thorned and grasping.

Matthew didn't speak again. He kept moving with easy confidence—the kind that came from listening to a place long enough to know which of its secrets could be trusted.

And Zinnia?

She followed, mind racing.

Her body ached. Her head rang.

She didn't know the rules of this world.

Didn't know how to pass.

Didn't know how to hide.

She only knew one thing for certain.

Standing still was how women like her got caught.

So, she walked.

The trees gave way to a clearing where a cottage rose from the earth—nestled against a moss-covered slope, half-eaten by ivy, chimney trailing lazy smoke into the black sky. The thatch roof was patched with care. Bundles of herbs hung from the eaves, each one bound tight with red thread.

A neat stack of firewood waited by the door. Beside it, snare traps and a longbow leaned against the wall. Light flickered softly behind coarse curtains.

Matthew stepped forward and pushed open the door. It creaked in protest.

Inside the air wrapped around Zinnia.

It was warm—not only hearth-warm, but soul-deep. Firelight spilled across uneven floorboards. A low table bore knife nicks from years of use. Jars filled with god knows what lined the walls. A heavy cauldron hung over the fire, steam curling upward.

The scent hit next—rabbit stew, thyme, woodsmoke, and something earthier beneath.

Her stomach growled, loud and undignified.

"Help yerself." Matthew gestured to the pot. "Wild carrot and rabbit. Shot him this mornin'. Saucy bastard tried to bolt."

"Sounds like my kind of rabbit."

She limped toward the hearth and ladled herself a bowl. Steam curled into her face. Heat kissed her numb fingers. It smelled divine. She could've cried.

She didn't.

Instead, she ate in methodical bites, eyes scanning the room between mouthfuls.

No Bible. No crucifix. Just a charm above the door—twisted rowan, black thread, a raven's feather. Etched runes marked the mantel in fine lines.

"You live out here alone?" She licked the stew from her spoon.

"Aye." He shrugged off his coat and hung it by the door. "Don't much care for town. They come when somethin's broke—but won't look me in the eye when it ain't."

Zinnia nodded to the charm. "That's a protective ward."

"It is."

He watched her—curious.

She was from another time. That much was clear.

And beneath that certainty, something else stirred. Low and slow, unexpected and inconvenient.

He tossed another log into the flames. Sparks leapt, and the fire leaned toward her. The blaze stretched—not high, not wild, but as if it recognised her. The air rippled, and for half a heartbeat, the stew in her bowl grew hotter.

Zinnia held her breath.

His gaze flicked to the fire. Then back to her.

The flames settled.

The room didn't.

She continued to eat, savouring the hot, earthy, unexpectedly good meal—watching him over the rim of the bowl.

"You're not worried someone might call you a witch?"

"They have. Still do."

"And yet here you are. Not burned. Not drowned. Not a warning nailed to a church door."

"I don't give 'em reason to light the pyre."

She raised a brow. "You live alone. Hang bones. Brew things. That's a death sentence in three acts."

He crossed to a shelf and poured something dark into a clay cup. "I'm a healer. Been one since I could name poison from cure."

"That doesn't exactly stop the pitchfork crowd."

Matthew took a sip and gave a humourless smile. "No. But savin' their young slows 'em down."

They sat in silence.

Zinnia finished the last of her stew and set the bowl aside. Her body still throbbed, but the heat had taken the edge off.

She looked at him. "So, what were you doing out there tonight? Really?"

"I walk the forest."

"At night?"

"It's when the hidden things speak."

"That's not an answer."

"It's the only one ye're gettin'."

She sized him up. Shirt clinging faintly with heat and sweat. But his face? A solid wall. No cracks. No tells.

She was still woman enough to admit he was a fine-looking male. If her hormones weren't fried, they'd be singing hubba hubba in three-part harmony.

"You always this cryptic, or am I just blessed?"

Matthew's mouth curved into something not quite a smile. He said nothing.

She got up, took the dish to the table.

She was too tired to be tough. Too raw to pretend she didn't want warmth more than answers.

"Is there somewhere I can crash?"

"Crash?" His brow knit, confusion flickering behind his eyes.

"Yeah—somewhere to sleep."

He took the lantern from its hook. "This way."

She followed. The short hallway was all old beams and creaky boards. Shadows clung to corners—she was pretty sure they'd lived here longer than he had.

Another charm hung low on a crossbeam.

"You make these?" She brushed her fingers close, not quite touching.

"Some. The rest… were here a'fore me."

She gave him a sideways glance, but he didn't elaborate.

He pushed open a door.

The room was small but solid. A patchwork quilt, faded but clean, covered the bed tucked beneath a sloped ceiling. A low chest sat at the foot, and above the headboard hung a dried sprig of lavender, brittle with age but still sweet on the air.

A ceramic basin and glazed pitcher waited on a three-legged stool, water clear with mint leaves floating on the surface. A cloth and towel had been folded beside it.

A pale linen nightgown lay draped over the chest.

"That for me?"

Matthew didn't meet her eye. Just gave a single nod. "Figured ye be wanting to wash the earth off."

"You always keep spare nightgowns lying around for strange women you find in the woods?"

"Only the ones dressed like travelling jesters."

"Touché."

He set the lantern down inside the doorway.

"It's not much. But it's warm. And it's safe."

Safe. It felt like a lie dressed as a prayer—or maybe a dare she was dumb enough to believe.

She stepped inside, walking over to the chest.

Her hand brushed the linen gown. Soft. Clean. Homespun, but well-made.

"Thanks."

He turned to leave.

"Matthew."

He paused but didn't turn around.

"Why are you helping me?"

"Because ye look like someone the world already tried to burn."

He didn't wait for a reply.

Just walked away. Footsteps soft as dusk.

She didn't breathe for a beat.

Not because it was sweet—but because it was true.

And hearing it out loud made her realise, he saw her.

She dragged her muddy shirt over her head with a wince.

The fabric stuck where it shouldn't have. Her skin protested.

She dipped the cloth into the basin and carefully wiped away the layers of blood and grime.

She tugged the nightgown over her head.

It slid over her shoulders, soft, clean and warm.

She crawled into bed, the quilt heavy across her body.

Her muscles still ached. Her thoughts still raced.

This wasn't an accident.

She'd been thrown.

Marked.

Hunted.

And whatever was out there knew she was here.

The Veil had tried to keep her.

The forest had let her pass.
The magic inside her had started to whisper.
She wasn't ready.
Which clearly didn't matter.
Fire wasn't the finish line.
It was the crucible.
Whatever she was becoming was about to be forged.

Three

"The dead never stay gone in the Bayou.
They sit on porches, smoke their pipes, and wait for you to listen."
— Old Cajun saying

Present Day—The Bayou

Pauline Broussard dreamed of her son.

Not the way she had found him, broken and still, the pistol cold on the floorboards.

In the dream, he looked as he always had—shoulders broad, face open, the boy she'd raised into a man.

But his eyes—God help her—carried sorrow older than the swamp.

They sat at her kitchen table, scarred from decades of meals and arguments, where Zinnia used to bang her spoon like a drum. A single candle flickered between them.

"Maman." His voice cracked as he reached for her hands. His palms were warm, though she had buried him years ago.

"I'm sorry for how I left you and Zin."

Pauline met his eyes. Grief had already taken enough from her—she would not give it her voice, too. Love, though? Love she could give without limit.

"You were weak that day, boy. Weakness ain't the same as wickedness. I forgave you the moment I found you."

His face crumpled. "I should have stayed. She needed me."

"She needed a mother and a father," Pauline corrected. "And the Bayou knew I was strong enough to be two people." Her grip tightened. "Don't you carry that guilt where you are. You hear me, chèr? Zinnia ain't been unloved a single day in her life."

Tears slid down his cheeks, vanishing before they reached the table.

"She's in trouble, Maman. I seen it. You have to find her."

Pauline's throat ached, but her grip never faltered. "You think I don't already know? My loa been restless since sundown. Tell me what else you seen."

"Chains," he whispered. "Throwing her through time. Seraphina will come for you. Her family is the key. Promise me you'll go."

Pauline nodded once. "You have my word. A Broussard don't let blood go wandering without bringing it home." Her gaze sharpened. "But there's more, isn't there? What else haven't you told me about my grandbaby?"

He hesitated, shoulders bowing as though even death couldn't lift the weight from them.

"Her maman… she was Les Revenantes."

The name struck her square in the chest. She had heard it whispered around Bayou fires and back-alley shrines—women who walked the Veil itself, guardians of the thin place between worlds. Gateborn. Cursed and sanctified in equal measure.

She had always half-believed the rumours. Never imagined they'd take root in her own blood.

"Les Revenantes? You certain, chèr?"

He nodded. "She wanted to escape it, Maman. Wanted a quiet life. But responsibility like that don't wash away."

Pauline thought of Zinnia as a girl—bare feet in the mud, laughter ringing wild, climbing trees she wasn't supposed to. All that time, she'd told herself the child was only Broussard.

But blood had a longer memory than denial.

"Then why does my grandbaby carry Hart and not her maman's name?"

"Because Lilly wanted her hidden. She thought a divided bloodline would run too thin to wake the old prophecies. Gave Zin a name buried deep enough no one in the Enclave would remember it." His voice broke. "A simple name for a simple life."

Pauline's face stayed composed, hiding the turmoil beneath. "So, the name was a shield."

"A shield," he agreed. "And a hope. But blood don't care about names."

"And you believed that would be enough, chèr?"

"She swore it to me, Maman. Swore our girl would never be dragged into that world. And I believed her." His voice faltered. "But when Lilly vanished, I knew why. And I couldn't bear the thought that me loving her had killed her—and left our daughter carrying the curse alone."

Her son had always been fragile in ways she couldn't fix. Soft where the world demanded steel. But this—this truth—explained the fracture that had broken him clean through.

Pauline straightened. "Zinnia may be Les Revenantes, but she's still Broussard. That girl carries two rivers in her veins—and rivers carve the land. Don't you forget it."

His eyes brimmed. "She's more than both of us, Maman."

Pauline squeezed his hands. "Then she'll live long enough to find out what she is. I'll see to it myself."

Resolve, heavier than grief, settled into place.

The candle guttered.

Her son faded, his fingers slipping through hers like water.

"I love you, Maman."

"I know, chèr. My heart is always yours. Now rest."

She woke with her heart hammering.

She rose at once. Old bones or not, Pauline did not waste time when the spirits came calling.

At her altar, she lit three candles—white for mercy, black for strength, red for bloodline. Smoke curled into the corners as she murmured in Cajun French, a prayer caught between sorrow and fire.

She poured dark water into her bowl, scattered salt, cayenne, and three sprigs of rue.

The surface rippled.

No wind—nothing but the stirring of spirits.

She braced her fingers on the bowl. She hadn't felt this kind of pull in years.

Her reflection vanished.

Zinnia's face appeared—wild-eyed with fear.

Pauline gripped the rim and began to chant, the old words she'd learned from her Tante Cécile. Half Catholic. Half something older.

"Hold on, bébé," she whispered. "Mémère's coming."

She crossed herself.

Then she packed dried herbs, gris-gris, her rosary, a knife older than she was, clean clothes, and bones.

She moved out onto the porch, placed the bag at her feet, eased her body into the rocker, lit her pipe—

—and waited.

***

Maison Bellarose

The Scriptorium reeked of burnt sage and frustration. Books sprawled open across the long oak table, runes bleeding faintly on vellum. The *Grimoire of Aveline* sat at the centre, its portal diagram etched into the vellum—a wound that refused to close.

Killian prowled the room, boots cracking in clipped bursts against the floor. His jaw was iron, his patience ground to dust.

"We've done everything outlined. The portal should have locked onto her. There's something we're missing."

Seraphina's fingers hovered over the pages, trembling slightly. Her eyes, ringed with exhaustion, scanned the symbols again—but still, they refused to unlock. She exhaled long and uneven, lowering her forehead to the table.

The answer was there. Mocking her with its silence.

A sudden prickle hit the back of her neck. She straightened slowly.

The lines on the page seemed to shift, or maybe she finally saw them clearly.

"Oh my god," she breathed. "I don't know why I didn't see this before. It needs blood."

Sebastian was almost too scared to ask, but he found the words coming out of his mouth anyway. "Whose blood?"

The air cooled as Saffron leaned close, her form thinning the candlelight.

"You're right. We need someone from her bloodline to mark the page. Pronto."

Samthrax let his chair drop forward. For the first time since Zinnia had been thrown into the void, he felt a spark of hope. "Okay. Let's go juice a relative—gently, of course."

Seraphina swallowed hard and braced her hands against the table.

"There is a slight problem. The only person I know who's still alive is Zinnia's grandmother, Pauline Broussard."

The name struck like a match.

Sage looked up, disbelief carving her face. She had known Zin most of her life. How had she never known that? "The Cajun witchdoctor?"

Sebastian swore, raking a hand down his face. "You cannot be serious. All the kids at school used to say she could hex a man bald for sneezing near her doorstep. She is literally a cautionary tale."

Killian stopped pacing. The storm in his eyes didn't ease.

"Broussard's reputation isn't smoke. I've seen her work. She doesn't suffer fools. Or witches."

Seraphina wasn't looking forward to what she had to do. She'd met Pauline only a handful of times—the woman was downright unnerving.

"She raised Zinnia. I don't even know if she knows the truth. And now I have to show up and tell her that her granddaughter is missing. Because of me."

Samthrax whistled. "Good luck with that. Word around demon world is that lady is about as forgiving as a gator with a limp. She'll eat you whole if she thinks you failed her young."

Saffron flickered, eyes fixed on her daughter. "I'll go with you. Pauline and I have crossed paths before."

Seraphina's brow arched. "What are you gonna do, haunt her until she forgives me?"

Samthrax's smile twisted dark. "I'd bet she's waiting for you and knows more than we do. But..." He tapped an imaginary watch on his wrist. "That's tomorrow's problem. Tick-tock, ladies."

Killian made the call. "The demon's right. Sera, you and Saffron go. Bring her back. She's our only chance of tracking Zinnia."

Seraphina shoved her chair back, heart pounding.

Pauline Broussard was the last person she wanted to face.

But she was their only shot at bringing Zinnia home.

***

Seraphina's boat bumped against the dock. She climbed the steps, pale with nerves. Saffron floated beside her.

Pauline continued rocking, pipe smoke curling from her lips.

"Took you long enough, chère." Her eyes flicked to Saffron. "An' you done brought company. Bonjour, Saffy. Been some time. Shoulda seen the resemblance—shame on me I didn't."

Saffron hovered nearer, her smile faint.

"It's good to see you, Pauline. I wish it was under better circumstances."

The three women fell into silence.

Seraphina's stomach knotted. Pauline's gaze cut through her, merciless and unblinking. She wanted to speak—to beg, to explain—but the words jammed in her throat.

Saffron flickered faintly, her smile faltering. Ghost-light couldn't carry the weight of regret, but she felt it all the same—the ache of leaving her daughter and grandchildren too soon, and the shame of dragging innocents into the family drama.

Pauline tamped her pipe. The motion was practiced.

The Bayou seemed to lean in, cypress branches groaning low as though it, too, waited on what would come next.

Before Seraphina could find any words, Pauline spoke.

"My boy came to me, said my grandbaby is in trouble—and that you are the key to that trouble being over." Her eyes never left Seraphina. "When she took up with you, petite, I was wary. I knew you was bound witch. But you helped her get clear o' that no-good man. I seen how much y'all meant to each other. That put my worry to rest."

She leaned forward.

"Now her power waking up. A power I knew nothing about until this night. The truth is crawling out her, and that poor baby is all alone in a strange place with no understanding." She paused.

"You're here because blood finds blood. And you need mine to find mine."

Seraphina nodded, relief warred with dread.

"You're right, Pauline. I hid myself and my children for years from magic. But my mother was taken, and I was forced back." Her voice tightened. "Zin's power is waking, and she's had no time to learn or adjust. She's a powder keg—and more powerful than either of us can fully grasp. We need you to come with us. Help us to track her."

Pauline stood and reached for her bag. "Already packed, chère. Her maman done carried more in her blood than I ever knew."

Seraphina nodded. "Came as a surprise to me as well."

Pauline turned to Saffron.

She hadn't looked too hard when they were both alive—another powerful woman keeping her distance, guarding her own.

But now? She saw her.

The bedrock strength. The grief that had shaped her without breaking her. Death hadn't dulled a thing. If anything, it had burned her clearer.

Whatever had passed between them in life didn't matter now. What mattered was this: Saffron had remained to stand watch and to guard the threshold with her daughter in the fight that was coming.

Pauline respected that.

"So, you stayin' on to help your fille through the dark comin' for her and hers?"

Saffron winced. "Yes, and I'm afraid that now includes your granddaughter."

Pauline nodded once. "Den we be in this together."

She stepped off the porch, bag slung over her shoulder, onto the waiting boat.

"Best we get moving, chère."

***

The between responded to will alone. It did not tear or part. It simply receded—as if yielding to something it could not name.

Brinnan entered the layer between seconds.

A space where linear time had no dominion.

The air enveloped his form, thick with moisture and decay. The scent of something half-alive curled into his fabricated lungs—brackish water, mildew, the slow digestion of things that refused to die.

He inhaled deeply, remembering the act though he no longer required it.

He enjoyed this freedom. Not for the eternity it offered—but for the severance. The weight of mortality had been stripped away. Consequence no longer masqueraded as meaning. Time had loosened its grip, and what remained of him had learned to move without being known.

Something had passed through here—recently.

The fabric hadn't finished healing.

He reached—not with hands, but with the part of himself that remembered what hands had once been.

A tremor answered.

Thin.

Frayed.

Still bleeding energy.

Not Zinnia—but an older current, still moving through the line.

The Bayou opened around him.

Cypress trunks leaned inward, dense and unmoving. Shadows clung to bark as if fused. Roots knotted through the water. Insects broke their rhythm as he passed.

The land did not recognise him.

But it knew he should not exist.

The thread dipped, brushing the water's skin. Beneath the surface, the swamp held its secrets. He moved between it all. His shape triggered no splash. His presence raised no wind. Even the moss refused to sway.

Ahead, a skiff glided through the stagnant wet, its outline wavering as though bound by a law the world was trying to forget. The dark water didn't part—it absorbed, swallowing sound, reflection, anything that might have made the vessel real.

Three women.

The first burned faint around the edge—light without source, flickering where the soul refused to finish departing.

Saffron.

She shouldn't still be here. The dead had no place in the passage between thresholds. Yet she hovered, luminous, pulling energy where none was offered. Interfering even in death.

The second moved the vessel without effort—one hand trailing slightly above the water's surface, guiding the boat by magic. Seraphina. His niece and forever a pain in his arse.

But it was the third who mattered most.

The thread coiled tight around her, and through it, Brinnan saw the bloodline—old, unbroken, moving cleanly through her veins.

Pauline Broussard.

He had misunderstood.

He'd thought Zinnia's power began and ended with Les Revenantes.

That the Gateborn legacy carried the whole of her design.

It did not.

That was only one side of the equation.

The other ran here—through this woman.

Zinnia's magic wasn't searching for balance.

It was reaching back—to its source.

By instinct.

A delicious turn of events.

Maison Bellarose emerged ahead—stone first, then silhouette.

Magic clung to its surfaces, layered and barbed. Spells traced the air in lines too old for speech. Symbols flared and faded, tasting those who approached.

The house did not guard.

It claimed.

Sigils sparked around Pauline, then withdrew. She was accepted.

Brinnan felt the house notice him—then dismiss him.

It could not raise an alarm for what did not exist.

He adjusted the shape he wore. The construct flexed and held—every detail calibrated for this layer of reality. Breath. Muscle tension. Heartbeat. All present. All lies.

Only the eyes remained untouched.

Emerald. Endless.

The only part of him that had not surrendered.

He did not linger.

He had what he needed. The timeline had shuddered. The next breach was already forming.

The thread was no longer dormant.

Zinnia's imprint bled forward through time.

She was becoming traceable.

Brinnan stepped back into the Between.

The current claimed him, accepting the return.

They were searching for her.

But he would reach her first.

Four

"Angels are not saviours.
They are soldiers, cursed with wings instead of choices."
— Unknown Revenante, forbidden scrolls

1695 – Lancashire

Zinnia woke to warmth. Not the emotional, cozy, fresh-baked-cookie kind. No, this was woodsmoke and leftover rabbit stew, the kind of warmth that soaked in and dared the cold to try again.

Which, right now, was exactly the kind of passive-aggressive hospitality she could get behind.

Her body ached like she'd been pulled through her own grave and told to walk it off.

Zinnia groaned as she rolled over in the too-soft bed, nightgown clinging to her damp skin, and stared at the wooden ceiling. She sat up, muscles whining louder than rusted hinges. She blinked. Took in the unfamiliar walls.

Where the hell was she?

Then yesterday slammed back into her.

Right. Not a fever dream. Just her new nightmare.

Voices drifted in through the walls.

One gruff and familiar—Matthew.

The other belonged to a woman.

Husky. Warm. Laced with honey and sarcasm.

Zinnia couldn't make out the words, but she'd bet good money she was the topic of discussion.

The bed creaked beneath her as her bare feet hit the floorboards that had probably seen more history than her entire Ancestry.com profile.

She glanced down.

The nightgown left absolutely nothing to the imagination.

Crap.

She grabbed the quilt and wrapped it tight. Once her dignity was secured, she padded through the cabin and pushed the door open.

Matthew sat on the porch, arms folded, wearing the expression of a man already regretting his morning.

The woman perched on the rail, every inch of her claiming the space as hers. Golden curls fell in soft waves over her shoulders, skin almost luminous in the morning light. The pale blue cloak hung loose, revealing linen and leather that were far too fine for 1695.

Her eyes—enormous, crystalline blue—cut straight through Zinnia.

Zinnia suddenly felt very human.

And very underdressed.

She'd give her left tit for a pair of jeans and a T-shirt right about now.

Matthew did a double take when he looked at her. That quilt had no business being wrapped around her like that. He shifted in his seat, crossing his legs casually, doing his level best to ignore the sudden problem pressing against the front of his pants.

"Mornin', lass. Sorry if we roused ye. This here's Divina."

Zinnia dragged her eyes away from him. She needed to get a grip— this man was dangerous to her equilibrium, and she didn't know him from a bar of soap. Instinct said secrets. Plural.

She faced the woman.

And met a cool, dispassionate stare.

"Nice to meet you, Divina. What brings you to the middle of the woods at the crack of dawn?"

"You."

"Me?"

"Yes."

Divina crossed her booted feet and watched the emotions play over Zinnia's face.

Confusion, check. Wariness, check. Annoyance, double check.

"Okay, is this where I play fifty questions to get answers? Because cryptic is starting to wear on my nerves."

Zinnia glanced pointedly at Matthew. He grinned back, unashamed, leaning in his chair with the kind of lazy confidence that said he knew a showdown was coming and planned to enjoy the view.

She should probably provide him with popcorn.

"I suggest you ask the right questions then."

Zinnia tugged the quilt tighter, resisting the urge to launch herself at this woman feet first. "Alright, blondie. Who are you, and why are you here?"

Divina tilted her head.

Defiance wasn't the point. It was a diversion. A way to keep control when neither of them actually had it. She wasn't here out of loyalty or mercy. This was punishment—divine orders wrapped in spite. Babysitting a Gateborn through magical puberty was her sentence, not her choice.

"Hmmm. Long story," she drawled. "Where would you like me to start?"

"At the freak'n beginning," Zinnia snapped. "Because my patience is circling the drain. Just an FYI."

Matthew covered his mouth, a cough disguising a laugh. He had no idea what a "freak'n" or an "FYI" was, but he understood the warning in her tone well enough.

Divina didn't spare him a glance. "You could say it was a committee decision. Definitely not my own."

She watched Zinnia's jaw tighten, the pulse in her temple jumping. That fuse was short.

Zinnia gritted her teeth, dangerously close to erupting. She fixed Divina with a glare that could've stripped paint. "You're not answering."

Divina smiled faintly. "And yet you're still listening."

Zinnia drew in a breath and counted to three in her head.

Divina felt the heat of her irritation rise off her.

Fine. If she wanted answers, she'd give her the truth.

That should make things far more interesting.

Divina straightened, folding her arms in challenge.

"I'm an angel. Technically. Sent to teach, guide, and protect you. Mostly from yourself. And from anyone else stupid enough to come sniffing around."

She let that land before continuing.

"I'm here because I screwed up. Wings-on-the-line kind of penance. And trust me sweetie—saving a clueless-as-hell Gateborn was not on my celestial to-do list."

Zinnia's mouth hung open. Words? Nope.

An angel.

A literal one.

She'd been hurled through time, dumped in 1695, and now she had a sarcastic parole officer with feathers.

Oh. For fuck's sake.

She snapped her mouth shut. "An angel. Seriously?"

A shrug. "Don't look so impressed. I'm more fallen than flying these days."

"Oh, I'm impressed," Zinnia muttered. "Just not favourably."

She turned on Matthew. "Is she for real?"

"Aye, lass. That she is." He leaned forward, elbows braced on his knees. "I ken this is a fair bit to swallow, what with ye being from another time. And I ken fine that Divina can rub folk raw. But we were both sent to ye, to see ye safe. Will ye let us do that?"

Sent to ye.

The words scraped.

She wasn't a mission. She was a woman ripped out of her life with no bloody roadmap.

And they expected her to just suck it up, buttercup.

"You talk like this was all decided without me."

"It was." Divina wasn't sugarcoating it—she didn't have time for that. "That's what a divine path looks like sweetheart. Welcome to yours."

Zinnia wanted to scream.

Divine path. Could her life get any more ridiculous?

Probably.

She'd rather mainline coffee. Then schedule a damn lobotomy.

"Your people skills could use some work."

"I'm not here to comfort you or blow smoke up your arse," Divina shot back. "I'm here to keep you breathing."

"Forgive me if that doesn't inspire confidence."

Matthew leaned back, calm radiating off him in a way that made Zinnia want to throw things.

"Ye can hate the way o' it, lass, but truth stands whether we like it or no. We are what's been sent, and ye've little choice but to trust it for now."

"Trust?" The word seared. "I woke up in a century that burns women for having opinions. You're an enigma, and she's an angel with an attitude problem. Forgive me if it's not high on the list."

Divina's scrutiny pinned her in place.

"Then move it up the list. You're alive because something in the universe still thinks you're worth the trouble. Don't waste that on thick-headed stupidity."

"You're assuming I care what the universe thinks."

"It has a way of humbling you when you don't."

Zinnia hated every inch of this situation. She was firmly in the red zone now—about to go off the Richter scale.

Matthew stood. The old floor groaned under his boots.

"Enough. It's been a long morn already. Both o' ye could argue the colour off the sky, and I've no wish to hear it a'fore breakfast."

His attention shifted to Zinnia. "Eat. Ye've the look of one who's fought through hell and forgot she's still flesh."

That hit harder than she liked.

Then he turned to Divina. "And ye. Give the lass a breath a'fore she bolts."

"Peace doesn't last long for people like her."

Zinnia's head flew up. "People like me?"

"The kind destiny keeps on a leash."

"Then you're in for a hell of a wake-up call," Zinnia fired back. "I'm no one's pet."

Divina's brows lifted. Maybe this assignment wasn't going to be as dull and tedious as she'd feared. A flicker of grudging respect stirred.

Zinnia turned on her heel and stormed inside. The door slammed, cutting off the morning chill.

Divina watched until the latch clicked home. "She's nowhere near ready for what's coming."

Matthew didn't answer straight away. "She's standing. That's start enough."

"You always did aim low."

"And ye've never learned when to hush."

Divina snorted. "Which is exactly why I'm in this predicament."

***

Present Day – Maison Bellarose

The boat ride had been silent except for the water against the hull—each lost in their own thoughts.

By the time they reached the jetty, the mist had lifted, and the house rose through it.

Pauline stepped onto the worn path first.

The ache in her body went deeper than travel.

Every step stirred the old pain in her hips and back—age, yes, but also the kind that knew when magic was watching.

It pressed against her skin in both greeting and warning—old power, controlled power. The garden was trimmed within an inch of its soul; not a single vine dared cross where it wasn't meant to. Even the air shimmered with discipline.

This house knew who entered.

She'd grown up hearing whispers about the Crescent Enclave—but standing here, instincts prickling, she finally understood the awe behind those stories.

The Bellarose didn't live surrounded by wealth—they *were* wealth, wrapped in bloodlines and secrets. The kind of magic aged like fine wine—fully aware of its own importance.

Inside, chandeliers scattered morning light across polished floors. Seraphina led her past portraits whose eyes followed every step.

Pauline kept her chin high. Let them stare.

The weight of her bag grounded her—the familiar rattle of bones and charm against cloth. She was used to smoke and salt and swamp-hum. This place was all cold polish and order.

They reached a pair of carved doors, runes etched deep and glowing faintly under the wardlight.

Seraphina pushed them open.

The scriptorium spread out before them. Shelves of ancient tomes lined the walls, not a speck of dust in sight. Gold inlay traced through dark wood; charms hung precisely where they needed to be and nowhere else.

Pauline didn't intimidate easily, but this here was a lot.

"Now this ain't the Bayou."

Killian looked up from the central table, where he was poring over yet another grimoire. He took in the diminutive yet infamous Cajun woman who had walked in. There was no denying her familial connection to Zinnia; there was also no denying the power that emanated from her.

"No, it's not, Pauline—but it has its advantages. We're grateful you came. I'm Killian."

"Pleasure Killian. My grandbaby's missing. Nowhere else I'm meant to be but finding her."

Killian inclined his head in agreement.

The bones in Pauline's bag stirred.

Two figures sat cross-legged on the floor, papers scattered around them in careful disarray.

Oh, hell. Twins. Bound by prophecy—and not the good kind.

Zinnia. Lord have mercy, what have you walked into this time, chère?

The girl spoke first, her voice warm and open. "Hi, I'm Sage and this here is my brother Sebastian, but we mainly call him Seb."

Her brother didn't bother to hide his appraisal.

Pauline's attention moved between them as she reached deeper with the instinct she'd been born carrying. Their bond glowed faintly—one half shadow, one half sun—pulsing in opposing rhythm. Harmony balanced on the edge of collapse.

"Nice to meet you both." The bones in her bag grew restless. "Prophecy rides your shoulders, don't it?"

Sage nodded. "Yes. But right now, we don't have time to work that out."

Seb watched her, a flicker of cold sweat gathered at the base of his neck. He could see why kids whispered about this woman; her eyes saw more than most people wanted known. "Knowing doesn't make it easier though."

"No, it don't chèr. It just means you walk careful. Power like yours ain't gift or curse. It's burden. Feed it wrong, it eats you alive."

Sage leaned forward, a tug of interest flaring warm in her chest.

"And what feeds it right?"

"Choice." Pauline rested a hand on the back of a chair. "But it don't come cheap."

The doorframe creaked.

"Well, this is cozy. Are you planning to introduce me to the witchdoctor, or do I have to announce myself? I'm practically family, after all."

Pauline turned.

She'd seen plenty in her years on this earth, but never a red-skinned demon dressed as if he were heading to the opera.

He rested against the doorway, the kind of self-assured stance that said rules were meant for other people.

His grin sat somewhere between charm and warning.

Killian didn't bother to hide the sigh that passed through him.

"You're tolerated, Samthrax. Let's not confuse the two."

Pauline measured him in a single sweep. "Family, huh? Dat what they're callin' demons these days?"

Samthrax took her in. The old woman stood rooted and unflinching. No wonder the others stepped careful around her.

He let his grin spread. "Only the charming ones. You must be Pauline Broussard. I've heard the stories—the woman who hexed a preacher's heart for lying in his own church." His head tipped, eyes bright. "Can't decide if I'm impressed or terrified."

"Terrified's safer." The demon's smile didn't move her. She'd seen prettier things crawl out of graves. "You bound?"

"I am." He spread his hands, wrists glowing faintly where the sigils lay buried under skin. "Housebroken. Spell-checked. Eternal good-behaviour clause. I'm practically a public service."

"You talk a lot for someone livin' on borrowed time."

"And you judge too fast for someone who's never been to hell."

Tension crawled up Sage's neck. The air had that charged weight, the kind that came right before something exploded. Samthrax hadn't been this annoyingly upbeat since the battle.

Pauline's magic pushed outward.

The demon answered in kind.

Neither yielded.

Sage's nerves snapped first. "Okay—maybe don't start a turf war. We *just* cleaned the wards."

Seb leaned forward, grin fighting to escape. "Let them. It's been an uneventful morning."

Sage shot him a look that could've fried circuits. He only shrugged. If things exploded, at least it wouldn't be his fault this time.

Pauline studied the demon again. The confidence wasn't reckless. It was practiced—the kind that came from surviving things meant to kill.

"You got yourself locked up in the Shadowkeep for bitin' off more than you could chew."

"I did." Samthrax crossed to his favourite chesterfield sofa and made himself comfortable. A faint wave of heat rolled off his skin as he exhaled. "I made a poor choice. Tried to snack on one of the ancestors. Woke up in a cage surrounded by the nightmares I used to make fun of. Humbling experience."

"And Seraphina let you out?"

"Yep. With caveats, of course." He held up his glowing wrists.

Pauline snorted. "Redemption ain't free, demon. You think servin' a pretty witch bought you outta what you are?"

He tapped one claw on a fang. "You say that like you know something about sin and second chances."

For a long beat, neither looked away—old power measuring old damnation.

Pauline's voice dropped lower. "I know plenty about both. You stay on the right side of that binding, we'll get along fine. Step off it, and I'll drag your carcass back down myself."

Samthrax's eyes gleamed, a flash of respect under the arrogance. "You've got teeth, old girl. I like that."

"Keep talkin', I'll show you how sharp they still are."

Sage stifled a laugh. "I think she wins this round."

Killian cleared his throat, clearly out of his depth. "May I remind you all—we have work to do."

Samthrax stretched into the chair, riding the last flicker of challenge. He lived for moments like this—seeing how far he could push before someone snapped. Killian's command didn't bother him; authority never did.

"Sure thing bossman. You want coffee before or after we save the world?"

Pauline watched him sprawl, her loa prickling. The arrogance didn't trouble her—it was the ease beneath it. The certainty that no one here could truly kill him.

There was affection in him too, toward the others. That was unexpected.

"You can make coffee?"

"The best you'll ever have."

"Then start with mine, chèr. I wanna see if your brew's as dark as your soul."

He grinned. "Now we're friends."

"Don't bet on it."

When he stood and moved toward the counter, she didn't mean to track his movement—but she did.

Whatever else he was, he belonged to this house now.

And she would learn soon enough which side of it he served.

Five

"Some legacies are not passed by hand, but by wound.
The deeper the silence, the louder the inheritance."
— *Coven proverb, exact origin unknown*

1695

Zinnia couldn't sleep.

She'd tried. For hours. Staring at the ceiling. Then the walls. Then the dark line where wall met floor, shadow and timber bleeding together.

Every nerve twitched with the what-the-fuck of it: magic, witches, angels, demons, time travel.

She lay on her back, hands tight around the edge of the quilt. Not for warmth. Not for comfort. Just to feel something real. Her palms ached from the grip. Her skin buzzed, the way a lightbulb does before it pops.

Enough.

She threw the blanket off. Swung her legs down. The floor slapped cold against her feet. It travelled up her legs fast enough to make her hiss. She reached for the red cloak Matthew had left hanging over the chair and pulled it around her shoulders.

It made her feel like Red Riding Hood, dropped into the wrong damn story.

Let's hope the wolves keep their teeth to themselves.

The hood fell deep enough to hide behind. A small mercy—because right now, she didn't want to be seen by herself, let alone anyone else.

She moved out of the room, careful not to wake the house. Every board underfoot knew someone else's weight, and she didn't trust them not to protest hers.

Shit, she hadn't crept out of a house since she was a teenager.

The cabin door creaked open in one slow arc.

Cold rushed in.

It pressed against her face, her fingers, the tops of her feet. Mist dragged low across the clearing—pale and wide, creeping over the ground in lazy sheets. It curled around her ankles, damp and clinging.

She stepped outside.

Behind her, the door shut with a small click.

The clearing stretched open, ringed by trees standing watch like sentries. Zinnia found the path without thinking. The night teemed with unfamiliar sound—too many noises she didn't recognise, and too many missing that she should.

She didn't care.

Out here, she could move.

Her mind churned. It kept circling the same fear: *what if no one comes?*

She wanted to run. Hard. Fast. Until the woods blurred, her lungs burned, and the questions in her head finally stopped trying to tear themselves into words.

Seraphina. Where the hell are you?

Get me out of this goddamn nightmare.

Cold crept under her skin as she followed the narrow path, pressed between trees that leaned too close, their bark flaking and dark with old moisture. Branches tangled overhead, swallowing the sky. Roots buckled through the earth, slick with moss and decay. Every step sank slightly, the forest floor soft with centuries of mulch.

She pushed deeper.

Brambles scraped the hem of the cloak, catching and whispering for her attention.

The smell of loam thickened. Something small moved in the brush nearby.

Fear should have come by now.

It didn't.

Whatever part of her that handled panic had switched off the moment she'd crash-landed here.

What filled its place was focus.

Focus on getting the hell out of dodge and back to where she belonged.

Zinnia slowed and inhaled.

She lifted her head, instinct pulling her left—toward a narrow break in the trees.

There they leaned harder, bent at unnatural angles. The space between them formed a tight corridor. Too narrow for carts. The brush underfoot was low and soft, flattened by more than animals.

A trail.

A well-used one at that.

She hesitated—long enough to wonder if this was the part in the story where the girl makes the stupid choice.

The pull tightened, insistent and wordless. Her feet moved before her better judgment could argue.

Zinnia stepped onto the path and followed it into the dark.

She didn't know how long she'd been moving when the night sounds changed—voices.

What the hell?

Zinnia quickened her pace, angling toward the sound.

She should have turned around and run the other way.

Women like her didn't walk toward chanting in this timeline. They ended up swinging from trees or becoming a human bonfire. She knew that.

Still, her feet moved.

The thicket thinned ahead. Light bled through the trees. Lanterns, maybe. Or torches.

Shadows swayed with the glow—broad shapes moving in measured sequence.

Zinnia faltered. Her breath snagged in her throat.

Curiosity scratched at her skull.

The path curved again. The sound grew louder, the cadence practiced and sure.

The mark at the back of her neck flared to life.

She couldn't go back.

Something ahead had already decided she belonged.

And something in her had already agreed.

Zinnia kept to the treeline at the clearing's edge. The earth beyond was black and bare, packed down by generations of feet that had walked this pattern before.

Twelve women moved in flawless unison.

Barefoot. Hooded. Each carried a small iron-tipped staff.

Heel. Toe. Press.

Heel. Toe. Press.

The staves struck the ground as one, the sound echoing like a second heartbeat.

The sigil revealed itself as her vision adjusted.

Twelve women. Twelve points.

Each movement drove the lines deeper, the symbol unfolding in glowing gold increments. Zinnia couldn't read it—not fully—but her body could. The mark seared, a hot line cutting across her shoulders.

The thirteenth woman stood at the centre.

Unhooded.

She wore deep green, arms bare to the elbows, palms stained dark. Her face was lifted to the sky, long dark hair spilling down her back, voice confident as the chant poured from her mouth.

The others did not speak.

In absolute silence, they completed the sigil, staves striking again and again until the shape pulsed with contained power.

Zinnia didn't move.

Geezus.

This wasn't some half-arsed candle circle.

This was disciplined. Drilled. Power shaped by repetition and obedience.

If I had a shred of self-preservation left, I'd be halfway back to the cabin.

Her feet didn't get the memo.

One of the women—tall, older, hair loose beneath her hood—halted mid-step.

Her head turned.

Not toward the circle.

Toward the trees.

Toward her.

Zinnia stopped breathing.

Shit.

The woman said nothing. But the pause spread like a ripple. One by one, others slowed.

Until the thirteenth lowered her arms.

And turned.

Zinnia's world screeched to a halt.

The mark on the woman's inner left wrist ignited in perfect tandem with her own. Same crescent. Same burn.

Les Revenantes.

Zinnia's knees wanted to give. She locked them, pulled up her big girl panties and stepped into the clearing.

No one moved.

The sigil held beneath their feet.

Zinnia turned her back to them, lowered her hood, and exposed the mark at the nape of her neck.

She heard surprised gasps before turning back to face them.

She half-expected some kind of magical slap for entering where she didn't belong.

But it didn't come.

She met the woman's eyes.

And to her absolute shock—

They filled with tears.

...Okay.

That's weird.

The circle cleared, every hooded woman vanishing into the trees without so much as a twig snap.

Not one word.

Not even a dramatic stare over the shoulder.

They were simply gone.

All but one.

She remained standing at the centre of the sigil, bare arms streaked with whatever they'd used to draw it.

The crescent gleamed at her wrist, a perfect mirror.

This wasn't a coincidence.

That much she was certain of.

But that didn't explain the way this woman was looking at her. Disbelief, threaded through with recognition.

Zinnia folded her arms tight across her chest.

Say something. Anything.

Nope, got nothing.

The woman stepped forward, making the space between them

shrink.

"My name is Lilly."

The woman waited, eyes fixed on her, as if the name should mean something.

It didn't.

Zinnia cleared her throat.

"I'm Zinnia… The mark you have, you're Les Revenantes, right?"

No reply.

Zinnia planted her feet and willed her body to behave.

There was heat building behind her eyes, and she had no idea what the hell it was attached to.

"You're from my bloodline. You knew who I was the second you saw me, didn't you?"

Still no answer.

"Cat got your tongue lady. Or am I not speaking clearly enough for you?"

Every instinct screamed for distance. But stubbornness dug in harder. She hadn't stumbled into a full coven to walk away empty-handed.

Lilly couldn't speak.

She wanted to. God, she wanted to.

Her mouth refused to cooperate. She'd rehearsed this moment for years—rewritten it in a hundred private drafts. None of them began like this.

Now, with her daughter right in front of her, her tongue felt thick.

Zinnia was taller than she'd imagined. Stronger. Beautiful in a way that stole the air from her lungs.

Her voice held no trace of the baby Lilly had left behind—and none of the patience Lilly might have prayed for.

But this was her daughter. There was no mistaking it.

So much time, and this was what remained—a stranger standing ten feet away, unaware of who she was.

Lilly wanted to reach out—wanted to touch her daughter's face, memorise every line. But her arms stayed at her sides, stiff and useless.

This was what she'd earned.

Zinnia drew back, almost imperceptibly.

Lilly felt it before it happened—the backward tilt, the body preparing to bolt.

"I know you don't recognise me."

Zinnia's brow furrowed, struggling to make sense of whatever this new weirdness was.

Words tore free, scraping against everything she'd buried.

"You wouldn't. You were… you were but a babe when I let you go."

And in an instant, the whole world was all ears waiting to hear what came next.

"I'm your mother, Zinnia."

Her stomach rolled. Her mouth tasted like copper. She didn't know if she wanted to scream or throw up.

Mother?

What the actual fuck was this woman saying?

The word hit with no context, no history, no memories to pin it to. Just impact.

Her mind tried to comprehend it and failed. Spectacularly.

She should say something. Ask something. Demand answers.

Instead, she stood there with her whole identity unravelling under her skin, thread by fucking thread.

She had a mother.

Of course she did.

Babies don't appear out of vapour and dumb luck.

But her mother had been a blank space on forms. A question she'd stopped asking Mémère because even she had no answers.

Her father had taken his own life before she was out of the cradle, leaving her in her grandmother's care.

That absence had carved itself deep into her soul—why he hadn't loved her enough to stay, why her mother had vanished from both their lives.

But her grandmother had loved her fiercely. Still did. Still stood as her greatest champion.

And now this woman was standing in front of her in 1695 no less trying to claim that title and expecting Zinnia to just accept it?

Hard no. Fuck right off.

Too many feelings, none of them useful.

She kicked them back where they came from and grabbed her go-to.

Rage.

At least that one knew the rules.

Lilly stayed where she was, watching the storm roll across her daughter's face—grief, fury, disbelief—and waited to see which one was going to stick.

Anger felt inevitable.

She couldn't fix the past. She couldn't reclaim the years they'd lost.

But she could stand here now.

Before Zinnia could get a word out—and before Lilly could take a single step forward—the air split with holy wrath.

Wind tore through the clearing. White light burned down through the canopy.

Wings cut through the branches—brighter than snow, louder than judgement—wrapping tight as a figure dropped into the clearing.

Boots hit earth with a thump, all righteous fury and feathers.

Zinnia raised a brow, talk about unwanted dramatic entrances.

Divina. Hair tangled, expression thunderous.

Perfect.

The celestial being guaranteed to make this flaming wreck of a situation even worse.

"Thought you had to earn those back?" She didn't bother filtering the acid. Everything inside her already felt brittle. Might as well snap out loud.

"That's simply a metaphor, sweetheart." The coat dusting was performative. So was the smile. Her eyes measured Zinnia, precise and unsparing.

"Being stuck down here with you lot? That's what I must do to earn my way back into the good graces. It's been… titillating thus far."

Disapproval rolled off her in waves.

Her eyes slid to Lilly.

The look sharpened.

"From the smell of tragedy radiating off you both, I'm guessing you dropped the M-bomb?"

Zinnia kept her mouth shut. Teeth locked. She was barely keeping her thoughts in line as it was. Adding Divina's running commentary wasn't helping.

Lilly didn't bother hiding the exasperation. Divina's tone, her smugness—none of it had changed.

As if the guilt weren't already crushing enough, now came the angel with a mouth full of razors.

"You assume correctly."

Divina's next barb was prepped for release. It died halfway to her tongue when the emotional backdraft rolled through the clearing.

The brutal twist of empathy punched into her.

It was the instinct she disliked the most.

She dragged in a breath. This wasn't just strain.

It was grief, duct-taped to hope, stapled to guilt. The kind of grief that tasted metallic in the back of her throat. Exposed and unresolved, sitting between mother and daughter like a third presence neither could look at directly.

Divina could feel the wreckage right to the soles of her feet. She hated when someone else's pain made it through her armour.

She resisted the urge to vanish back into the sky.

"Christ."

Not a prayer. Just prognosis.

This assignment was heading to hell in a handbasket. And she was holding the bloody handle.

Six

"Those who fear prophecy will always fear the prophet."
— Enclave proverb, struck from the Canon

The Council Beneath the Dome – Present Day

The chamber was not meant to host secrets.

Killian had ensured that himself—spells in the walls, mirrors that reported on reflections that never were, oaths scored into parchment and sealed in sacrament.

No room for private plotting.

But power always found its shadows.

And Yvane had carved these shadows long before Killian rose to his polished pedestal.

He would never sanction what she was about to set in motion.

So she hadn't invited him.

Let him play diplomat.

She would keep the realm intact.

Nine councillors gathered in the side chamber hidden beneath the Enclave Hall.

Above them, the Looking Dome stirred—its surface clouding, then clearing.

Yvane did not waste time on ceremony.

Results were the only currency that mattered.

Her agent entered through the side arch—cloaked, hooded, hands gloved in rune-scribed leather.

One councillor stopped mid-reach.

Another lowered her eyes.

Two others did not look at the agent at all.

The hood fell back.

Blightmarks threaded her cheek in dark, drifting lines that crept and redrew themselves as if undecided.

Her eyes held a winter that did not thaw.

Her voice slid across the chamber.

"I've found him."

Varas leaned back, fingers steepled beneath her chin. She enjoyed broken things. Often wondered how she might break them further.

"Brinnan?"

A single nod.

"He has embraced the shadow. Fully. The Umbral rites are complete."

Salen appeared bored. Which meant he was listening.

"Shadow Ascendant."

The agent stepped forward. Her presence didn't beg. It commanded.

"He is hunting the Gateborn. Not to destroy her—but to consume her whole."

A hairline seam spidered across the Dome's inner surface.

For a fraction of a second, the image within it misaligned.

Then it resealed.

No one acknowledged it.

Maltren leaned forward, the burnished side of his face unreadable by design.

"To what end?"

"To open the Veil permanently. To collapse all barriers between what was, what is, and what must not be."

No one spoke while they digested the information.

Yvane broke the silence.

"And Zinnia?"

"She lives. The mark strengthens. She is bound to her inheritance whether she accepts it or not. The Gateborn lies dormant within her. Brinnan intends to wake it on his terms."

Salen clicked his tongue. "He'll unmake her."

"He'll do more than that." Maltren's fingers tightened against the table. "If the Veil breaks…"

One corner of Varas's mouth curved without warmth. "Then we strike first."

Yvane folded her hands neatly before her, as if this were nothing more than housekeeping.

"She cannot be allowed to fall into his grasp. Nor into Killian's. His sentiment will be our undoing."

Salen steepled his fingers, thumb rubbing once along the ridge of a signet ring.

"So we are suggesting what precisely? That we… end her?"

The agent looked to Yvane.

Awaiting permission.

Yvane nodded again.

"We make a necessary sacrifice."

There was no objection.

Varas tilted her head slightly. "And Killian?"

The smallest smile touched Yvane's mouth.

"He still believes in salvation. He will understand when it's done."

She tapped the obsidian once.

Beneath the table, a hidden sigil engaged.

The Looking Dome clarified—vision drawn directly from the agent's sight.

A forest.

Zinnia—cloaked, the mark on her neck blazing.

A woman before her.

Then—

Wings. White light cleaving downward.

Yvane leaned forward a fraction. The Dome's reflection cut across her face, sharpening the planes of it.

"Observe the angel. Intervene only if she obstructs the outcome."

The agent bowed her head. "Understood."

As she turned to leave, Yvane sent her final command telepathically.

Should Brinnan get there first, stay close.

If he falters, finish it.

Her power comes to me.

The agent did not reply.

She simply left.

***

Maison Bellarose – Scriptorium

The locator grid pulsed faintly on the table—thin lines of gold crawling outward from the bowl of dark water, mixed with Pauline's blood.

Nothing held long enough to read.

Killian leaned over the runes, arms braced on the table, calculation settling across his features.

The magic in the room adjusted itself around him the way disciplined things did around authority.

Sage hovered near her father, rocking lightly on her feet, unable to stay still. Her stomach tightened, the kind of squeeze that warned her a deadline had already passed.

Please. Give us something.

Seb sat opposite, pen poised, recording each fluctuation in a shorthand only he could decipher.

Pauline's thumb circled the mouth of her gris-gris pouch.

"Her blood's fightin' somethin'," she murmured. The surface of the bowl twitched in uneven bursts. "It ain't refusin' the spell. It's reachin'. But somethin' else is holdin' on."

Seraphina didn't look up from the grimoire. "Temporal displacement disrupts continuity. We need a stabiliser."

"It's not like we aren't trying." Sage gritted her teeth. The locator flared—then died. Mocking them. Heat gathered behind her eyes, she refused to let it free.

Trying clearly wasn't cutting it.

Killian maintained concentration.

Come on, girl. Give us a thread.

The locator pulsed once more.

The ring on Killian's hand started letting out a loud metallic whine and glowing red.

Killian straightened at once.

Conversation stopped mid-breath.

"Someone's in the side council chamber, which should never see use without my summons."

Seraphina's fingers tightened around the grimoire. "You warded the council's auxiliary room?"

"I warded every room they didn't want me in."

A jitter of pride and horror at her father's spying skills tangled inside Sage.

"Is that... legal?"

"No, but necessary."

Killian pressed his finger to the top of the ring.

The projection slammed to life instantly—ripped straight through the spy-wards he'd seeded years ago.

The side chamber under the Dome.

Nine councillors seated at the obsidian table.

And an agent—hood down, face visible.

Samthrax, midway through making a fresh batch of coffee for the masses, whistled.

"And that would be a blighted one. Me thinks your buddies don't like you much bossman."

Killian couldn't disagree. If this was who they'd pulled out of the hole, something serious was moving behind his back. Which also meant they needed to find Zinnia like yesterday.

The agent spoke.

"I've found him."

Yvane's expression remained carved stone.

"Brinnan has embraced the shadow fully. The Umbral rites are complete. He is hunting the Gateborn. Not to destroy her—but to consume her whole."

Saffron placed her hand on Seraphina's shoulder.

Even Samthrax didn't joke.

This wasn't a rescue anymore. It was a race.

Pauline itched to reach through and throttle them herself. How dare they go after her grandbaby. It would be a cold day in hell before they got their hands on her.

Killian absorbed the information.

His suspicions were confirmed. Fucking vultures.

The agent continued.

"She is alive. Her mark strengthens. Brinnan is closing in."

The council murmured.

Then Yvane delivered the blade:

"She cannot be allowed to fall into his grasp. Nor into Killian's. His sentiment will be our undoing."

Sage stayed locked on the councillors, tracking every nuance, every curve of a smile that didn't reach the eyes. A cold drop rolled down her spine.

"Does she mean just Zinnia?"

The dark beneath Seb's skin moved. Too fast to leash. Words poured out.

"No—she means us. She means we'll get in the way."

Killian's anger bled outward.

The sigil lines beneath his hands thinned, gold paling to ash at the edges.

A fine crack snapped through the lacquer of the table and sealed as quickly as it formed.

"Dad…" Sage touched his arm.

His hand covered hers for a moment; his attention never left the grid.

Yvane looked at each councillor in turn.

"We make a necessary sacrifice."

It was delivered the way one authorises a ledger adjustment.

Pauline scoffed. *Politicians were all the same.* "Over my dead body, chère."

The projection jumped—showing Zinnia in the forest. Cloaked. Mark flaming gold.

Sage swayed a little. "Oh my God, Zin."

Seb's hands clenched against his thighs. "Okay, she is definitely not in Kansas anymore, Toto."

Killian lifted his hand and the image froze mid-frame.

"No. That looks very much like England to me. Past England."

Samthrax, who had moved on from playing barista to poring over older grimoires, moved closer to the image. "I know where that is. Our girl's in the late 1600s. Which means unfriendlies towards witchy poos."

The twins spoke as one. "Our girl?"

Samthrax eyed them both in amusement. "That's what you took from what I just said?"

Saffron snorted. "Well, it is a little hard not to get caught up on that detail, however, let's focus on what you're seeing here. Explain."

Samthrax waved his clawed fingers toward the image. "That's Hedgemoor Wood. Ashwick Vale. Lancashire."

Killian studied the terrain, the tilt of the trees—every inch matching a place etched into old maps and older memory.

"You're sure?"

"Hundred percent. Place is cursed as balls and twice as dark. When I was playing hellspawn in my youth, it was the place to be."

Pauline didn't need the Loa to spell it out. One look at that forest, and her gut wanted to pack up and leave home.

The place was unclean. A sour tang coated her tongue.

"Mmm. I'm gettin' some real bad juju off it. Somethin' there don't sit right."

Everyone murmured agreement.

The locator grid kicked hard.

Gold scattered across the runes, then imploded. The bowl lurched against the table, cracking through the centre. Water and blood spilled into the carved lines, steam lifting as the sigils drank.

The distortion behind Zinnia elongated, straining against a boundary none of them could see. Testing the membrane between worlds. Pressing. Learning.

Seb's pupils flared wide. A thin line of shadow leaked from the corner of his eye, trailing down his cheek before sinking back into his skin.

"It's looking at us."

Silence rippled through the room. All eyes locked on Seb.

Sage's heartbeat misfired once, then refused to settle. They'd all seen his shadows lash out before—but this had been automatic.

Please don't let it take him the way it wants.

Pauline's first instinct was to shield him. "Child…" Her own shadows drew inward, her magic stepping back as if acknowledging something new in him.

Saffron drifted closer. She studied her grandson with dread she kept smothered.

Samthrax's easy grin slipped away, the heat that clung to him deepened—enough to curl the paper nearest his elbow.

"Now, that's a development." He watched Seb the way predators watch other predators—measure first, decide later.

Killian's focus locked on the fading shadow-mark along his son's cheek. *Noted.* A line had been crossed. He filed it with the same precision he gave threats and promises.

Seb wiped at nothing; his fingers trembled against his cheek, the cold settling deeper. His stomach sent *empty now* signals; he swallowed them back down. "What the hell was that?"

Right now, Seraphina was a mother trying to be a strategist.

A strategist trying not to scream.

"That my son is something we talk about later. For now, we move forward. You're sure it saw us?"

Seriously, could her life get any more complicated. Her son was now bleeding shadows, and her best friend was being stalked by something Eldritch which had just clocked them!

Seb nodded. He kneaded his shoulders, trying to loosen them. They wouldn't budge.

"Yeah. It locked on."

The locator grid buckled. White flared across the table. Then everything cut to black.

Pauline's hand rose to her throat. "She's bein' tracked."

Killian's fist slammed down.

"So, she's not just lost in time. She's standing in a place that wants her."

The beams creaked overhead. The wards dimmed, almost cowering.

The projection flickered once more—Zinnia turning quickly, eyes

59

wide—before tearing down the centre in a clean, impossible line.

Light leaked out.

Then nothing.

Seven

"Abandonment wounds stay quiet—until the moment they don't."
— Les Revenantes family proverb

The Between folded inward around Brinnan, awareness stirring at the outer limits of his sight. A presence tugged against the fabric of the place—one that didn't belong inside the fractures of time.

He halted his momentum.

The disturbance hovered at the fringe of perception—brittle. Uninvited.

He let it infiltrate him. The Umbral rites had hollowed new corridors inside his mind, and the Between answered along those recesses.

The agent stepped from the rift with disciplined restraint.

Her shoulders stayed high.

Her jaw never unclenched.

Council scent clung to her—fear masked beneath duty, blightmarks alive along her skin.

She released a measured sweep of magic, a thin wedge cutting through the dark in search of his residual distortion.

Her spell brushed the space he had occupied seconds earlier and found nothing.

Brinnan let the moment lengthen, noting the minute correction in her stance—the tension pulling along her spine.

She believed she was stalking a trace of him.

She did not understand the trace was studying her.

Brinnan absorbed her pattern, letting the details roll through his mind.

Her pulse struck in regulated beats—Council conditioning.

Her magic advanced in clipped increments—disciplined, contained.

Her thoughts pushed forward in short bursts—measuring steps, checking the dark.

She was searching for something she could not fathom.

And she had been sent to stop him.

Annoyance brushed his periphery.

The interruption was nothing more than an insect vibration inside the fault-lines of reality.

Did these fools truly imagine they could interrupt what had already aligned?

He let his focus tighten.

The Between responded immediately.

Still unable to detect him, she stepped deeper into his territory.

The agent's posture faltered.

Her weight tipped back a fraction.

One hand flexed at her side for no clear reason.

She didn't understand what she felt, only that something was off.

The Between no longer flowed around her. It pressed.

Her wards flickered under the strain.

A thin crack ran through the air around her, not visible, but present in the way her magic trembled.

The realm rejected her.

It always rejected the living, but this reaction carried another warning.

She was not alone.

Brinnan advanced without moving.

The Between obeyed.

Sound drained from around her.

Her boots met nothing—no resistance, no rebound, no confirmation of ground.

She inhaled.

The breath left her in a sharp break.

It ghosted white in front of her.

Confusion struck; sequence slipped.

Temperature had no jurisdiction here unless something imposed it.

He had.

Panic sparked through her in erratic bursts.

Her training forced her to rein it in, but she couldn't suppress the next breath—shallow, uneven, betraying her.

She reached for a phase-step.

Brinnan registered the spell as it gathered—a compact orbit of runes turning at her dominant hand, bracing to shear sideways through the plane.

He touched the forming construct with a single fragment of will.

It ruptured.

The runes inverted and tore apart before she could pull back. The recoil snapped through her arm and folded her forward, spine bowing under the impact.

Terror rose—silent, contained, honed to a lethal edge.

She still couldn't see him.

Her eyes cut through the dark, chasing movement that refused to stabilise. She pivoted in a tight circle, scanning for origin.

Her wards thinned.

Her magic lost cohesion, breaking apart in uneven surges.

The last anchor to linear time loosened.

Brinnan watched the moment of comprehension break open in her mind—a single, fragile recognition:

Something had found her first.

Her mind seized, hunting for a coherent thought.

None stayed whole long enough to matter.

Brinnan turned inward, unsealing the channels.

The Between answered, shadows bending in recognition.

He reached her without crossing the distance.

Alarm detonated through her aura.

Her consciousness buckled against the pressure—an instinctive recoil, exposed and terrified.

She threw up a shield on reflex. But the barrier dissolved the moment he touched it.

What steadied her scattered, sliding across the floor of the Between in loose shards.

Her pulse battered the inside of her skull.

He pushed deeper.

Her legs failed.

Sight fractured.

One future.

Then another.

Then a dozen more.

Outcomes tore through her:

Her death in Council chambers.

Her death without record.

Her death in shadow, swallowed before she could scream.

She tried to resist.

Her mind refused to obey.

He widened the breach.

Further paths tore open—roads that diverged, merged, broke again.

Her identity splintered across too many outcomes for one mind to contain.

She reached for the present, but it wouldn't stay fixed. It warped beneath her feet. It rebuilt itself without logic.

Then the truth arrived.

She had never been anything more than an instrument.

Disposable from the moment they sent her.

Yvane would sacrifice her as soon as the job was done.

No loose ends.

Her thighs locked, useless against the tilt of the Between.

She tried to hold a thought—any thought— but they dissolved in the surge of competing futures.

Brinnan allowed the understanding to land before he guided her toward the one thread that remained unbroken across every possibility.

Zinnia.

Her mark rising.

Her bloodline waking.

Her power reaching.

Her path converging toward him.

The agent felt the inevitability settle against her soul.

No denial left.

No defiance.

No sanctuary in any timeline she had clung to.

Her remaining resistance gave way.

Brinnan stepped into the emptied centre of her. Knowledge unfolded through him in layered strata, each piece aligning without friction. Everything she carried opened.

The Council's design surfaced first.

They wanted Zinnia gone, cut down before she completed the rise.

But Yvane had other plans—she wanted her awake.

An uncontrolled Gateborn held enough force to rupture the order of things. Yvane intended to steer that rupture.

Another name surfaced.

Pauline Broussard.

Fear wrapped tight around Pauline's name. The agent carried the residue of it—Council chambers grew dense whenever Pauline was mentioned. The kind of power under that woman's skin unsettled them. What she might ignite in the girl unsettled them more.

Brinnan took the knowledge in without response.

Pauline reduced to a minor fluctuation. Nothing structural.

Killian followed.

The Council had excluded him from their plans. Sentiment compromised him. He cared for the girl. He cared for his people. The agent's mind held whispers of meetings where Yvane questioned his loyalty, where others agreed in silence.

Confirmation layered over confirmation: they were not unified.

Cracks ran through them.

Nothing more than weak seams, ready to give.

Brinnan let the variables align until a single inevitable outcome clarified.

Zinnia's power was accelerating beyond their projections.

The Council was scrambling.

He would not allow them to reach her first.

She was his convergence, not theirs.

A flicker brushed the edge of the Between.

Zinnia's mark, bright against the dark.

The person beside her triggered a second resonance, softer but distinct.

Lilly.

Alive.

Moving within the girl's orbit.

So. The mother had returned.

A variable unaccounted for.

A realignment passed through the fractures of the realm. Zinnia's timeline drew at him again—insistent, pulling against the gravity of his own ascension.

He acknowledged it.

A subtle recalibration.

The Between adjusted, aligning toward her exact coordinates.

The agent hung suspended between moments, emptied of direction.

Training alone kept her upright.

Nothing inside her reached forward anymore.

Continuity dissolved.

What remained of her drifted.

Brinnan regarded her as one might assess an instrument stripped of function.

Nothing in her remained useful.

No line tied her to anything of consequence.

He withdrew the force that had kept her upright.

Her legs gave.

The Between intercepted her descent before impact, holding her suspended in a weightless arrest.

She stared ahead.

Eyes open.

Sight empty.

Breath continuing only because the body refused to quit.

What she had been minutes earlier no longer cohered.

The realm thinned around her, easing her toward the low drift where discarded travellers accumulated.

Brinnan didn't follow her into that descent.

She offered nothing further.

The turbulence surrounding him levelled once the interference dispersed. The Between smoothed back into equilibrium, leaving only the steady ascent of his own expansion.

A new summons hit him.

Zinnia.

Her mark flared through the instability of the past, reaching across time the way flame hunts oxygen.

Brinnan turned toward the signal.

The Between tightened into a single vector.

At last, convergence.

***

Zinnia dragged both hands through her hair and paced a track across the clearing, breath tearing from her lungs in uneven pulls she couldn't get under control.

Heat flared at her neck where the mark kept firing.

Each throb slammed through her nerves, sharpening everything—anger, confusion, the ache behind her eyes since Lilly opened her mouth and blew Zinnia's entire life open in one damn sentence.

I'm your mother.

The words kept circling.

Kept cutting.

What the fuck.

Zinnia stopped pacing long enough to stare at the woman.

Lilly didn't move. Didn't speak. Didn't dare step closer.

She met Zinnia head-on, contained in a way that felt deliberate.

And infuriating.

Zinnia forced herself to stay upright. Her shoulders felt welded in place—like if they dropped, the rest of her would follow.

"Do you know what it does to someone growing up without answers? Without anything? Just questions and dreams and this—" Her hand shot to her neck, fingers digging into the mark that refused to settle. "This thing waking up in me and no one telling me a single fucking thing?"

Divina shifted from foot to foot, caught between stepping in and staying well clear of the emotional storm playing out in front of her.

Irritation pricked. A reminder she was here because the cosmos had a twisted sense of humour.

Lilly's composure broke.

Tears slipped free, silent and constant, her whole face trembling under the weight of grief she'd carried for too long. She absorbed Zinnia's pain without shielding herself from it.

Zinnia felt none of the comfort that was probably meant to offer.

"Say something. Anything." Her hands curled into fists until her knuckles shone white.

"Because right now, I'm standing here wondering if you even wanted me. Or if abandoning me was just the easiest version of whatever destiny bullshit you were tangled in."

Humour—her usual armour—refused to show up.

No snark.

No deflection.

Just the unhealed wound of a girl who'd grown up believing she wasn't worth staying for.

And hadn't that bled into every goddamn relationship she'd ever had.

The mark flared again, hotter this time.

The forest reacted instantly—branches tightening overhead, soil tugging inward, wind stirring with intent.

Zinnia didn't look away.

Her attention remained fixed on the woman who should have been there her entire life.

"Tell me why you left, and no circling the pig's arse. I want it straight."

Lilly's mouth curved slightly. Steel lived in this girl. The realisation hit with a bittersweet mix of pride and grief.

"You were never the mistake, Zinnia. The legacy was."

Zinnia snorted. "Could've fooled me."

Divina chuckled at the moxie. Damn. She was starting to really like this one.

Lilly didn't rise to the barb.

"My bloodline isn't just magic. It's a duty you don't get to outrun. I tried anyway. I tried so hard. I wanted a life that wasn't built on doors between worlds and prophecies I had no control over. I wanted your father. I wanted you."

Zinnia felt the truth in her words. It only made everything inside her detonate faster.

"I thought if you grew up far from all of it, maybe the legacy would stay quiet." Lilly pressed a hand to her sternum.

"You're not full blood. Sometimes that dulls the line. Sometimes it doesn't. I prayed it would."

Zinnia barked a humourless laugh. "Newsflash, praying did squat."

Lilly lowered herself onto the nearest rock.

"I hid you. Your name. Your blood. Everything that could make the Council look twice. I thought if you grew up Broussard, if you carried the Hart name instead of Les Revenantes, you'd be safe."

Her head shook slowly.

"I didn't leave because I didn't want you," she repeated.

"I left because staying would have painted a target on you so bright they'd tear the world apart to reach you. They were already watching me. Questioning why my mark hadn't passed on. I couldn't let them see you. Not even once."

Her eyes brimmed, she let the tears fall.

"I gave you a chance at a normal life."

Her voice faltered on *normal*.

"And in doing that, I broke every part of mine."

"So, you left to save me. And it still fucked everything up."

Lilly let out a deep sigh. "Yes. And I will carry that until the day the

Veil takes me."

Zinnia's voice dropped. "I don't know what to do with any of this."

The confession slipped out before she could stop it.

"I don't know how to carry all of this and still be—"

Her words stalled.

"Still be me."

Her knees gave and struck the ground as if the world had lowered itself on top of her. She dug her palms into the dirt just to feel something solid.

"I spent my whole damn life wanting you. Wanting a story that didn't hurt. Wanting parents who loved me enough to stay."

Her head dipped.

"And now you're here and I don't know what the hell to do."

Her daughter was breaking in front of her—and Lilly felt it piece by piece.

The strength she'd relied on for decades slipped.

The urge to reach for Zinnia nearly dragged her forward, but she squashed the impulse, terrified that one wrong movement would undo the ground they stood on.

No child should have had to be this strong.

The thought hit with brutal clarity.

Her doing.

Her sin.

Her consequence.

Lilly's fingers flexed at her sides.

Zinnia needed truth, not escape.

Needed space, not smothering.

Needed to choose whether this connection would live or die.

"Please," Lilly breathed, barely audible. "Don't carry this alone."

The forest shifted again, responding not to Lilly, but to Zinnia's pain.

This was the part Divina hated.

Not the prophecy crap.

This—human emotion melting all over the damn place.

She watched Zinnia draw inward, the mark blazing bright enough to stain the clearing gold.

A warning.

A gigantic problem.

Shit.

Divina stepped forward, stopped, stepped again. Held herself back with visible effort. Her jaw clenched hard enough to ache.

"Okay, she's about three sobs away from going nuclear."

Her wings pushed under her skin, clawing for release.

She crouched beside Zinnia—not touching her, not daring to—close enough to intercept the explosion if it hit.

"You don't break alone," Divina let the promise land heavy between them.

Not alone.

The thought stripped the last layer of control Zinnia had left.

Her body shook.

Tears hit the dirt.

Heat drove outward from the mark in rolling bursts.

The clearing tightened around her, the world knew what was coming and it was bracing.

Zinnia pressed her forehead to the earth. "I can't—I can't hold all of this."

Power coiled under her skin, frantic and rising.

Lilly moved.

"I've got you."

The vow escaped before she could stop it.

She dropped to her knees beside her daughter, close enough for their marks to ignite in tandem.

It was time.

Lilly raised her wrist. The crescent flared the instant it neared Zinnia's neck.

When the symbols aligned, the wind ripped through the clearing, corkscrewing around them.

Power gripped the three women, refusing to release them.

Lilly pressed crescent to crescent. The contact reverberated through the earth, fissures racing outward through the soil.

The ritual rose unbidden. Words poured out—rhythmic, command-heavy.

The awakening had already taken root.

The Veil thinned to gauze.

The forest bent toward the epicentre.

Heat stung the air, lifting in hard waves that shuddered through the ferns, rattled branches, dragged the light into a tight orbit around Zinnia's body.

Lilly kept chanting.

Divina planted herself at Zinnia's back, boots grinding into earth, hands raised—ready to absorb or redirect whatever tore free. The ritual current crawled over her nerves like charged wire; she bared her teeth.

"Come on, kid. Don't let this eat you."

Zinnia screamed.

Not a mortal scream.

A Gateborn scream.

The kind that splits stone and leaves nothing untouched.

She was ripped in multiple directions at once—past scraping along her nerves, future prying at her ribs, something older levering at her shoulders—all of it insisting she rise.

Her magic convulsed along her bones, frantic and directionless.

Her pulse became a weapon.

Her breath scalded her lungs.

Lilly's voice pushed through the storm:

"Let it out. I will not lose you again."

The forest bowed to that promise.

Trees bending until their crowns kissed the ground.

Force blasted outward, flattening the grass.

The space around them detonated in gold—pure, searing, consuming. Light poured from Zinnia's neck in a violent column, driving upward, shredding leaves into a spinning storm.

The clearing didn't simply flare.

It ignited.

A Gateborn awakening—unrestrained, unfiltered, un-fucken-stoppable.

Zinnia lifted from the ground, spine arched, hair suspended in the current, the crescent burning white-hot.

Divina staggered but held.

Lilly locked her grip and drove the chant deeper, anchoring, insisting, refusing to let the power tear her daughter apart.

The Veil thrashed.

Reality shook.

Magic flooded every crack of the world.

And Zinnia—finally, brutally, irrevocably—rose into her power.

Eight

"If the land feels it, the hunters already running.
Best you start running too."
— Witch Hunter-era folk saying

The cottage lurched on its foundation.

Matthew froze mid-sip.

The floorboards groaned beneath an impact that didn't belong to this century.

Gold split the wards he'd carved into the walls.

The charms snapped against their nails, clacking wildly. Dust shook loose from the rafters. His chair skidded an inch across the floor. He caught the table's edge as another blow tore through the room.

Zinnia.

Her mark flooded the land.

Not a whisper. Not a flicker.

An explosion.

Shite.

His pulse misfired, stumbled—then bolted.

She shouldn't be triggering yet. Not without someone to anchor her.

Adrenaline shot through him.

Enough to haul him forward whether he was ready or not.

Thinking stopped. His entire chest twisted around a single truth:

She was in pain.

And if she burned through her tether before anyone reached her—

He couldn't finish the thought.

She needs someone there. Needs someone to put hands on her shoulders and drag her back into herself.

Someone who won't run.

He grabbed his coat without getting his arms through the sleeves, shoved the door open so hard it slammed against the stone, and ran. The forest shut around him, ground shaking under each step. The old magic of the vale hissed under his skin, alive in a way it hadn't been for centuries.

Her power hit again.

If the Veil tears, this whole timeline goes with it.

"Zin—" The name barely made it past his teeth.

The woods blurred as he forced himself deeper, pushing past whatever stood between him and that terrible pulse.

He could feel her fear.

Her emergence.

Hold on, lass. Don't lose yourself.

His foot hit uneven ground; he stumbled, caught himself, kept moving. The tremors rolled through the earth again, harder now. Leaves shook loose from the branches above him.

Another wave crashed into him.

He pitched forward, barely catching himself.

This was more than Gateborn power.

"Hold on," he rasped, forcing the words into the cold air, breath shredding in his throat. "I'm comin'. Just—hold on lass."

The earth heaved beneath his boots.

Every bloody witch hunter in the shire is gonna be searchin' these woods.

A pyre is not your future, lass.

I am.

And he ran like hell.

***

The crystal on Yvane's desk dulled to nothing.

A flat void where a trained operative's mind should have been.

She studied the dead crystal in silence, the realisation sliding through her with cold precision. She reached out with her mind to confirm what she already knew.

No response.

No landing point.

Just nothing.

Brinnan had found the agent and erased her.

Not a simple death.

Death left residue.

Death echoed.

This was total absence.

A level of Umbral control outside the limits she had calculated.

Her fingers hovered above the crystal, assessing angles, consequences, the scale of her mistake.

She measured everything.

Brinnan had outpaced her.

He had grown into something she no longer fully understood.

That failure scratched at something beneath her composure.

And he had stripped a Council-trained blighted agent clean—one chosen specifically because she was powerful and a breath away from demonic.

Her strategy tilted.

Only a fraction.

Enough to expose the flaw.

She had overestimated herself.

And the agent.

The admission landed without mercy. She had believed she could keep the pathways narrow, the players contained, the outcomes predictable.

She had misjudged what Brinnan would become without restraint.

She recalibrated.

Brinnan would know Zinnia was awake.

He would know where she had landed.

He would sense the timeline thinning, bending toward convergence.

But another detail rose beneath that:

A ward inked into her wrist tingled once—distinct and unmissable. She glanced down.

The Gateborn mark had surged.

And someone bound to the original line had activated beside it.

This signature had been dormant for years and was blood-linked.

Lilly Les Revenantes.

Alive.

And with the girl.

Her pulse remained level. Her mind did not. Connections rearranged themselves with ruthless speed.

Lilly had vanished years ago.

With her, the visible trail of the bloodline.

They had believed the mark dormant, unpassed.

Yet here she was—in another time—with the very child who carried it.

A mother anchoring a Gateborn coming online.

A variable she had neither anticipated nor priced for.

Her plans edged out of alignment, but not beyond reach. Momentum still favoured her if she moved fast enough.

She turned toward the unused runes across her desk—contingencies she hadn't spoken aloud, crafted for outcomes only she was ruthless enough to enact. No other Council member needed to know how many she had prepared or what each demanded.

She touched a single rune.

It activated instantly, hungry for purpose.

Phase two.

If Brinnan had surpassed her expectations, she would adjust accordingly. If Lilly stood with the girl, she would account for that too. Variables expanded. Outcomes shifted. The board remained hers.

Lilly altered the parameters.

Zinnia was rising.

Her power was raw, unbound, and resisting containment.

The Council would want control.

Brinnan would want consumption.

Pauline would want her blood back.

Yvane wanted victory.

The awakening shifted the balance.

It did not remove her from the game.

There were still alliances she could fracture.

Still pressure points she could weaponise.

Still paths she could force into compliance.

Control was not gone.

It had simply become expensive.

She set the crystal aside, its emptiness no longer useful.

Her mind closed on one razor-edged truth:

She had underestimated Brinnan once.

She would not do so again.

***

The Between carried Brinnan forward in a clean, obedient line, its corridors yielding, its darkness opening around the thread that bound him to Zinnia. Her essence tugged through the fractures with bright insistence, guiding his path with a magnetic pull.

The realm acknowledged her.

It acknowledged him more.

Then the awakening struck.

A violent influx tore through the aligned corridors, ripping them apart. Shapes folded inward, pathways jammed against one another, the entire structure convulsing in a single recoil.

Brinnan halted mid-transition as the thread shattered into noise.

Zinnia had risen.

Her power ran wild through the Between, scorching shadow-lines and breaching chambers untouched since the rites carved themselves into the framework of him.

The place strained, its instinct uncertain for the first time since he claimed mastery over it.

He held still, letting the waves break around him, measuring the force.

This was more than Gateborn.

The rupture threw a second pattern across the dark.

Not Zinnia.

Older.

Focused.

It wasn't only Lilly's bloodline resonating through the fractures; Broussard moved with it—earthbound, deep, hoodoo-rooted.

The mother had stepped in, lending structure to the rise, preventing the girl from tearing herself and the Veil apart.

That bond had weight.

Not enough to concern him.

But enough to delay him.

Brinnan pressed deeper into the noise, searching for the thread again—only to feel another presence cut across the realm.

Male.

Power-bearing.

Not mortal.

Not ancient either.

Something in-between.

Magic coiled around the signature—wild, unrefined, driven toward Zinnia with reckless determination. The man moved fast, driven not by power but by purposeful intent.

Intent could become interference. Interference could become obstruction.

Brinnan catalogued him without urgency and continued searching.

Then the fourth presence cut in.

Pure and unwelcome.

Angelic.

Her signature cut straight through the Between, untouched by its rules, beyond shadow, beyond him. Where her presence imposed itself, the realm refused to close. The darkness parted around her, not in reverence—

in recognition of authority.

She alone could sever him from the rites.

She alone could reach the core the shadow could not protect.

A rare thing stirred—fast, electric, undeniable.

The recognition of a limit.

A place his mastery couldn't reach.

Her nearness to Zinnia was not an inconvenience.

It was a problem.

Brinnan reached again, pushing against the disruption.

The Between resisted, the awakening still tearing through its chambers.

Shadows bent.

Fractures realigned.

A route flickered open—a jagged, unstable connection leading toward the clearing.

He followed it.

Zinnia's rising signature pulsed in bright waves. The girl was reshaping the balance around her. The place adjusted in real time, recalibrating its centre of gravity toward her power.

The male moved closer.

The mother braced the girl.

The angel stood guard.

Every piece converged around her.

Brinnan stepped through the distortion.

The path obeyed.

Whatever stood with Zinnia—

whatever shielded her—

whatever believed it could claim her first—

He would arrive all the same.

She was awake now—and the awakened did not belong to the light.

***

The scriptorium had fallen into the kind of uneasy quiet that followed too many hours chasing answers.

Books lay open. Runes sprawled across the tables.

Sage worked through theories with Seb, pretending she understood half of what he was saying.

She swung between hope and dread, never long enough in either to find footing.

Samthrax flipped through grimoires he clearly planned to bully into cooperation.

Seraphina revised ward sequences under her breath.

Killian tracked and mapped each probability the way other men mapped prayers.

Pauline sorted gris-gris components into neat piles, humming low to keep the Loa happy.

A fragile imitation of normal.

Then power hit.

Every ward along the walls lit at once.

Gold bled through the cracks between stones.

Pauline's Loa kicked awake, crowding her skin, vibrating at a pitch she hadn't heard since the night her son came to her in a dream.

The first wave wasn't Zinnia—it was bigger, deeper, old enough to pull the Veil inward.

Then came the second.

That one was Zinnia.

"She's risin'."

Samthrax pushed off his chair in the same instant; his demon-sense tore straight into the current, analysing and recalibrating. His mind raced through everything he knew of Gateborn ascensions, and none of it matched this.

Saffron drifted closer to the table. "That's definitely more mojo than we were expecting."

Seraphina walked up to Killian and wrapped her arms around him, the twins groaned pretending the show of affection was doing them harm.

She didn't care—she needed to be held.

Killian rested his chin on the top of her head, eyes never leaving Pauline and Samthrax. Feeling the magic was one thing. Interpreting it was another. It appeared these two were the only ones able to do so.

Another pulse tore through the scriptorium—violent enough to make the wards around the ceiling flare.

Pauline caught it instantly.

And recognised the truth inside it.

Lilly.

She was alive.

And she was with Zinnia.

Her vision blurred for a heartbeat—not with tears, but with fury and relief striking so hard she forgot to breathe.

So, she wasn't dead after all.

She was there.

Helping Zinnia rise.

A fissure opened in her chest—old grief uncoiling, pulling the memory of her son into the present.

His story should never have finished.

That struck harder than the event itself.

Samthrax was the next to catch the layered signature. His eyes widened, the demon in him stretching forward.

"Ah hell, Zin's not just Gateborn."

Sage's thoughts scattered. Every time she believed she'd hit the limit of revelations, the universe dumped another flaming pile of destiny into her lap.

"What do you mean by that?"

"She's Les Revenantes and Broussard." Samthrax tapped his temple once in disbelief. "That's a double-line ignition. Hoodoo and Gateborn rising together. No one gets both. No one survives both. Unless—"

Killian felt the suckerpunch.

"Unless she was made for it."

The shift was unmistakable.

A fulcrum had formed in Zinnia. And fulcrums did not bend. They broke worlds open.

Saffron's glow trembled. "But who is anchoring her? None of us can reach her."

Another pulse.

This one clean—devastatingly calibrated.

Pauline cleared her throat.

"That would be Lilly, her mother."

Cue shocked silence.

Sage was starting to get whiplash from all the shit she didn't know about the people in her life. "Her—what? Isn't she dead?"

"Apparently not, chere." Pauline made a mental list of what she wanted to say to that woman when they met—and they would.

Seb's shadows lashed once against his sneakers. "Zin's mum is in the past with her? How the hell—"

Another tremor jolted him, dragging his shadow with it. It wanted out—wanted to answer whatever Zinnia had become.

The thought did not sit well.

Samthrax ran a clawed hand through his hair. "Oh, this is bad. This is so bad. Two bloodlines igniting at once? You realise Brinnan will feel that from wherever he's slithering through?"

Killian recognised the opening for what it was. This was the opportunity they had been waiting for; they could follow it all the way to her.

"Track it."

"Sure but understand bossman—that wasn't an awakening. That was a door blowing off its hinges. She just told every creature with a scrap of sensitivity that she exists."

Saffron felt herself grow lighter—dangerously so. "Then Brinnan isn't the only one who will come."

The runes gave a single, sustained note that rattled the ink bottles on the table.

Pauline braced both hands on the table's edge, fingers biting into the wood.

"My grandbaby is risin' with a power she shoulda never had to shoulder alone. And her mother—her mother—is right there holdin' the line."

Seraphina straightened as renewed energy cut through her exhaustion.

"On the upside, Zinnia may have bloody near short-circuited the whole universe, but it has at least given us a way to track her and bring her home. We just have to get there before anyone else."

Samthrax cracked his knuckles with grim amusement. "Well. This is gonna be one hell of a family reunion."

Zinnia's scream tore across time, striking the chamber hard enough to rattle glass.

Sage jerked back from the table. Seb's pen dropped. Pauline's Loa drove against her skin like a drumline.

Zinnia was awake.

And everything that had been circling turned toward her.

Nine

The clearing hadn't recovered.

Neither had Zinnia.

Her heartbeat didn't match her body.

It was too fast. Too big for her ribs.

Every thud of the mark came out of sync, knocking the rhythm off-line.

She tried to breathe. Her lungs sent a *bugger-off* signal.

Heat gathered in her palms. In her throat. Behind her eyes.

She pushed herself upright. Her hands sank into ripped soil that still held the shape of where she'd fallen.

The world felt too much, too loud, too close, too everything.

Her vision dragged when she turned her head, lagging behind her by a fraction that made her stomach pitch.

"Okay," she rasped. The word tore on the way out. "What the actual hell did I just do?"

She felt like she'd been dragged through the universe's worst idea of a factory reset. This definitely rivalled being sucked through the portal and thrown back in time.

In fact, this shit won by a landslide.

She needed a coffee. Generously laced with good ole Irish.

Better still—a big arse tub of chocolate ice cream and someone to tell her what she'd just broken.

Lilly sat a few feet away, frozen between reaching for her and not daring to. Her own mark trembled against her skin, the aftershock still moving through her. The kind that comes from holding a line no one had held in decades—if ever.

She watched Zinnia the way she'd imagined doing for years.

Every rise of her daughter's chest tore straight through her.

She's burning through the world, and I wasn't there to teach her a damn thing.

She shoved the guilt deeper and let it bite.

Divina flopped down behind them.

Her mind spat the truth before she filtered it:

This is exactly why angels don't get assigned to prophecy brats.

One minute they're human, the next they're rewriting natural law and I'm supposed to pretend this is within workplace guidelines.

Zinnia dragged her eyes to Lilly—because the universe enjoyed a good emotional sucker punch. "I'd appreciate an explanation, because pretending this is normal is not gonna fly."

The mark roared again.

Zinnia gritted her teeth.

"And heads up—I don't feel enlightened. I feel like the magic equivalent of a grenade missing the safety pin."

Lilly absorbed it—not physically, but in the centre of herself.

She's terrified and I did this. I left her in the dark.

"Zinnia, you are slowly settling. The power will—"

"Will what?" The question ripped out of her, hot and impossible to leash. "Decide I'm worthy? Decide it's bored? Decide to stop playing hacky-sack with my organs? Because honestly, *Mum*—" the word hit her own ribs harder than the awakening did, "—the customer service on this bloodline is bullshit."

Divina barked a short laugh before she could help it.

Yeah, this feral kid's gonna survive.

She watched the light around Zinnia's throat.

"She's not stabilised. You two need to wrap this up, because she's going to blow the whole damn sha-bang if she keeps spiralling."

Zinnia braced her hands on her knees, head hanging, chin resting on her chest.

That would be the understatement of the century.

"Spiralling? I think you mean fucking losing it."

Her vision skipped.

"I can feel everything." The confession broke loose before she could stop it. "The ground humming. The trees listening. The whole damn world staring at me and I don't know what the hell to do with any of it."

Lilly inched closer cautiously, reading the swell of power from Zinnia's body the way one read a storm about to break. "You don't have to know yet, you only have to allow."

Zinnia looked up at her then, eyes burning. "Allow? I can literally feel time opening. Past. Future. Shit that I have no idea about."

"I know, but you need to go with it, stop fighting it."

The world shifted enough to remind her it wasn't done with her.

She gripped the dirt, grounding herself before it dragged her under again.

Divina swore under her breath. "I was not properly informed about the hazards of this assignment."

Zinnia forced her head up, panting. "That makes two of us. What's happening to me?"

Lilly lowered herself onto her knees in front of her. "Your power is learning you. You're learning it. It's a negotiation."

Zinnia barked a laugh with zero humour in it. "My arse it is. It feels like it kicked the door in and claimed squatters' rights."

"I'm right here. I'm not letting you go."

"You don't get to lose me twice, mother."

The ground heaved again.

Light spilled from Zinnia's neck.

She clenched her jaw, fighting the pull rising under her skin. "Something's watching." A shadow brushed her awareness in a way nothing human ever could. "I think I'm being hunted."

Divina's head snapped toward the tree line, instincts spiking.

This just keeps getting better.

"Yeah. I feel it too. And if it's who I think it is—we're out of time."

Zinnia swallowed. "Brinnan?"

"Brinnan," Lilly confirmed, quiet and certain. "And he's not the only one."

***

The shock rolled through Ashwick Vale.

Animals went wild.

Chickens burst from their coops.

Dogs dropped to their bellies and whimpered.

The cattle scattered across the fields, breaking hedges and trampling crops.

Inside the village square, the church bell swung once—untouched.

The sound rang through the square.

Mothers froze mid-step. A child dropped her doll.

Every villager felt it.

Witchcraft.

Jonas Hale—witch finder by oath, survivor by spite—jerked upright from the stool he'd been perched on. The tremor hit him straight in the spine.

His hand closed around the pendant at his throat.

That was power. The likes of which he had never felt.

He swept his gaze across the square.

Old Widow Crampton clutched her rosary so hard the beads snapped.

The baker dropped his tray of rolls without noticing.

Jonas felt the second wave before it came.

He braced.

The surge tore through him, rattling his teeth, lighting every nerve with the echo of something vile. The earth answered it—soil shifting, roots forcing upward in restless coils.

This was no common witch.

He barked an order without looking at who he addressed. "Fetch the others."

Boots scattered in different directions.

Jonas lifted his face to the tree line bordering the village. A faint wash of gold spread through the trunks.

His skin tightened along his arms.

A corner of him—buried beneath scripture and scar tissue—felt something closer to awe.

He crushed it flat.

His journey as a hunter had begun when he was a boy. Dragged along behind his father with the rest of the village.

The woman hadn't looked like a monster.

But that was part of the witchcraft, being able to walk amongst ordinary folk and pass as one.

She'd looked small. Barefoot. Terrified.

Begged for water before she begged for God.

Someone had shouted that she'd cursed the crops.

Someone else swore she'd spoiled a child in the womb.

No one agreed on what she'd done.

Jonas remembered the screams, as the fire consumed her.

Remembered the smell of burning flesh.

That night, he learned the lesson that he lived by.

When power appears, stamp it out.

He checked the weight at his belt—knife, rope, iron enough to make him feel righteous.

The third strike came.

Strong enough to bow the tops of the trees.

Jonas staggered.

Every hunter in the region would feel that.

Every ward.

Every creature that fed on magic.

The witch wasn't hiding.

She was blazing.

And that made her easier to find.

This was what he'd trained for.

What he was born for.

"Get the torches," Jonas commanded. "Get the stakes ready."

No one argued.

The villagers poured into the street.

All terrified.

***

The power under Zinnia's skin didn't ebb; it reorganised.

Tightened.

Paid attention.

Every instinct she had screamed that remaining still was a mistake.

Awareness spread outward whether she wanted it to or not.

Beyond the trees.

Beyond the slope of the vale.

Thin impressions brushed her senses—weapons, sweat, leather pulled tight in anxious hands.

Too many points of attention coming in fast.

They had felt her.

The understanding clicked into place, quiet and irreversible.

Staying here was not an option.

Lilly felt the shift at the same time. Zinnia's magic wasn't erupting anymore.

It was aligning.

Mapping exits.

Pulling at distances like doors left half open.

Divina widened her reach, angelic perception stretching beyond mortal range.

Minds tipped from fear into action.

Torches were pulled from hooks.

Boots found roads.

They were already being boxed in.

Hunters. As in plural.

Zinnia dragged in a breath and forced the power down. It wasn't enough to mute it. She needed to buy some time.

I've turned this place into a bloody beacon.

"We can't stay here."

The words came out even despite the chaos clawing at her insides.

Lilly nodded.

Divina tracked another flicker at the edge of her perception and filed it under *immediate action required.*

Move or be surrounded.

And she was absolutely not fighting a mob of witch-burning zealots before breakfast.

Zinnia shifted her weight and nearly triggered another explosion before wrenching it back under her skin, swearing under her breath as the mark burned in warning.

"We need to cloak that magic. Now. Playtime's over."

"You think I'm not trying, blondie? Give a girl a break."

"I said *we*. Stop bellyaching and stand still."

Divina stepped in close and unfurled her wings. The feathers lit with precise runic patterns. She folded them around Zinnia, enclosing them both, shutting the clearing out.

Warmth sank into Zinnia instantly, easing the frantic edge of the storm inside her.

Her power sank into semi-obedience.

Her shoulders sagged. Tears slipped free before she could stop them.

Divina's eyes were closed now, murmuring in a language Zinnia didn't recognise, hands holding her arms firmly.

When it ended, the wings withdrew. The light dimmed.

"This won't last, but it'll keep us hidden long enough to move."

Divina did not enjoy how slim that margin felt.

Power this volatile hadn't crossed her path in centuries.

She'd seen warriors with less at stake crumble.

"Let's haul arse."

No one argued.

They stepped away from the centre of the clearing.

Behind them, the awakening finished burning through the clearing. What it left behind would linger.

Ahead, the forest stood indifferent.

And somewhere beyond it, men were already closing in.

***

Matthew didn't feel the hunters first.

He felt the forest *lying*.

Paths that had opened for him earlier now hesitated.

The old tracks beneath the leaves no longer agreed on which way they led.

Zinnia's power still rang through the vale—fainter now, folded inward, but unmistakable to anyone who knew how to listen. It tugged at him from somewhere ahead.

Thank God, the lass was still thinking.

Jagged emotions washed over him.

Matthew paused at a shallow ravine and let his awareness drift.

He tasted iron on the air.

Old prayers muttered with clenched teeth.

Fear pretending to be courage.

Too many heartbeats for a single patrol.

Someone competent had organised them.

Jonas. And that annoyed him.

He'd wrapped his cruelty in method and called it discipline.

And lasted longer than he should have.

Matthew shifted his stance and felt the land answer, slow and resentful. The vale had never liked hunters. Never liked men who brought fire and destruction into places that survived on ambiguity.

Matthew let the shape of himself blur—enough that a human eye would slide away from him rather than land.

Voices drifted closer.

Excited in that brittle way men got when they thought God was watching.

Idiots.

He slipped downhill, boots barely touching earth, and brushed a hand against the bark of an oak that remembered older bargains. The tree groaned softly, roots tightening, ground subtly re-angling itself.

The first hunter hit it moments later.

A curse split the air as a man went down hard, weapon clattering, fear breaking rank. The sound rippled through the group.

Someone swore. Someone else hesitated.

Matthew didn't smile.

This wasn't sport.

This was containment.

He moved again, crossing their flank without crossing their sight.

Confusion bloomed.

Orders contradicted one another.

Someone shouted about signs that made no sense.

Excellent.

He felt a brief flare of attention from somewhere deeper in the woods.

Zinnia.

She felt him too.

Hold on, lass. Just a little longer.

Matthew reached further this time, threading probability through the hunt. A wrong turn here. A fallen tree there. Footprints leading nowhere. Echoes that didn't belong to any voice present.

The hunters spread thinner, losing cohesion.

One group pulled north, chasing a certainty that didn't exist. Another stalled, arguing.

Jonas—felt the loss of control and hardened against it.

Control was his religion.

Losing it pissed him off.

Matthew adjusted.

He let himself be *almost* seen.

A silhouette between trunks. A movement too deliberate to be animal.

Jonas latched onto it instantly.

Come on you scoundrel, here I am.

Matthew withdrew quickly, leading him away from the others, deeper into the tangle where the vale grew old and unfriendly. Where roots hid bones and paths closed without explanation.

Behind him, the hunt fractured completely.

Ahead of him, Zinnia's signature—still volatile, still dangerous, but moving.

He could work with moving.

NINE

Matthew vanished into the green, drawing iron and fire and righteous stupidity with him.

He'd bought her time. She'd have to decide what to do with it.

Ten

"There are places that do not hide you.
They remember you."
— Fragment from a Veilwalker field journal (author unknown)

Zinnia stopped walking because the ground stopped agreeing with her feet.

The sensation rolled up through her soles, resolute and unhurried.

This wasn't random.

Her mark answered with a low throb, a private confirmation. Alignment achieved. *Congratulations, Gateborn. Please proceed to your doom.*

Something tugged—not at her body, but at the narrow inner ledge where everything now seemed to queue up before becoming real.

Thought.

Memory.

Choice.

Time brushed along her inner axis in crooked, ugly layers.

She felt fear that wasn't hers.

Regret that hadn't happened yet.

A certainty that if she took three more steps the wrong way, someone would die.

Possibly her.

Which felt unfair, frankly, given the week she was having.

She turned, scanning the trees.

The forest had closed ranks behind them. Branches knitted tight where they'd passed, leaves settling into places they had not occupied moments before. The land preferred they not be found.

Ahead, the ground dipped, shallow at first, then steeper.

A crease in the earth, thin and dark, its contours too clean for chance.

Stone showed through the soil in a way that felt purposeful.

That hadn't been there a minute ago.

Or had it?

She knew this place.

Which was impressive, considering she had never been here, had never lived in this time.

Wasn't that a complete headfuck.

Behind her eyes, something fixed into position.

"There," slipped out of her, startling her.

She had no idea she was going to speak.

Apparently her mouth was now taking orders from a department she hadn't even met.

Lilly followed her line of sight and stopped short.

She couldn't see what Zinnia was responding to, not in any clear form, but something shifted all the same. The section ahead of them behaved differently. The closer Zinnia looked, the heavier the moment became, as though the earth itself had leaned back and folded its arms.

Divina felt it immediately.

Her instincts reordered without conscious input, ancient hierarchies aligning. Whatever lay ahead wasn't broadcasting power.

This was a place that had already decided who was allowed to notice it.

Zinnia stepped forward.

The strange thing was how much better that felt. The riot inside her didn't vanish, but it stopped tripping over itself. The closer she moved, the less the world demanded her attention. Thoughts that had been stacking on top of one another finally spread out.

The cut in the earth revealed itself as she approached.

Roots curled back from the opening as if they'd been asked to make room.

Stone emerged.

Black onyx veining the rock, quartz splintered through it in irregular lines that refused symmetry.

Zinnia slowed at the entrance.

Her power recognised the terrain and reined itself in.

In a way that felt almost respectful.

That was new.

Behind her, Lilly's stomach dropped.

Not fear for what waited inside—fear for what kind of design responded to her daughter like that. This wasn't shelter built to hide the vulnerable. This was architecture meant to *work with* what scared the world.

Divina let out a single breath.

Angels despised places like this. Not because they were hidden, but because they were honest about the danger.

Without pausing to ask herself why, Zinnia lifted her hand.

Something rearranged behind her eyes.

Gaps. Angles. Places where the world could be persuaded to look elsewhere.

She understood it the way one understands balance before falling: instinctive, unarguable.

Her fingers moved.

The air responded.

The cave's opening dulled at the edges, light losing interest in it, attention sliding away as if guided by a polite but firm hand. Anyone looking directly at it would see nothing worth noticing. A smudge of stone. A trick of dusk. The sort of thing the mind corrected and forgot.

Zinnia stepped forward.

Crossing the threshold felt like being removed from a room where everyone had been talking at once. The noise didn't vanish—it simply no longer belonged to her. The inward strain that had gripped her since the awakening began to ease.

Her mark sank.

The gold deepened, the heat retreating into something quieter, something that listened before it answered. For the first time since her power had torn itself awake, her thoughts lined up instead of bouncing off each other.

Halle-fuck'n-lujah.

We may survive today after all.

Behind them, the men continued in pursuit, intent marching forward in boots and prayers—but the sound skimmed past the cave's mouth without catching.

Lilly followed her daughter across the threshold.

The moment she stepped inside, the panic she'd been holding at bay morphed into something rawer. Relief hurt more than fear ever had. Her hand rose to her chest, fingers digging in. Aware with painful clarity of how close she'd come to losing her daughter again—and how even now that possibility was an ever-present concern.

Divina lingered at the mouth, watching the concealment hold.

Good enough to buy time.

Divina disliked relying on that phrase. It tended to expire at the worst possible moment.

She stepped inside and tranquillity filled her.

Unexpected and a much-needed respite.

Zinnia's muscles let go as the world finally stopped clawing at her.

"Okay, this should keep us off the radar long enough to figure out what comes next."

And far beyond the tree line, in places that paid attention to disturbances like this, something old adjusted its calculations.

Interest piqued.

***

Jonas Hale did not slow the hunt.

Slowing implied uncertainty, and uncertainty was how mistakes were made.

Instead, he shortened the distance between men, clipped commands down to essentials, forced the line forward.

He reclaimed what had been peeled away from the formation, pulling stragglers back into alignment with a glare and a wordless expectation of obedience. A few had arrived shaken, swearing blind they'd followed orders only to find themselves alone among trees that refused to look familiar.

Jonas did not ask what they'd seen.

Men responded to structure.

If the land had forgotten that truth, it would remember soon enough.

The ground continued in its contradictions.

Tracks overlapped where no boots should have crossed.

Prints doubled back without turning, impressions fading and reappearing as if the earth couldn't decide on which story it wanted to tell.

Jonas crouched and worked his fingers into the dirt.

He rose swiftly, irritated.

The ground wasn't the problem.

Interference was.

Too many men. Too much noise.

Panic inventing patterns and calling them signs.

"Hold the line."

The words should have snapped the moment back into place.

They didn't.

The dog balked first—growling, hackles raised, teeth bared at air that refused to justify the reaction.

One of the younger men laughed nervously; it died halfway through.

Someone crossed themselves and whispered a prayer meant for storms or childbirth.

Jonas didn't turn.

This was what came of relying on villagers who mistook fear for faith.

They lacked the discipline to recognise resistance when it dressed itself up as confusion.

The path narrowed. Then split. Then rejoined again.

Trees leaned where they hadn't leaned before, branches encroaching into space that had been clear not five minutes prior. The forest wasn't blocking them outright.

It was guiding them badly.

Jonas's anger cooled, giving way to understanding.

This was design.

The witches weren't just hiding *in* the forest.

It was helping them.

He recoiled.

Land was supposed to submit to godliness, not interfere with it.

He stood very still, aware of the men behind him adjusting their grips, glancing at one another, waiting for direction. Someone muttered about circling back. Someone else suggested the witch had slipped into hell itself.

Cowards always reached for spectacle when reason demanded endurance.

Jonas turned.

"We're close."

The lie fit neatly into place. He believed it enough to make it useful. The land resisted him, yes—but resistance proved proximity. Whatever twisted the paths, whatever bent the ground into riddles, it had done so *because they were nearing something worth protecting*.

That was what God wanted him to see.

And Jonas Hale had never failed to answer a calling.

***

Matthew felt the hunt bend before he saw it break.

That was always the moment that mattered—the instant before men noticed the rules had changed.

When confidence wobbled.

When conviction lost its footing and blame began looking for a target.

He'd pushed hard.

Not recklessly—never that.

But enough that the land had taken note. Enough that the Veil had leaned close, curious, like it always did when he threaded himself too deeply through probability.

He tasted it now, metallic at the back of his throat.

Ah. Bugger.

The vale didn't enjoy being bent this many times in quick succession. It tolerated guidance. It resented coercion. And Matthew had done something closer to the latter when he fractured the hunt earlier—split paths, inverted intention, fed the men enough to keep them moving in the wrong direction.

Necessary.

Still costly.

He slowed, letting himself pull back from the land.

The forest objected, then relented.

Behind him, Jonas was reorganising.

Matthew didn't need to look to know that.

He felt it in the way the hunt re-weighted itself. The man was competent in the ugliest possible way—he believed order was moral. Believed suffering was proof of righteousness.

Men like that didn't stop.

They adapted.

Which meant Matthew had to.

He let himself exist a little more solidly for half a breath.

Jonas noticed.

The hunter's attention swung toward the wrong cluster of trees with gratifying speed.

Matthew slid sideways through the undergrowth, pulling the man's intent with him, stretching it thin. He didn't hide the trail this time. Didn't scramble the signs. He laid them deliberately—broken branches at the right height, disturbed moss, the faintest echo of warmth where he'd paused.

Come on then, ye clever bastard.

The land resisted again, giving a warning rather than a rebuke.

I know, I know. Give me a bit longer mother.

He felt it then—the moment Jonas crossed from *hunting witches* to *hunting something else*. The shift wasn't conscious, but it was profound. The hunter's fear changed flavour.

Less righteous. More alert.

Predators recognised other predators by the tells.

Matthew almost felt sorry for him.

Almost.

He let the illusion end abruptly—tracks ended in nothing, the sense of presence vanished like it had never existed at all.

Behind him, the hunt fell apart again. Orders contradicted. Cohesion bled away.

Jonas would recover.

But not fast enough.

Matthew turned his attention forward.

There.

Zinnia's signature had changed. It wasn't flooding the vale anymore. The difference registered immediately.

Smart girl.

He followed it without hesitation, aware of the line he'd just crossed. He'd used more of himself than he liked. Slipped closer to habits he'd sworn off centuries ago.

Old habits. Older debts.

The Veil stirred, pleased.

He would pay for that later.

For now, there was a newly awakened Gateborn in a cave full of stones that knew how to keep secrets—and a hunter who'd realised the world was deeper, darker, and far less obedient than he'd been taught.

Matthew vanished into the green once more, leaving Jonas Hale with questions God had no intention of answering.

And ran toward the girl who had made the world sit up and take notice.

***

The women sat. Each lost in their own thoughts.

Backs to stone, spaced far enough apart to breathe without touching, held in that fragile pause where survival hasn't yet softened into trust.

The black-veined stone threaded through the walls radiated a soothing frequency.

It sank into their bones and told the danger to sit the fuck down.

Zinnia slid her spine lower against the rock, legs stretched out. Eyes closed.

The peace sliding into her after the shitshow she'd just lived through was overdue.

Lilly sat opposite her, knees drawn to her chest, arms wrapped around her legs. She realised she had helicopter mother written all over her. All she wanted to do was wrap her daughter up in bubble wrap and make sure nothing touched her again.

Or send anything that did into the nastiest oblivion she could find.

She was a Gateborn after all, powerful in her own right—yet her power was nothing compared to her daughter's.

So much for diluted.

Apparently, hybrid meant explosive.

She was so damn proud of Zinnia. Worse for wear right now, no denying that. They all were.

But she was strong. Sharp-tongued, unapologetic, honest. Lilly loved her all the more for it.

The rush of it nearly unbalanced her, too big and too sudden to process.

Divina had claimed the wall to Zinnia's left, her boots planted, head tipped back against the stone. The second her body made contact, the hyper-vigilance she hadn't been able to switch off finally powered down.

Oh, blessed be Mother Nature and her rare moments of competence.

The crystals embedded in the cave walls throbbed faintly—onyx swallowing light, quartz bending it—granting permission rather than illumination.

They were being held, softly, gently. Giving them somewhere to regroup and stabilise.

Zinnia dragged a hand down her face and opened her eyes. "The only thing left to make this joint perfect would be a cup of coffee, served with a chocolate croissant."

Lilly's mouth twitched despite herself. Zinnia clearly didn't realise that as a witch with immense power one could conjure exactly what one wants. "Darling your wish is my command."

Lilly rested her palm against the stone, eyes closing.

"By flame and grind, let coffee run hot,
With honey drawn sweet, a golden drop.
Let cream come thick, smooth, and bright,
And warm chocolate croissants appear in sight."

A battered iron pot appeared onto the stone between them, steam curling from its mouth, rich and dark. Cups followed. Cream. Honey. And finally—warm chocolate croissants wrapped in linen.

Zinnia's mouth hung open. The scent of the coffee made her mouth water. For one dizzy second, she felt what it might have been like to grow up with a mother who could make things better on command. She looked at Lilly and grinned. "Holy shit, can I do that too?"

Lilly laughed. "Yes, honey, you can."

Divina huffed. "Right now, I don't recommend it. You're more likely to summon the whole bloody coffee plantation."

She reached for a pastry. "Still. As the ever-grateful angel that I am—this is divine."

Zinnia poured the coffee and handed out the cups. Each added their own creamer and sweetener, blissfully aware that this moment of comfort could not—and would not—last.

"So can we build a fire too?" Zinnia asked around a mouthful of pastry.

Seriously. She had never tasted anything finer.

Mood: improving rapidly.

Divina looked around. Someone, at some point, had stacked old wood against the back wall—far enough in that a flame could breathe without choking.

She sparked it with a flick of her fingers. The flame caught small and unwavering, curling upward without smoke, light dancing across the crystals and disappearing into the cavern's vast throat.

The cave ran deeper than the hillside could account for.

Zinnia stared past the firelight, senses brushing into the dark beyond.

"So just to clarify—this isn't, like, a murder cave. Right?"

Lilly was sipping her black coffee. She tilted her head, feeling into it. "It's… happy we're here. Happy to help."

"That's a relief, I think I'm traumatised out."

Divina laughed outright then. "And we're right there with you."

The fire crackled softly.

Zinnia could feel the timelines closing in now that the noise had died down.

She decided exploration was not a good idea.

"I can still feel them," she admitted. "The… options. How things can go wrong."

Lilly's heart sank. This was an enormous responsibility to carry for the trained let alone the untrained. "How many?"

Zinnia hesitated. Her mouth twisted. "All of them."

And not one of them came with a solution. Just outcomes stacked like cards, waiting for her to lose the game.

Divina dropped the humour.

Her perception expanded past the physical.

Probabilities sorted themselves into viable and fatal.

The margin for error was minimal.

Dear heaven above, this was a new kind of Gateborn.

"Well," Divina's tone was brisk in a way that tried to pretend this wasn't horrifying, "good news is, you're not spiralling."

"Bad news?"

"You're cataloguing."

Zinnia groaned and tipped her head back against the stone. "I'm not a fan of this upgrade."

Lilly watched her. She wanted to apologise. For the blood. For the legacy. For the dark that had found her daughter so easily.

Instead, she said the only thing that mattered.

"You're not alone in it."

Zinnia opened her eyes and looked at both women.

"I know. And I'm really bloody grateful."

The fire pushed heat into the cavern, light moving across the rock in uneven sweeps.

For now, there were no demands.

Above, beyond the stone and roots and redirected attention, men with torches argued.

And Matthew made his way to the cave.

Eleven

"Those who write the rules rarely bleed by them."
— *Notes recovered from the Scriptorium archives, author redacted*

Present Day

The Scriptorium was a hive of activity.

Samthrax had whipped up lattes. Seraphina had arranged a table of snacks. No one named the symbolism, but it hung in the air anyway— normalcy as a shield.

Ideas ricocheted.

Half-finished, overlapping, abandoned mid-sentence as consequences caught up with them.

Now that they had a trace on Zinnia, the question wasn't *if* they could get her back.

It was *how many rules they were willing to break to do it.*

What they did know:

Tracking her the right way would announce them.

Not only to the Council, but to anything listening along the Veil's seams.

Tracking her the wrong way would get them all killed.

Or worse—leave them alive long enough to regret it.

Tracking her quietly… was their only real option.

Quietly didn't mean safe. It meant survivable if luck held and nobody hesitated.

"I'm thinking not sanctioned paths," Samthrax offered. "This cannot get caught up in red tape bullshit."

The demon in him was already halfway down three illegal corridors, tail giving away how much he liked the idea.

Killian considered Samthrax's words. "Fair point."

He stood at the edge of the locator array, attention split across a dozen probabilities that wouldn't resolve.

The trace they'd caught was real.

Zinnia wasn't static. She was moving. Adapting.

Which meant time was not on their side.

Sanctioned paths would light up brighter than a flare—get flagged and wrapped in enough magical admin to choke a dragon.

Unsanctioned routes were far quicker.

They were also the reason three entire retrieval teams had memorial plaques in the outer hall.

Seraphina didn't look up.

"Have to say, I'm with you guys."

She sat on the floor, biscuit in hand, chewing slowly while her mind tore ahead.

Loud meant exposed. Wrong meant dead. There wasn't a version of this that didn't take a chunk out of something—they just had to decide what they were willing to lose.

"I'm not opposed to bending rules." She brushed crumbs from her fingers on her jeans. "Especially the ones written by people who won't be on the ground bleeding when they fail."

Saffron caught herself enjoying that.

Rules had never saved the people who mattered. They only decided who got blamed afterward.

"That's new."

Seraphina grinned over at her mother. "I've grown."

Pauline recognised the turn and very nearly laughed.

Well, look at that. Took reality misbehavin' for people to realise permission was nothin' but another leash. Gateborn and Broussard rising in the same girl. The Veil twitchin'. And suddenly nobody pretendin' this was up for debate.

"You trace her proper, and you'll light up every hungry thing between here and whatever year she's landin' in. Not just the Council. Not just the Veil. All of it."

She let that hang.

"But if you follow what's leftover—the brush of her, the things stickin' to her—then we've got a chance."

Interest kicked up behind Samthrax's eyes.

That was clever.

Tracking residue didn't trigger the systems.

It was messy. Illegal-adjacent and absolutely his wheelhouse.

"Well, I'll be damned." Grinning now. "That's some premium-grade mischief, Grandma."

Pauline stared him down with the kind of look that had cut bigger things in half.

"Pauline'll do."

Samthrax chuckled and tipped an imaginary hat.

Growth was important. Personal development mattered.

But poking people? That was sacred tradition.

Sage was elated.

They had finally moved from theory into locked direction.

This was dangerous, elegant application that made her brain light up even as every sensible instinct listed the ways it could end badly.

A sliver of dread curled beneath the thrill.

Wanting it this much probably voided some universal warranty.

"And if the Council realises what we're doing?"

Killian had already followed every branch, measured every failure, and chosen the consequences he could live with. The rest were discarded.

"They won't until we've already moved, I'll make sure of it."

No one pretended there was still a safer option waiting to be discovered.

This was strategy. And commitment.

They would accept the reckoning later.

Sebastian was mid-thought—half-listening, half-planning—when the now familiar skin crawl began nudging in with quiet glee.

If you let me take the wheel, we can get back your friend. All you have to do is step back. I'll do the rest.

The voice slipped through the cracks of his mind, smooth and confident.

Don't pretend you're not curious.

Sebastian kept his face still. Kept his hands still. Anyone watching would see a kid listening. *Fuck off. You're not getting the wheel. Not ever.*

It pushed back hard, anger spiking at the refusal.

Then it was gone, leaving behind a silence Sebastian didn't trust for a second.

Samthrax noticed immediately. Darkness recognised its own.

Kid's carrying a huge monkey on his back. And not the fun kind.

Samthrax filed the detail away, already tracking the moment when it would matter. The kind of moment where there wouldn't be time to plan, only choose.

For now, none of that mattered.

Zinnia was alive, within reach, and that outranked everything.

***

Matthew nearly walked past the cave.

Not because he missed it—because the forest nudged him to keep going.

Everything around him encouraged motion, avoidance, forgetful-

114

ness.

He stopped. Irritation lodged under his skin.

The cave had told the land to lie, and the land had obeyed.

He stepped through the threshold and felt the listening quiet gather around him.

The crystal-threaded stone held a tone slightly beneath annoyance, mapping him unapologetically. He let it. He wasn't here to dominate; he was here because a girl had torn herself open to time, held on through sheer force, and kept the world mostly intact.

He was also here because he wanted to kiss some bloody sense into her.

Zinnia knew the moment Matthew arrived.

Her power recognised his but couldn't pinpoint it—more like slotting him into the new, too-large architecture of herself.

Definitely Veil residue clinging to him.

That was intriguing.

Oh, this man is so much more than he lets on.

Matthew stopped just inside the firelight, hands loose, stance neutral in the way of someone who knew exactly what he was choosing not to be.

"Lasses."

Divina had never been so glad to see Matthew, though she'd chew glass before admitting it out loud. They were barely holding the line here, and the man's training came with a long list of inconveniently useful applications.

She flicked a wing half-out in greeting. "Woodsman, took your sweet arse time. Nice of you to join us."

Matthew laughed. He didn't often get welcomed with both sarcasm and visible relief.

"Well now," he drawled, "when a Gateborn wakes an' cries her name to every bastard carryin' fire, I reckon traipsin' bold's a fine way t'get smoked."

He shifted his gaze to Lilly. "I'd hoped ye were still breathin'."

He glanced between mother and daughter. Noting the unresolved tension. That confirmed Zinnia now knew her lineage.

Lilly gave him a small nod. She was genuinely pleased to see him, even if his presence now meant things were worse than she'd hoped. She didn't know exactly what he was, but she'd always known enough not to ask.

He returned the courtesy.

Of more immediate concern—he was very obviously attracted to her daughter.

She didn't quite know how she felt about that.

Zinnia, for her part, was giving off sparks of mutual interest and exactly none of the caution her mother thought the situation warranted.

Lilly grinned, enough to make Matthew mildly uncomfortable.

"Good to see you, Matt."

Zinnia blinked at the familiarity.

Her brain caught on the name, the ease, the shared history.

My god. Does everyone but me know my bloody mother?

The past kept popping up, and she was always the last one to read the map.

Matthew barely had time to recover before Zinnia turned her attention on him directly.

"How'd you find us, pretty boy? This cave doesn't announce itself to outsiders."

Of all the descriptors he'd been assigned—dangerous, suspicious, magical pain in the arse—pretty boy had never made the cut.

He coughed, adjusted his coat, and gave her a flat look.

"Ye'd be right. I'm no outsider."

He didn't elaborate. No need to complicate things further right now.

"The rest can wait. Every zealot in the valley's lookin' yer way, lass. I'd sooner not end the week on a pyre."

That would be a crappy end to an already traumatic time travel experience.

Zinnia let the thought slip out before she could filter it. If she didn't laugh, she might scream.

And screaming felt harder to recover from.

"I'll be honest, spontaneous combustion sounds highly unappealing. Any alternative suggestions that involve fewer flames and slightly more not-dying?"

If humour was the glue holding her together, she was gonna apply that shit generously.

Everything inside her body wanted to move. But movement meant exposure, and exposure meant torches, and torches had a worrying history of ending in agony and crisping.

Divina turned in a slow circle, weighing the space with her usual lack of ceremony. The cave was responding to Zinnia. It wasn't hostile and that worked for now.

"My vote? We don't run blind. We stay put long enough to rest, then we plan how to get Miss supercharged home and survive the journey."

Zinnia snorted.

Lilly didn't laugh.

She was too busy bracing against the feelings rising in her—part fear, part awe, part impossible hope.

Home.

The word sat in her chest like something she'd lost—and accidentally found again.

She hadn't let herself want anything in decades. Wanting had led to loss, and loss had nearly ended her.

But this—this felt right.

"I'm with the angel. If we walk out now, we die dramatically."

She locked eyes with Zinnia. Her daughter was standing, barely, in the middle of something far too big for her—but she wasn't giving in.

"We wait. But we wait smart."

Zinnia leaned back against the stone.

Her body welcomed the contact. She tried not to think about how good it felt to be recognised without being consumed.

The crystal threads didn't stop working, either. Whatever they were doing to the world outside, it was still happening. She didn't have to push to notice it as it slipped between her thoughts.

The wards were active at the lowest level, minimal but effective. Beyond that, more waited, pending instructions.

"So," she ventured, mostly to stop her brain spiralling off into timelines it refused to explain, "if we're waiting smart, I'm guessing that doesn't involve me improvising anything with a dramatic glow and a steep learning curve."

Divina turned to her. Approval passed over her face with all the subtlety of a clipboard check.

"Correct. You improvising right now is how continents get rebranded. Last time someone winged it, Atlantis got a bit soggy."

Zinnia raised an eyebrow. "That was real?"

"Parts of it still are. Mostly underwater. Not our best day."

Zinnia filed that away under *do not screw up that majorly*.

Lilly watched Zinnia, cataloguing every small adjustment—the way she tested words before releasing them, the way her perception kept brushing the boundaries without tipping over. Zinnia was still keyed up, still on edge—but she wasn't drowning. That alone felt miraculous.

"We need subtlety," Lilly added, grounding herself in the practical. "Listening wards. Delay wards. Wards that essentially bullshit."

Zinnia grinned.

"Works for me."

The idea slid into place with disturbing ease.

She could sense where the cave's patience ended, where it would tolerate interference and where it would take offence.

"I can… feel where they'd go. I'm not pulling anything, just—seeing empty sockets."

Divina tilted her head, checking Zinnia's energy again. She was stabilising faster than expected.

"Then we wait a few more minutes. Let your system finish doing whatever catastrophic housekeeping it's halfway through. Then you show me the sockets, and I'll make sure nothing bites us in the arse."

Zinnia stretched her arms over her head, trying to loosen knots that had taken up permanent residence in her shoulders.

She thought of Matthew giving her a rub down.

So not the time Zin, concentrate.

"Right. Team effort. No triggering a jurisdictional inquiry."

"I'm still appealing the last one," Divina pointed to herself, "case in point."

Lilly allowed herself a smile at that. The two of them bickered like sisters.

Zinnia pushed her heels into the stone and sat up straighter, her senses loosening and spreading automatically.

The cave responded immediately—making room for exploration.

"Let's give this a whirl. I'm feeling optimistic."

Matthew stepped forward. "There's somethin' that must be done a'fore ye begin, lass." He clicked his fingers.

A gold field slammed around Zinnia.

Hard edges cut across the cave, lines carving themselves into a tight perimeter that boxed her in without touching her as symbols surfaced in quick succession, stacking until there was no room left for error. The construct finished forming with a final, decisive snap.

All three women gasped.

Matthew paced around her, boots scraping against the stone. Chanting in a tongue even Divina didn't track, syllables clear and precise. His hands rose only as much as needed, fingers adjusting the symbols by inches.

He never took his eyes off Zinnia.

Lilly froze. The final recognition hit too fast to hide.

Veilwalker.

That kind of magic didn't just walk free.

He was either one of the strongest allies they could ask for… or a catastrophic threat.

And it raised an entirely different question.

What the hell was he doing out of the Veil in 1695?

She didn't interrupt. The magic was holding, and the reaction from the cave was approval, not defence.

But her focus didn't leave him for a second.

Zinnia stayed perfectly still.

Her pulse absolutely didn't, and her magic leaned into his without asking.

Zero resistance, zero shame.

Apparently, it liked whatever he was doing.

Who was this man?

Matthew knew the moment was costing him. Every second he worked, more of what he was slipped into the open. Divina already knew. Lilly didn't. Not fully. Zinnia was too new to see it clearly, but that wouldn't last.

He would explain later. If they lived through the next hour.

He met Lilly's stare head-on.

"I'll tell ye all after. Know that I'm on yer side, and I need ye to trust me."

Lilly's magic pressed into his regardless, testing for fault lines, lies. She pushed harder.

He let her.

All she found was urgency, and honesty, he meant every word.

She turned to Divina, silent question already formed.

Divina nodded.

The tension bled out of Matthew's shoulders now that the immediate threat of two Gateborns turning on him had passed. One hybrid was already pushing his tolerance for risk. Two would have been deeply inconvenient.

"A'right, lass. Yer ready. I've settled yer workings to lower the risk o' disaster."

Zinnia's eyebrow crept upward.

Is that what that was?

Because it felt phenomenal.

God, imagine him in the sack.

Her brain immediately staged a full production involving bad decisions and historical costuming.

Matthew cleared his throat. Barely contained amusement flickered through the link.

Ah. I should likely tell ye—I can hear yer thoughts. It won't last. For now, we're linked till the wardin's done.

Heat flooded Zinnia's face. A warning would have been polite. Or humane. Or literally anything.

Next time you invade my head, try knocking. She fired back.

"Alright," she forced out loud. "Here we go."

Zinnia lifted her hands.

The section in front of her changed.

The cave's attention thinned in specific locations, openings becoming obvious all at once. Gaps where something could exist without resistance.

Places the world already expected to be occupied.

Matthew's focus tightened immediately.

He moved closer.

"Ye see 'em."

Not a question.

"Good. Don't fill 'em. Just acknowledge."

She nodded, hands still raised. The urge to act pressed hard, demanding release.

She ignored it.

Control first.

Manners mattered, she knew that instinctively.

The connection between them held.

And against her better judgement—

She didn't hate it.

Top of Form

Bottom of Form

Divina moved, wings half-manifested, eyes tracking the invisible architecture Zinnia was holding open. She paced the perimeter with professional suspicion, testing each pocket of nothingness with careful pressure. Some resisted. Some welcomed. One snapped.

"Hmmm." She rerouted it with a clear twist of intent. "That one's wired for deception. Leave it. It'll hand us to the Hunters."

Matthew gave a sound of agreement.

Lilly stayed back, watching the three of them work.

The problem wasn't what Matthew was doing.

It was how little the cave objected to him.

She could feel the Veil's fingerprint all over Matthew now.

Unmistakable once you knew what to look for.

The rules he wasn't bound by—exile or escape, it didn't matter.

You don't move between worlds and expect it to leave you untouched.

Zinnia exhaled and tightened her focus. Her hands made fine corrections, shaving the edges of what she was maintaining. The cave took the adjustment and did not object.

Matthew drew a breath through his teeth.

"Aye. That'll do it."

Her attention locked on him.

"Do what?"

"Make e'eryone nearby right certain they've better places to be."

That… sounded ideal.

The lattice stabilised without flare or flourish.

Outside, the movement changed—voices tripping over themselves, footsteps losing momentum.

Zinnia eased back against the stone. The charge in her bloodstream began to ebb, leaving her lightheaded.

"Please tell me that counts as subtle."

Divina folded her wings with a satisfied snap.

"Congratulations. You've successfully gaslit reality."

Lilly exhaled slowly. The vigilance she'd been running on since the forest drained out of her in one clean swoop.

"Now we can rest."

Matthew stepped back, severing the link. The absence hit harder than Zinnia expected.

"Aye, we rest." His eyes stayed on the dark beyond the firelight. "This has bought us more time only."

"And after?"

His mouth curled. The humour wasn't deep, but it was real.

"After, lass, we start breakin' rules properly."

The fire crackled.

The cave remained neutral.

And, for now, the valley lost interest.

Twelve

"The Between remembers those who take without permission.
It doesn't forgive them."
— *Veilway proverb, origin disputed*

1695

Brinnan emerged from the Between.

He didn't come from the front. That path was for bodies and panic.

He entered along the fault beneath the hillside, tracing the current of magic embedded in the rock—closed to anything it didn't recognise.

The back wall of the cave opened wide enough for him to pass.

The wards held their shape. The newest ones twitched—uncertain, testing for a category that fit him. The earlier workings did not react at all.

They knew his kind.

He crossed the threshold without sound.

The cave had begun adjusting itself around the girl. Stone angled subtly toward her. Light pooled where she sat. Space made allowances.

It had marked her as significant.

It did not extend that courtesy to him.

The difference registered in small ways—a thinning of warmth, a minute contraction in the walls, a reluctance in the air itself.

He stood beyond their range of notice and watched.

Zinnia had stopped resisting.

The magic running through her no longer met friction. It moved cleanly from thought to action, beginning to respond rather than overwhelm.

That was the shift that mattered.

Not power.

Participation.

The Veilwalker remained within striking distance. He would complicate matters. The magic in him wasn't ornamental—it was built for use.

The angel tracked constantly, her awareness sweeping in disciplined arcs. She did not relax even when she appeared to.

The mother had already committed to the long war. Her protections were not flashy; they were layered and deliberate, positioned to endure rather than dazzle.

Brinnan measured them all.

Competent. Dangerous.

Temporary.

None of it was unexpected. None of it changed the outcome.

Let them train her reflexes.

Let them give her vocabulary.

Let them mistake containment for mastery.

He would wait while they built her into something coherent.

Then he would remove the frame.

Patience was not passive. It was leverage.

When she finished integrating what she had become, he would take the whole of it—her power, her life. The imprint she left behind.

The Veil would not need to be conquered.

It would simply lack an alternative.

Outside, the zealots scraped for justification, hungry for a witch who would bleed.

All they needed was the right kind of trail.

A misplaced footprint.

A whisper carried in the wrong direction.

A sign that looked like proof to men already desperate for it.

He could leave that much behind.

Idiots were so easy to manipulate.

He turned from the chamber. The magic parted for him before he asked.

The cave let him go without resistance.

When he left, the cave swallowed the air.

And tried to forget what it had just let in.

***

Present Day

The jolt didn't announce itself. It moved up through the floor, humming into the soles of boots, sneakers, bare feet—everybody *felt* it.

"Shit." Killian looked across the room at Samthrax, who was staring too hard at the wall.

"You feel that?"

Samthrax didn't answer. His eyes rolled white as a fine filament slipped out of him—barely visible, searching, tasting the air.

When they snapped back into place, something feral flickered underneath.

"That came from the Between."

Everyone in the room spoke at once.

"Brinnan."

Killian's pulse spiked. Brinnan was the thorn he was itching to tweeze. His temple gave a traitorous throb. If this kept up, he wasn't going to stroke out—he was going to explode.

"He's found her."

Samthrax stood, pacing off the agitation that news left in his blood. Or maybe he'd had too much caffeine.

"Yep. Operation DEFCON Holy-Shit just went live."

Sage dragged the trace array back up. Fingers moving fast.

"He wasn't pinging. We would've seen it."

"He doesn't ping," Samthrax muttered, already plotting ten forms of demonic retribution. "Ascension wiped that out. He can shape his own visibility now. He could walk through a Council sanctum and they'd thank him for the intrusion."

Pauline closed the grimoire she'd been skimming.

"We got t' do somethin'."

"Agreed," Killian planted both hands on the table, knuckles whitening. Energy bounced off strategy. "We don't have time to—"

"Forget time bossman, we don't have the *tools*," Samthrax cut in.

"You try engaging Brinnan with trace spells and noble intent, and you'll be naming body parts for a coroner with no reference chart."

Silence followed that.

Seraphina turned to Samthrax. Already bracing for regret.

"You spent years in the Keep Sam. Is there anything down there that gets us what we need—without nuking the balance?"

Saffron choked. Not easy for a ghost.

"Have you lost your damn mind? There's a reason *our family* holds the key to the Shadowkeep. That place isn't a solution, it's the consequence."

Samthrax turned, shock plastered all over his face.

"Did you just call me Sam?"

Seraphina sighed skyward.

"Freudian slip."

She looked at her mother.

"Mum, I'm not letting Zinnia die because we're worried about upsetting family doctrine. Not happening."

Back to Samthrax.

"So, is there anything?"

He barked a laugh.

"There're a few things. I spent my incarceration getting very well acquainted with what your ancestors like to lock up."

He tapped a fang with one claw.

"But you're not gonna like what I suggest."

Saffron was done with patience.

"For god's sake, spit it out."

"The *Veilwatch Grimoire.*"

Saffron's reaction was immediate. Loud, and not subtle.

"You want to unleash that? Are you cracked? That book's not a shortcut—it's a blood offering with footnotes. And you expect us to trust *you* with that power out in the open?"

Samthrax snapped right back.

"For hell's sake, I have bled for this family. Protected every single one of you. And I still get treated like I'm trying to smuggle hell in through the basement. I'm *leashed.* I couldn't betray you if I wanted to."

He stepped forward, eyes burning red.

"And the worst part? Even if the leash broke, I'd still stay. Because for the first time in centuries, I feel like I'm *worth something.* Stop judging me for what I used to be. I'm not asking for forgiveness. I'm asking for *trust.*"

Sebastian surprised everybody by speaking up.

"He's right, Grams. He's earned that much."

Nobody spoke.

For a few stretched seconds, the room was lost in thought.

Seraphina stared at Samthrax across the table.

Of all the things to hit her, it was the memory of him trying to teach her demon poker last week—half-cheating, full charm, sleeves too loud to be legal.

She caught herself smiling. Bloody hell. He was growing on her.

Killian's tongue pressed against his molars.

Somewhere along the line, the demon had stopped being a liability and started feeling like one of them.

Trusted? Not quite.

But close enough that Killian felt the sting of that possibility, and it unsettled him.

Sage watched the way Sebastian looked at Samthrax. He'd already let the demon into his inner circle. And Seb would need someone soon. Someone who laughed at the dark.

And Samthrax, for all his bullshit, was the right fit.

Pauline eyed Samthrax. The kind of stare that could peel a soul apart if it had anything to hide. She found no lies, and that was good enough.

Saffron made an annoyed noise somewhere between a sigh and a curse, her incorporeal hands flaring out.

"Fine. But the second that book turns on us, I *will* possess someone long enough to end it."

Killian gave it a moment before stepping in.

"Someone explain this Grimoire. I've never seen it in any sanctioned archive."

"That's because it's unsanctioned," Samthrax offered, smug and unapologetic.

He *loved* that word. It sparkled with opportunity.

Killian sighed. Somewhere in the back of his mind, the Council protocol manual burst into flames.

"What's in it?"

He knew he'd dislike the answer.

Saffron replied with the tone of someone giving a warning label, not a list.

"Wards. Countermeasures. Spells scrapped when someone remembered we had morals.

And one tether spell. Experimental. Designed to link a caster to a soul signature—wherever they are. Whenever."

She looked at Samthrax like she could burn a hole through his face.

"And I assume *that's* why you recommended it."

Samthrax grinned, fangs catching the light.

"Damn right, Mumma Bellarose. It'll find her fast, like yesterday fast."

Seraphina watched her mother struggle with the need to slap ten shades of crimson off Samthrax.

Geezus did he have to be so openly irritating?

She rubbed her hands down her jeans, brain kicking hard against the consequences that were about to be invited upstairs.

"Alright then let's go get it."

If this was the only way to reach Zinnia before Brinnan did something irrevocable, legality was officially out the back door.

Seraphina turned, marched to the far end of the Scriptorium, and stopped in front of the bookshelf.

She pulled two books free and stepped back.

The shelf yawned open, revealing a staircase choked with old power—the kind that says 'enter here to die stupidly' in every horror film ever made.

She looked at Samthrax. "Come on."

He grinned. "After you, Princess Deathtrap."

She didn't need hand signals to flip him off. Her face did the job just fine.

The path down glowed faintly under Seraphina's steps, recognising her as the key.

Samthrax was humming *House of the Rising Sun*, badly.

She shot him a look.

"You could maybe not antagonise the jail while we're in it?"

"I'm not *antagonising*," he drawled over his shoulder, walking backwards down the stairs. "I'm radiating mutual respect."

She didn't respond.

He displayed his questionable survival skills on the daily.

The deeper they went, the more the walls changed.

Smooth gave way to etched.

Etched gave way to clawed.

Symbols older than written language curled up the stone, some pulsing in brief, twitching spasms as they passed.

The vault door came into view.

Seraphina placed her hand against the iron.

Lines twisted across its surface, smooth and deep. Each groove adjusted to her presence, recognising lineage before letting go.

The door opened without sound.

Samthrax stepped in first, heading straight for the back corner.

A pedestal table sat under a shroud of gloom. And on it—

The *Veilwatch Grimoire*.

The space around it buzzed louder than bees chasing honey.

Dozens of other objects lined the vault walls—trapped, cursed, angry—but none dared flicker toward it.

They knew better.

The Grimoire held a faint, unstable sheen, bound in something that wasn't quite leather, sealed in spells that refused to sit still.

Every time Seraphina looked directly at the cover, her vision snagged and blurred.

They really should've slapped a warning on it—may cause ocular seizures.

Samthrax placed one clawed hand millimetres above the surface.

"It knows we're here."

Seraphina stepped up beside him.

"Grab it."

"Don't boss me. I'm a demon, not your familiar."

"Seriously?"

"Sorry, I'm on edge."

He closed his hand around the Grimoire.

The pedestal didn't explode.

The ceiling stayed up.

No one turned into a swarm of snakes.

Samthrax exhaled with dramatic dignity, vaguely relieved.

He tucked the book under one arm and turned to her.

"See? Totally safe. Barely cursed."

Seraphina rolled her eyes.

"Let's hope you haven't just jinxed us."

They moved upstairs quickly, partly to escape the extreme creep factor and partly because getting to Zinnia was now a matter of urgency.

The Shadowkeep sealed with a deep boom behind them.

Back in the comfort of the Scriptorium, Samthrax dropped the Grimoire onto the table.

It landed with a sound that didn't belong to this century.

It seemed to have a heartbeat.

Sebastian stiffened.

His shadow deepened—literally—whatever lived under his skin leaned forward.

Looked closer and licked its lips.

He stepped up to the Grimoire without realising he'd moved.

He looked at it.

It *looked back.*

How was that possible?

Then it opened on its own.

Pages fluttered once, twice, then stopped—right on the tether spell.

Not a word had been spoken.

Pauline crossed herself out of reflex.

Sage made a sound halfway between a gasp and a curse.

Saffron glided closer. She needed to witness the coming disaster personally.

Killian didn't move.

Samthrax let out a slow breath.

"Well. That's either very good news... or the start of unexplainable horrors."

Sebastian couldn't stop staring at it.

He couldn't have walked away if he tried.

Killian cleared his throat.

"Alright. What does the spell need?"

Saffron drifted to the edge of the circle.

"A soul signature match. Which we have." Her eyes slid to Pauline.

"And a blood bond strong enough to find the thread."

Pauline lifted her chin.

"Obviously I'm both."

Samthrax tilted his head, impressed.

"You sure are, hoodoo mama."

The look she gave him could have fried an egg on a winter's day.

Sebastian had zoned out. Everyone and everything slid into the background.

The Grimoire sang to him, a low, primal invitation—he felt drunk on it.

The pages fluttered again.

Like they'd noted his presence—and approved.

Pauline moved forward, already drawing the blade she kept strapped beneath her dress.

The scent of iron spiked.

The book drank it in without touching it.

The spell ink brightened.

Samthrax stepped back. Muttering something like, "Please don't explode."

Killian looked at Sebastian. "You good son?"

When he didn't answer, Sage moved closer nudging him.

Sebastian looked at them both briefly, nodded and went back to the book.

Sage checked the spell structure crawling over the page.

"It wants two things. A caster with direct connection to the Veil… and the offering."

Her voice tripped. "Sebastian. It's asking for you."

The shadow inside him stretched. Hungry. Ecstatic to be seen.

Pauline laid her bleeding hand against the page.

The blood sizzled.

Symbols aligned.

The spell activated.

Sebastian felt the pull get stronger.

No one told him what to do.

The book had already chosen.

His fingers found the spell's invocation mark, index and middle. He pressed down.

He couldn't breathe.

The spell yanked him into the tether line, dragging him hard across distance that didn't behave like distance.

He *saw* Zinnia.

Not her face. Not her body.

Her pattern. Half-burned and trying to recalibrate.

The Veil knitting around her. Forces shifting. Interference.

And beneath it all—Brinnan.

Watching and waiting.

Sebastian screamed without sound. The tether held.

His body felt too hot, his brain felt swollen. Instinct told him to pull out—run—break connection.

He forced his mind to clamp down, to shape the pull. To *name* it.

Zinnia. Zinnia. Zinnia.

The Veil kicked back.

Magic clashed across his skin like it didn't want him inside its system.

His shadow surged.

Power met resistance and did not yield.

And just like that—the tether locked.

He dropped, legs gone. Caught by Killian before he hit the floor.

The Grimoire closed itself.

The mark on the page branded black, into the table.

Samthrax fingered his horn.

"Well. That's definitely the worst way I've ever seen someone locate a friend."

Pauline bound her hand.

Saffron was shaken.

Sage looked like she might throw up.

Seraphina was praying under her breath.

Killian wanted to bubble wrap his kid.

Sebastian looked up, his voice wasn't what came out first.

The shadow inside him sang it lullaby soft.

"She's still alive. But not for long."

***

Something breached the dark.

Zinnia felt it close around her—ears ringing, every hair lifting.

The familiar connection ran straight through her body.

Sebastian.

Relief punched into her chest, all nerve and no grace. She didn't need a face.

The thread was his—stubborn and full of teenage angst.

She reached back immediately.

Wait. What was that?

There was something else inside him—not dominant but entwined.

It moved when she touched him through the link.

Coiled. Slick. *Hungry.*

Her magic reacted. No conscious command.

It locked down around her core, lit the cave in a hard burst, layered protection between her and the thing riding shotgun in her best friend's son.

The tether wavered, then held.

The other thing slithered back behind Sebastian, hiding in plain sight.

She could feel the smug confidence; it made her want to evict the fucker immediately—if she only knew how.

They knew about the prophecy, about how volatile Seb's power was. But this—

This wasn't what she expected.

Did the others know?

Zinnia pulled back. Molars grinding hard enough to spark.

Relief fought nausea. That was her Seb—but what else had its hooks in him?

Matthew felt the electrical surge arc through Zinnia via his own body, which confirmed what he had suspected.

The veil had bonded them.

Which was a risk he couldn't afford.

Yet gods help him; he didn't want to break it.

"Ye right lass?"

Zinnia pressed her palm to the wall to keep from falling.

She barely got the words out. "They found me."

Divina's eyes locked on Zinnia. "Who?"

She really didn't like the sound of being found.

"Seb. My friends from my timeline."

Divina relaxed. "You saw them?"

"Yes." Her voice cracked. "He was reaching for me. It's him. But it's not *just* him. There's something else. In him."

Lilly, mid-conjuring a set of mattresses to prevent numb backsides, stopped.

"Explain."

Zinnia looked up. "His power isn't his. Not all of it. Something dark's in there. It *saw* me when he reached through."

Matthew already hated himself for what he was about to ask.

The current he'd felt was the same power he'd brushed once before—shortly before his exile.

It had nearly killed him.

"Would he be a twin, lass? From the Graves line?"

If the answer was yes, hell wasn't coming—it had already booked a seat.

Hybrid Gateborns were bad enough.

But the twin prophecy?

That was extinction-level.

"Yeah. He is. His mum's Bellarose and his father's Killian Graves. They're good kids."

Matthew staggered back and sat down hard.

"Holy shite. This is beyond dire."

"What are you talking about?"

She knew it was bad. But not fall-over-yourself bad.

"If the old records hold, the next Graves-born twin's meant to house the Return. An' if yer lad fits that mark, lass—then he's no' just a risk. He's prophecy made flesh. Is that no' right, Divina?"

Divina's wings shot wide, tension written clean across her.

"One catastrophe at a time, please."

Of course she'd known. She'd been *assigned* to this reality.

Which included going back to the present and dealing with that shitshow once she got there.

So much world saving, so little time.

Matthew took in Divina's agitation.

She'd never been able to lie worth a tinker's damn, and this time was no exception.

"Ye bloody well knew."

No point denying it. "Yes."

Matthew was usually a voice of reason, trained into a brutal type of discipline.

But right now, he wanted to drag the whole truth out of the bloody Angel.

She was still hiding something. Obvious as hell.

Lilly let out an impressive whistle. "Alright. Enough. It doesn't matter."

She turned to Zinnia. Her voice softened. "What else, honey?"

Zinnia closed her eyes.

She found that shutting out the visual helped with the inner sensory.

As curious as she was to watch a showdown between her hunky woodsman/not woodsman and the angel, her mother was right, time was of the essence.

She reached for the connection, feeling Sebastian under it all—trying.

Wanting to help. Loyal to the bone.

But the darkness in him followed her every move.

She threw shackles around it. Partly for shits and giggles, mostly because instinct said do it.

The response was a hiss of anger, but instant retreat.

Alright. I'll remember that when I get back.

"They're trying to get me home."

Divina caught Matthew's glare.

He wasn't going to let this go.

She focused on Zinnia.

"Then we better make damn sure that thing can't use him as a key."

No sooner were the words out than Lilly was already locking the boundary tighter.

Zinnia trusted they could stay ahead of it.

"They're not the threat. But what's riding with them is. And it just tagged this place."

Divina tucked her wings and sat on the mattress, mouth flattening into a hard line.

"Then we're on the clock."

The cave shuddered, deep in its stone.

Zinnia squared herself.

Time to prepare—for all of it.

Thirteen

"The loyal blade waits not at the table, but beneath it—unsheathed,
should the hand of power falter."
— *From the Sealed Codex of Internal Measures (Council Archive 1.14.03)*

Yvane sat alone in her office, fingers hovering above the blighted agent's shard.

She'd been mid-sentence in a report when three wards ignited across the eastern lattice—wards she'd laid herself, long ago.

The conclusion was immediate.

The *Veilwatch* Grimoire.

And with that, the game changed.

It had been erased in every way that mattered—locked behind consensus, archived in fear, kept off the Council's official record, marked untraceable by anyone who hadn't built their own contingency.

Yvane had.

Because some things didn't stay buried. And she'd needed to know when this one surfaced.

The tracer spell she'd buried in the weave had activated, waking after more than a decade dormant.

It rippled across her skin, creating goosebumps in its wake.

She moved quickly, cutting off the alert before it could reach the wider network.

Whoever had touched the Grimoire hadn't done it by accident.

Yvane didn't believe in accidents.

Which meant someone had both access and intent.

She stood slowly, smoothing the line of her tunic with one palm, as if that could iron the implications flat.

She stared at the shard again, fingers lowering but never making contact.

This was the kind of reroute that stayed invisible until the casualties piled up.

And invariably it was never the right bodies.

She turned to the chamber doors, already composing what she'd say. Which version would land best. Which truths were still too large to serve.

The Council didn't need the whole of it.

What they needed was momentum.

And she knew exactly how to deliver it.

***

The Council Side Chamber

The door sealed behind them with a finality that didn't need a lock.

Nine chairs around the obsidian table were occupied. Killian's remained empty.

Yvane had placed herself at the head, robes crisp, eyes crisper.

The chamber reeked of treason.

She cast a dispassionate eye around the table.

Maltren folded his hands, the movement like the man himself. Precise to a fault.

Varas leaned back, mouth curled into a conspiratorial line. She thrived on drama.

Salen held her gaze, openly assessing. He was a weapon dressed in patience.

Rowena sat opposite Yvane. Unassuming as always. The council mouse.

The others waited patiently for Yvane to reveal why she had called an emergency meeting.

None of these fools notice the moment they stop thinking for themselves.

She had to keep the illusion of consensus alive.

She laid the single shard of crystal on the table—blackened, cracked, still humming with residual heat.

The Council's missing agent.

"This was found at the perimeter of the Between. It's all that's left."

Yvane savoured the internal recoil.

The room realised what it meant. Fear always did wonders for focus.

Maltren unfolded his hands, leaning forward just enough to release pressure from his spine. "The blighted one?"

"Yes."

"How certain are we?"

Yvane swallowed her irritation.

She considered reminding him his seat came from her vote.

"I've checked that it carries her essence, there is no doubt."

Uneasiness spread through the room.

No one touched the shard.

Maltren's fingers curled beneath the table. The agent hadn't simply died—she'd been undone. That kind of power didn't belong in this world. It belonged to prophecy. Or nightmare. Or salt-washed bones left outside the rites.

Salen cleared his throat, one hand dropping to his knee to stop the restless motion.

"How close did she get?"

"Too close I would say."

Salen bit the inside of his lip as his pulse spiked.

He'd always used pain to stop panic from gaining ground.

Brinnan would destroy the world if left unchecked. These threats were escalating. Containment wasn't strategy anymore—it was survival.

"He unmade a blighted?"

"He did more than that." Yvane tilted her head. "He silenced her entire legacy."

She moved through their thoughts without breaking surface.

Exerting enough pressure to test the yield.

She needed to know who still bent when asked.

At this stage, a fracture in unity would be… inconvenient.

Only the mouse remained unreadable.

Everyone else? Rattled and compliant—exactly as intended.

Varas let out a slow breath through her nose. Casual on the surface. But inside, her thoughts ran cold. *Silencing a legacy* wasn't just an act of war. It was a rewriting of natural law. She glanced at the others. No one was openly reacting.

Rowena studied the shard.

Her heartbeat slowed.

Yvane had placed it deliberately. Like a stone dropped in water. Testing current. Watching where the cracks would spread.

She felt the brush of Yvane's mind, soft and searching.

Her protections held—subtle enough to deflect without raising suspicion.

She said nothing. She needed to know who followed first.

Varas crossed her legs with the kind of elegance that made people forget she could gut them with a glance.

"We have seriously underestimated Brinnan."

Yvane tapped her fingers on the obsidian.

Plotting.

"It would appear so."

The room fell to thought. Every member circling the same unspoken truth:

Each second of inaction handed ground to the one creature none of them could leash.

"And the girl?" Maltren asked. "Zinnia?"

"Awake. And growing into the full force of the Gateborn and the Broussard."

The room combusted—voices colliding, chaos gaining traction.

A hybrid? No good ever came from their kind.

She needed to be eliminated.

Brinnan could not—must not—get to her first.

Yvane slammed her perfectly manicured hand down onto the table to regain control.

Silence descended.

"Enough, Brinnan's already moved to intercept. The family lines have started to converge. If she's not pulled into alignment now, we lose her. Or worse—he takes her whole."

Alignment was a polite word.

It covered restraints. Severance. Magical nullification.

And, if necessary, removal.

The Council had used softer language when they'd erased bloodlines before.

History preferred euphemism.

So did tyrants.

Rowena felt the lie slide beneath the truth.

A little too easy. A little too rehearsed.

She kept her expression neutral.

This was the game Yvane played best—tell enough truth to keep the blood from boiling.

Lie just enough to redirect the blade.

"She's not aligned to anyone." Salen pointed out, but even as he said it, tension braced hard behind his sternum. The girl wasn't a risk because she'd chosen a side—she was a risk because soon, she wouldn't need one. He'd seen what happened when systems cracked under magic this ancient. Not even doctrine would hold it back if it got loose.

"She could be," Yvane countered. "With the right nudge."

Varas raised a brow. "And let me guess. You're offering to give the nudge?"

"I'm offering to save what the rest of you refuse to take seriously."

She forced herself to sound cooperative and reasonable. "Brinnan is no longer bound by physical form. Ascension has unmoored him. The Council is three moves behind, and Killian is compromised."

Maltren cracked his knuckles. "So, what do you propose?"

"Custodianship," Yvane was setting the trap. And they were walking into it with smiles.

She continued her pitch. "We retrieve the girl. Bind her power under Council law. Educate her in containment. Control the convergence before it reaches its apex."

"And Killian?" Rowena asked the question as if it was a matter of curiosity. Not strategy.

"He'll be informed. After."

Varas barked a short laugh. "So, we're staging a soft coup?"

"No." Yvane interlaced her fingers, her mouth curving into a smile. "We're preventing one."

No one objected.

They should have.

Rowena kept her gaze soft, her breath even.

Inside, micro explosions of panic were taking place.

She watched how Yvane's fingers never strayed far from the crystal shard.

Power was her kryptonite—she always wanted more.

When the motion came, it came unanimously.

No objections presented or recorded.

Rowena lifted her hand with the others, maintaining her role.

She remembered the last time a vote had been a landslide.

Killian's father had argued that day.

Had trusted the institution.

He'd been dead inside a fortnight.

They had no idea she had been recording.

Every session.

Every word.

Every deviation from sanctioned process.

She now had enough to burn them.

The session adjourned with clipped instructions and rehearsed calm.

An extraction team would be assembled.

Assets prepared.

Time compressed.

Rowena left last.

The corridor beyond the chamber was cold and empty.

She reached into her cloak. Not for a comm rune. Too traceable.

This crystal was older.

Gifted to her by Killian's father, Alaric Graves.

Her thumb brushed its top. Sending the call.

"It's time," she murmured to the stone.

"He needs to see what's coming."

***

A high, relentless tone rang behind Killian's eyes—as insistent as an abscessed tooth.

Confusion swept through him.

This wasn't just any call—this was his very dead father's signature. One he hadn't heard in a decade.

The signal shrilled again.

He rubbed his temples, wishing the great Alaric Graves had chosen a calmer frequency than this high pitched, soul-drilling whine.

His father had designed it during Killian's teenage rebellion. He'd always answered. Otherwise, it left him with a migraine from hell.

He raised one hand, cutting the air in a deliberate arc—anything to shut the bloody thing off.

The stone in the west wall split open.

"Incoming," he shot over his shoulder.

His suspicions on the visitor were validated seconds later, when Rowena stepped through. Her robes swept the floor, her face unreadable.

Alaric's crystal floated behind her shoulder.

Black-gold edges. Flawed cut. Obsidian core.

It followed her in, hovered midair, and began to spin.

No one spoke.

A trigger note rippled out and the projection began.

Sound and image fractured into the air: The council chamber. Nine seated. Yvane at the head, laying the blighted shard onto the table. Every word clear.

"This was found at the perimeter of the Between. It's all that's left."

Maltren's voice followed. "The blighted one?"

"Yes."

Killian's anger crawled up from his boots—checking every vertebra on the way up. Sparking the dark legacy that ran deep in his veins. Shadows peeled from his fingers, coiling halfway up his arms before he wrestled them back.

Fucking sheep, the lot of them. They had no idea what they were invoking.

Rowena stood silent as the recording played, eyes fixed on Killian.

She'd seen what he could do. Respected the hell out of that family tree. And if she was honest—he terrified her. The way he carried that much darkness without drowning in it? That was beyond discipline.

The room listened as Yvane turned the council with her version of the truth. Reframed the girl. Twisted the language.

Brinnan.

Zinnia.

Custodianship.

A coup beneath protocol.

By the time the vote was cast—unanimous—Killian's hands had curled into fists at his sides.

The crystal dimmed, hovered a beat longer, then dropped into Rowena's palm.

"I couldn't let it go unseen. Yvane claims you're compromised, she has her own agenda. I don't have proof yet. But I feel it. They're already preparing to extract the girl."

Killian turned his full attention on her. The room receded. Her head throbbed as his power pushed for truth, uncompromising and absolute.

"When?"

"Killian stop. I am not your enemy." She rubbed her aching temple. "Tomorrow morning. They're assembling the team now. They'll come in under Clause 47C. Dominion law."

He pulled back—but only after he'd scraped through every atom of her.

Her honesty held.

It was the only reason she was still breathing.

"For fucks sake." Killian turned to the others.

Thought wasn't the problem—velocity was.

There were too many outcomes, and not enough time to vet the right one.

"Our timeline has just changed."

He reached out, took the crystal from Rowena's hand, and let the weight settle into his own.

"You were supposed to return this when dad died."

"I did," she replied. "It came back. Perhaps I keep it—with your blessing?"

His mouth nearly twitched at her request. Nearly.

"If I let you hold this, Rowena, it's with the understanding that you use it only when it serves Graves. Nothing else."

"I believe the facts speak for themselves, Master Killian. Used once in the decade since Alaric passed. Check it."

She wasn't about to let him run her down—and she sure as hell wasn't about to let him know how hard her heart was hammering for challenging him directly.

A chortle cracked from across the room, followed by a palm against a thigh. "Well, bossman, I do believe you've just been told to stop being a shithead."

"Shut up, demon."

He had no doubt Samthrax would give him a stroke before the Council ever did.

Rowena finally took in who else was there. Killian had consumed her focus—until now.

He was formidable enough, but the power in this room short-circuited her senses.

The Council knew the Bellarose line. Knew the Graves line. They understood bugger all about the Broussard bloodline, and Rowena would bet good coin the woman with the bayou edge and the *fuck with me you die* expression was exactly who the rumours spoke of.

Then there was the demon. She'd only ever seen him through the looking dome in Council chambers. In the flesh, he was worse. Tall, sharp-toothed, far too pleased with himself. Jovial on the surface—but the threat underneath was impossible to miss.

This wasn't a team.

It was a front line.

Brinnan was the war.

Yvane and the rest? A speed bump.

A flicker of cold skipped across her skin.

She'd chosen well.

Thank the gods she hadn't bought into the hype.

Killian turned the crystal over in his hand, registering the history it carried.

His father's pattern still clung to the stone. Nostalgia bit hard.

He handed it back to Rowena.

Her palm closed around it.

"Keep it."

That earned the smallest tilt of her head. Respect. Gratitude.

"Thankyou. You'll know the moment they move."

Killian studied her for the span of a breath. It was clear she'd abandoned the illusion that neutrality was a virtue. It was also clear having an insider took out a lot of the guess work.

"Be careful."

It wasn't a plea. It was fact between two people who knew what it cost to play this high. "Yvane's ruthless. If she figures out what you've done…"

"She'll kill me," Rowena finished. "Let her try."

Killian felt his mouth curve upward at her show of defiance.

She placed a hand on Killian's arm. "Go with grace."

He inclined his head. "And you."

He opened the portal with a flick of his fingers. Warded three times over for silence and stealth.

Rowena stepped through without looking back.

The stone sealed behind her.

Killian addressed the room.

"We need to plan."

Fourteen

"Strike a mother, and the world remembers why it fears daughters."
— *Veilwatch marginalia, author unknown*

1695

Brinnan watched them take the bait he'd laid—zealotry made for excellent choreography.

Shattered branches. Runes scrawled in ash along the bark, crude enough to look witch-born, symbolic enough to feel dangerous. He'd crushed bitterroot underfoot on purpose—letting the scent cling, sour and earthy, enough to raise suspicion.

He'd dragged torn lace through offal and tied it to a thorn bush.

He left strands of hair plaited into nettles.

A trail of broken-heeled prints that vanished into stone.

Everything pointed toward flight. Panic. Witchcraft.

He wanted them certain.

And they were.

Jonas Hale would see exactly what he needed to:

A girl running.

A coven hiding.

The hand of hell curling around some ancient hole in the earth.

The cave couldn't protect its guests from him.

Brinnan had already twisted the layers meant to keep them hidden.

Confused the bindings.

Spoiled the intent.

He found the strings and broke them one by one, drawing the zealots to the back entrance.

He enjoyed how simple people were.

***

Jonas Hale led five men through the moss-slick mouth of the cave, eyes wild with purpose.

He'd followed signs that appeared to be placed by the devil himself.

Irrefutable proof that Witches were in the forest.

And God had seen fit to deliver them to him personally.

"Keep the line tight."

Jonas drew his blade, fingers brushing the consecrated cross at his neck—silver worn thin by prayer and paranoia.

"There be sin inside. I can smell it."

The passage narrowed.

Light crawled through the stone. Symbols surfaced, vanished, returned.

The letters weren't right.

They didn't belong to any alphabet born under heaven.

One of the younger men muttered something about hell's tongue.

Another crossed himself and spat.

The cave began to turn their bodies against them.

Eyes watered without cause.

Tongues curled around an unknown bitterness.

Fingers tingled, then went dull, then tingled again.

Thoughts arrived out of order. Names detached from faces.

Intent slipped a half-step behind action.

One man broke. Dropped his torch and bolted back the way they'd come, mumbling a psalm with wet panic in his voice, and a brown stain spreading down his pants.

Jonas caught the stink and sneered.

Cowards didn't belong in sanctified work.

"Keep moving, ye piss-yellow bastards," he barked. He moved to the back of the line—if anyone run again, he'd drive them forward with the blade. "God walks with the righteous. This is his hand guiding us. Nothing here'll harm ye unless ye let it."

No one believed him.

But they kept going.

The hum in the walls got louder.

The first man stepped too far ahead.

The stone near his shoulder shifted.

There was a sound like wet cloth tearing under tension.

His scream died halfway through its first breath.

His chest caved, then ballooned grotesquely, ribs forcing their way through skin at impossible angles.

His spine arched—

then jackknifed. Vertebrae tore free one after another, ticking across the cavern floor while the rest of him twitched upright, refusing the message.

Skin sloughed from his face. His jaw wrenched loose, teeth spraying in an arc that skittered across rock and leather. One eye burst. The other withered where it sat, cooking in its own fluid.

The wall finished its work and went still.

What fell at Jonas' boots had once answered to the name Caleb.

Jonas stepped back—an instinctive retreat his pride didn't have time to intercept.

Silence rushed in to replace the screaming that should have followed—and didn't.

Another man gasped as the cavern floor tore open along a line that had not existed seconds before.

Roots surged upward—thick, ridged, bristling. They drove through his torso in a single thrust. His back bowed as they fixed themselves deep inside him.

Blood never reached the ground. It reversed direction midair, drawn back into him, siphoned through the roots as if gravity had changed its mind.

His skin slackened, then began to separate in long, obscene lengths, slipping from muscle and bone while whatever remained inside him jerked and spasmed.

His heart convulsed against its cage.

It tore free, flopping once in blind insistence before the roots pulled tight and pulped it between them.

They reeled him in piece by piece, drawing meat and splintered bone back into the wall that had claimed him.

What little remained crumpled inward and dropped.

The passage knit itself closed.

Correction complete.

The third man bolted.

The cave disagreed.

The ceiling slammed down with a noise between a snap and a slap.

When it lifted, he was gone.

Only half a boot remained, turned on its side, and a dark smear already fading into the floor.

Jonas didn't move.

Three of his men were gone.

The reek of blood chased thought. Copper clung to the back of his throat.

In front of him, Mark and Elias weren't breathing right—each taking ragged pulls through clenched teeth, eyes blown wide, lips gone white and cracked. Both locked onto the stone ahead, watching it the way prey watches killing fields.

Jonas grinned.

"Well, lads," his voice cracked, half-prayer, half-fever. "We was right."

They weren't chasing shadows. They weren't deluded.

This was witchland and clearly hell-marked.

Mark's eyes flicked to Jonas's knife. Elias saw it too.

Running meant turning their backs. Staying meant facing forward. They chose the direction that didn't end with steel between the shoulders.

Weapons at the ready. Relics gripped hard enough to split skin. Every part of them braced to maim or be maimed.

They reached the inner cavern as the sun outside died on its feet.

Zinnia felt them before she saw them—three heartbeats she didn't recognise, banging around at the back of her senses.

Male. Armed. Dumb.

She turned.

There they were.

Sweaty, wide-eyed, radiating male entitlement and holy conviction in equal measure.

Well, shit—was that an actual pitchfork?

Her patience was running on fumes.

They were staring at her like they'd walked into a devil's parlour.

To be fair, they'd probably never seen a woman with tattoos or a man's haircut.

"Fellas, trust me when I say you don't want to do this."

Zinnia almost felt bad for them.

"This is your moment to leave."

But she could already feel it—

they weren't going anywhere.

Jonas took one pace in, boots scraping the stone. "Three o' mine are dead an' this place did it."

"You walked into a sacred space with violence in your heart. What did you expect?"

"You're not holy. You're not even human."

Behind him, Elias rebalanced his weight.

Not watching Zinnia—watching the older woman instead.

And Lilly didn't move.

She carried the composure of someone who knew pain—and had never once been beaten by it.

"Go back the way you came."

Zinnia's fumes had dried up. She was officially out of patience.

"You don't want this fight."

"Don't tell us what we want, Witch."

Jonas spat the words, venom and certainty tangled together. "God has tasked us with ridding the land o' yer evil."

Elias was done waiting.

He moved—fast.

This was what he'd come for. What he'd rehearsed in the dark, again and again, when no one was watching.

The pitchfork drove into Lilly's side. He wasn't ready for the resistance—he'd imagined it would slide in like his knife through churned butter.

Instead, the haft jerked hard in his hands. He let go. The tool hung there, awkward, embedded.

The sound she made wasn't a scream.

It was a breath that stopped halfway in.

Lilly's knees dipped, muscles misfiring, body trying to decide if this was real.

She stayed upright out of habit alone.

That shouldn't be inside me.

The thought arrived distantly, as if it belonged to someone else.

Pain followed late, blooming outward from the metal buried in her flesh.

Her hand came down automatically, pressing the wound with

irritated precision.

Of all the stupid ways to go—

Blood soaked through her fingers.

And beneath the shock, as the burn intensified and her world started turning black, her mind fixed on a harsh truth: she wasn't walking this one off.

Zinnia's vision didn't blur—it bled.

Red burst behind her eyes—blinding, corrosive—hammering against the inside of her skull until thought shredded.

The cave dropped out from under her. Words went with it.

She didn't reach for the power.

It roared up and claimed her.

It tore up through her chest, splitting her open from the inside— structures grinding, fibres ripping.

The lock hadn't been picked.

It had been blown apart.

Her arms snapped into alignment, tendons standing out like cables pulled too tight. Fingers locked. Her body straightened in a violent correction, teeth knocking together hard enough to bite her tongue.

Her mouth opened.

No breath. Just current.

The man who stabbed her mother ceased to exist.

One second he had mass, form and heat.

The next he failed to hold together.

His body came apart in midair—skin shearing, muscle separating, ribs blowing in an outward spray that struck the cavern walls all at once. Blood dispersed into mist before gravity could claim it. What remained hit the floor in pieces too small to recognise.

Zinnia's hands shook.

The force inside her did not.

It wanted more.

Cracks burst across the ground beneath her feet—thin, searing, threaded with light that shouldn't exist in this world. The ceiling split open, not physically, but *dimensionally*, revealing nothing and *too much* at the same time.

Matthew stumbled back, swallowing hard as acid climbed into his throat.

He'd seen rifts before.

He'd seen gateborn lose control.

He had never seen the likes of this.

"Divina—"

"I know," she was moving. Her boots skidding on blood and the gods only knew what else. "Get her."

They flanked Lilly, half-dragging, half-lifting her body out of the centre.

Zinnia was glowing now.

Not with light—but with density.

The air couldn't get around her.

Magic escaped through her pores, scalding as it broke free.

Her aura had stopped being metaphor.

It was real. Loud. Killing the oxygen.

Divina's arms screamed from the effort of hauling Lilly out of the blast range.

"She's splitting the *veil*," Matthew's voice landed just left of panic. "She's *tearing it open*—"

"Yes, Captain Obvious, thank you for your insight."

And this is how reality ends—inside a cave, with one pissed-off hybrid.

There wasn't a hope in hell they were strong enough to stop her.

Zinnia's eyes opened wide and white and endless.

The closer you got to her, the harder it was to *be*.

Thought unravelled. Memory skipped tracks. Everything lost its shape.

She raised one hand.

Jonas Hale never had a chance.

She reached into the air and pried it open.

The veil peeled back with a shriek that wasn't sound.

Time dipped.

Gravity buckled.

Jonas was hauled forward unceremoniously.

He twisted.

Raged.

Spat every god he had ever prayed to.

And then he was gone.

So was the last man.

The air screamed shut behind them. The split sealed.

You could've heard a pin drop.

Zinnia's entire being burned as the adrenaline crashed. The power settling into a gentle rhythm beneath her skin—but her body trembled from being a conduit for whatever the hell that had been.

She had taken lives without hesitation.

She didn't feel triumphant.

But she didn't feel remorseful either.

And that scared her more than the gore painting the walls.

She rolled her shoulders, circled her neck. Breathing in deep gulps to collect herself.

Finally, she came back enough to register the others.

Lilly was on the ground, cradled by Divina.

Matthew was looking at her like she'd grown horns.

Divina was the first to speak.

"What the fuck was that?"

Zinnia looked at her hands.

Then up.

"I wish I knew."

Her legs were made of rubber—she moved anyway. Each step closer stripped away another layer of bravado.

Blood was everywhere. So much. Her brain scrambled, trying to remember how much a person could lose before it was over.

It looked like more was outside her mother's body than in it.

She dropped to her knees beside Lilly.

"Mum." She really liked how that word felt. She wanted more of it. Not less.

"Hey. Don't you dare check out on me now."

Her hands hovered uselessly, caught between the instinct to touch and the fear of doing more harm.

Something deep inside her screamed that she should've been able to stop this.

She looked up, eyes wide, panic raw.

"Divina. Fix her."

Divina's hands glowed faintly, pressed slightly above the wound. Her jaw was set in a way that meant she was concentrating hard.

"I am," Divina's focus never lifted. "I've been doing nothing else since you tried to break the world in half."

"So, I was supposed to let those morons get away with bloody near killing my mother?" Zinnia looked at her incredulously. "I'm not going for sainthood—the dickwads deserved it."

"I'm just saying there are other ways to protect people that don't involve losing control."

Zinnia sighed. She couldn't argue with that. Didn't mean it sat well.

"She's bleeding a lot."

"Yes, she is." Divina adjusted her grip, light shifting under her palms. "The fork missed the heart by millimetres. Punctured the lung. Tore through soft tissue. Some of the damage I can't just wave away."

Zinnia's alarm spiked ten notches. "What does that mean?"

"It means she's alive," Divina finally glanced up. "And it means this will take time."

Matthew crouched on Lilly's other side, hands slick with blood. The farm tool lay discarded a few feet away, bent from where he'd wrenched it free mid-cataclysm.

"I pulled it free when ye went off like judgement day," his voice sat somewhere between apology and confession. "Weren't much else I could do."

"You did fine." Divina was glad he had done that gruesome part—she was fine on the healing, not so much on object removal. "You did exactly what you were supposed to."

Zinnia leaned in closer, forehead nearly touching her mother's.

"Okay. You're gonna be fine. I won't accept anything else."

Lilly's eyelids fluttered. Her mouth twitched.

"So bossy." Her voice barely made it past her lips.

Zinnia laughed. It broke out of her—ugly and wet and unstoppable. Relief split her in half, flooding over everything else. She pressed her face briefly into Lilly's shoulder, careful not to hurt her.

Divina exhaled through her nose and reasserted command over herself.

"Luckily stubborn runs in the family. That's doing half the work for me."

Zinnia looked back at her, eyes red-rimmed.

"What else can I do?"

"You can stop tearing holes in existence, for a start." Divina's hands didn't stop glowing, light threading deeper now. "I've got this part."

Zinnia grimaced. "Guess I'm lucky you do emergency triage, huh?"

Divina's mouth tilted. "Yes. And if you keep using magic the way you were, that's all I'll be bloody well doing."

Zinnia sobered at that. The flicker of defiance fizzled under the reality of everything she'd just done. She drew her power inward with deliberate care, tucking it away like it might bite if handled wrong.

"Sorry," she murmured. "I guess I lost it."

"Yes, you did."

Then, softly, just for her:

"And we will be talking about that later."

Zinnia was not looking forward to that conversation.

Matthew sat back on his heels, eyes flicking between the two women.

He knew what power cost on the other side of release.

He also knew it was the damage left behind no one trained you for.

"We can't stay here, it's no' safe."

"No," Divina agreed, adjusting her position slightly without lifting her hands. "It's not. But we can't move Lilly yet."

"Then we move as soon as Mum can." Zinnia's eyes dropped to Lilly, watching the slow rise and fall of her breath. "And next time someone brings a farm implement into our family drama—"

Lilly's fingers twitched, weak but unmistakable, curling slightly around Zinnia's sleeve.

"—you don't overreact," she murmured.

Zinnia grinned through tears. The sound was still caught in her chest, but it was there.

"Can't promise that."

She looked toward the mouth of the tunnel—the one the men had come through but hadn't gone back out.

"There more of them?"

"No." Matthew shook his head. "I made damn sure there were no surprises waitin' in the dark."

"Checked while ye were still… lit up."

Divina's brows lifted. "Lit up? Understatement. She was more glowie than a literal angel." "Yeah, well." Zinnia blew out a long breath, her spine starting to catch up with the strain. "I was having a moment."

"Let's shoot for fewer moments." Divina rolled her eyes, but her mouth gave a half-smile. "Clean-up's a bitch."

Zinnia glanced around at the carnage.

Yeah. Fair point.

"Noted."

Lilly shifted slightly in Zinnia's arms. Her eyes cracked open again, slivered with exhaustion.

"I knew you were more."

Zinnia didn't know what to do with that.

So she nodded. And tucked it away somewhere she'd unpack later—when everything stopped trying to kill her.

Divina sat back at last, pale and spent. She'd done all she could—and it had taken its toll. Her hands dropped into her lap, the magic bleeding off her fingers like condensation.

"She'll be fine after some sleep."

Zinnia let her head fall back against the cave wall, the stone cool against the nape of her neck.

"Good," she exhaled. "Because I'm about one millimetre away from melting the next person who so much as sneezes at us."

"Let's hope that's no' me, lass," Matthew muttered dryly.

Zinnia gave him a tired wink. "You're safe, woodsman."

"I'll be takin' first watch. Get ye some rest, lasses."

Matthew sank onto the mattress Lilly had set aside for him, positioning himself to face the tunnel—blade in hand.

No sooner had he spoken than Zinnia's eyes slid shut, pulled under by exhaustion so heavy she couldn't fight it. Nor did she want to.

Divina followed a moment later, curling one arm protectively around what remained of her strength.

Matthew stayed awake. Back to the stone. Eyes on the dark.

He replayed what he'd seen until the noise in his head went quiet.

And only the damage remained.

Fifteen

"The easiest soul to steal is the one already doubting itself."
— from the Meditations of the Shadow Ascendant (Volume IX)

Brinnan felt the tear beneath the skin of reality—an unseaming that answered the sabotage he'd worked into its roots.

The hunters had done more than distract.

They'd provoked.

He'd anticipated disturbance. Maybe a scream or two.

He hadn't expected *her* to break it open.

The distortion fed into him—warm, serrated, loaded with motive.

On the other side, the long-forgotten things began to stir.

Slithering toward the weakest point, starving, misled.

They always mistook damage for permission.

He almost wanted to let one through.

But no—those weren't for this stage of the game.

This wasn't perfection.

It was potential.

She'd reacted in rage.

And rage never asked for instruction. It didn't calculate or preserve. It *took*.

That made it the most honest kind of key.

Better still—she had no idea what she'd touched.

The breach bore her fingerprint now—and everything that brushed it would remember her.

He smiled.

The inevitable violence thrilled him.

So much potential in untrained instinct.

He tasted what lingered—heat, grief, fury—unfinished, leaking.

The residue stayed with him.

Alive and exquisite.

He studied the others to confirm what he already knew.

The angel had gone straight to triage. Predictable. That species of purity always defaulted to function over feeling.

The woodsman had dragged the body clear, trying to keep pace with what he couldn't translate.

Neither had tried to stop her.

Wise move.

He discarded them. Their narrative had already ended.

Jonas Hale?

He'd been cast as bait and played his part with all the subtlety of a firebrand in a church. But watching him vanish into a pocket of existence his god had no scripture for? That had been delicious.

A private reward.

The true outcome stood trembling in the centre.

Saturated with what she'd unleashed.

Surrounded by people who would never unsee it.

She would carry this—not the kill, the clarity—and it would come back in solitude, replaying itself in new tones.

He wouldn't have to break her—she'd do it herself.

The Council would feel it soon.

Yvane, sooner.

Still clinging to her graphs and doctrines, mapping the girl as if she were a process—

as if lineage could be charted, as if blood obeyed sequence.

She hadn't recognised the threshold cracking beneath her feet.

But Brinnan had.

He felt the other pieces stirring now. Pauline. The tagalongs.

Scrambling to intercept what had already become uncontainable.

Let them.

The girl was a force stepping out of its own shadow—

volatile, unrepentant—

and finished with permission entirely.

***

Yvane's eyes opened.

Something had leaned against the perimeter she trusted most.

The room's balance had been upset, leaving behind an unease born only when an intruder passed through without asking.

She sat up fully, extending her attention inward, deep into the weave she'd laid into the foundation beneath her rooms. Every layer of her domain was set to trigger under duress.

The wards answered with a violent aftertaste—struck hard enough to stagger her.

Whatever had come through hadn't negotiated or tested.

It had hit and kept going.

That pointed to one conclusion.

She swung her legs from the bed, cold marble against her feet grounded her in ritual, giving her the illusion that structure still equalled control.

Across the chamber, the viewing pool waited, bound beneath its glyphs.

As she approached, the surface of the stone vibrated against her senses.

She released the lock with a flick of her fingers. The basin turned in on itself. Its gloss went black, devouring light, drawing depth without direction.

She expected her reflection. The system always returned that first as an orientation point.

But the pool skipped the courtesy.

In its place—residue.

"Show me."

Mishandled energy always left a stain—especially when it was born of impulse instead of design. The pool gathered it greedily, stitching a narrative from disturbance and excess.

Zinnia appeared radiating from the inside out.

Impressive and terrifying even by Yvane's standards.

There it was. Ungoverned amplitude and reach.

The girl's interior state spilled outward in a devastating arc.

Yvane felt the flick of admiration and crushed it.

Admiration implied parity. And this wasn't reverence. It was assessment.

She catalogued it carefully, the way surgeons chart nerve damage—methodically, without declaring the loss.

She leaned in, taking in each detail.

The stretch of the Veil. The vermin crawling behind it, sensing instability.

She watched the seam tear wide. Below, the starved things surged upward with the desperation of insects trapped beneath glass, vying for escape.

Two men were hurled through with no grace, no mercy, removed by a decision made too quickly to carry doubt.

She charted the sequence.

Initiation. Breach. Disposal.

The method lacked refinement, but the outcome spoke clearly enough.

The rift closed. The men, the choice, the cost—entombed inside it.

What lingered in the aftermath was proof.

Yvane straightened. Composure returned as thought began its real work.

That level of ignition should never have been possible.

Gateborn. Broussard.

Singularly, those lineages demanded regulation.

Together, they demanded something else entirely.

Legacy meant nothing if it wasn't *instructed*.

And yet—there the girl stood, breaking through with *will* alone.

Pure, undiluted, and wasteful in its current state.

This level of power? Invaluable.

She didn't need to destroy the girl. She needed to *contain* her.

Then transfer. Split. Isolate.

Extraction would have to be slow. Piece by piece. Anything else risked failure.

But if Zinnia could be pulled into the Council's hands—secured and looped inside the correct rituals—it could be done.

With precision and permanence.

She turned from the water. Plans already rewiring themselves.

Nothing that unstable stayed free for long. Nor should it.

And she had never been patient for its own sake.Top of Form

***

The cave hadn't forgiven them.

Zinnia woke in the wreckage of her own consequences. Consciousness slammed back into her body with the grace of a wrecking ball, immediately flagging her skeleton as unfit for further operations.

Add to long-term problems list: skeleton—useless.

Her first coherent thought landed and refused to budge.

Mum.

She sat up. Or tried to. Her joints screeched somewhere between an arthritic accordion and you've made a terrible mistake.

The ache wasn't physical—not exactly. It was the kind you get after pouring out everything you have and getting the universe's middle finger in return.

Christ, this magic shit was aging her faster than milk in the sun. At this rate, she'd be a twitchy, hairless cryptid by forty. Not even the sexy kind—the kind banned from public fountains and grainy security footage.

Her eyes found Lilly.

Less death-grey now. Splotches of human colour warming their way back in. Her chest rising and falling in that miraculous rhythm Zinnia liked to call life.

Relief swamped her—not just because Lilly had survived, but because Zinnia didn't want to lose the one thing she hadn't known she wanted until now.

All those lost years. All that blank space between them. Still unfixable—but maybe not unfinishable.

She wanted to try. She knew Lilly did too.

And no one—no one—was going to fuck with that.

Not God. Not Brinnan. Not whatever centipede-fingered horror was currently chewing through the connective tissue of existence.

Her attention drifted to the far wall.

Across the chamber, Matthew had made himself furniture. Back to the stone, hands easy, eyes fixed somewhere beyond her line of sight—until they weren't.

He turned and locked onto her.

Her whole system went red-alert. No soft flutter. No maybe-this-is-nice. It was a full-body punch of want that bulldozed every sensible thought she had left.

She'd known this was coming. Had circled it.

Apparently, the dial had skipped straight past curiosity to clothes are optional and so is dignity.

And he saw it.

The flicker of surprise in his expression was honest.

The heat that followed? Not subtle.

He smirked.

Bastard.

Pull it together, Zinnia. You are not a horny teenager.

Divina's consciousness clicked back into place with all the serenity of a professional watching two coworkers try to screw during a fire drill.

The scent hit first.

Seriously?

Someone was going to start humping the moss if she didn't intervene.

Exhaustion still rode her, but she boxed it up. That was a later problem. Right now, she had one unconscious woman, stable but fragile; two magically unstable hormone grenades eyehumping each other across a crime scene; and a closing window of opportunity to avoid imminent destruction.

Divine operations had run smoother during the Flood.

She cleared her throat. Loudly.

Both heads snapped toward her.

"Apologies for interrupting whatever your genitals had pencilled in for each other," Divina offered sweetly. "But unless you're planning to screw your way into another dimension, we need to leave. Our window's closing, and I'm not dragging your lust-struck corpses out of here."

Matthew felt the moment die an efficient death. The heat coiling low in his groin evaporated like holy water on a skillet.

He ran a hand down his face, trying to look casual—trying not to think about how quickly Zinnia had short-circuited his better judgement. She hadn't just gotten under his skin; she'd taken up residence and started hanging curtains.

She could also vaporise him mid-sentence if he said the wrong thing.

Which, strangely, didn't bother him much.

Still, this was not the moment to test whether magical foreplay counted as hostile action.

He turned to Divina, libido boxed, labelled, and shelved—for now.

"If ye've got a plan, now'd be the time to speak it. I've got naff-all in terms of safe ground."

Divina didn't answer. Not immediately.

It was the kind of pause you didn't want from a being who'd lived through six apocalypses. Which meant the options had veered into territory where even gods hesitated.

Matthew's gut tightened—impressive, considering it had been a knot since this whole thing started.

Zinnia kept her eyes on Lilly. Not looking felt like tempting the universe, and the universe got vindictive when it was bored.

Lilly's magic was faint. Unstable enough to leave a bruise on Zinnia's conscience.

If this went pear shaped, there'd be no one to blame except the three supernatural ticking clocks currently sharing a cave—a team you should absolutely not invite to your wedding.

She didn't dare look at Matthew. The connection—whatever the hell it was—hovered barely beneath the surface, like static before a lightning strike, and she didn't trust herself not to lean into it.

Divina exhaled slowly. Her celestial signature shivered through the air.

"There's somewhere I can take us. Somewhere beyond here."

Zinnia's stomach hit the floor with very little fanfare. That didn't sound like a trip to Starbucks. "The Veil?"

"Far older."

"Okay, that's… not ominous at all. You gonna elaborate, or is this a choose-your-own annihilation type deal?"

"It's called the Caethera."

Divina's tone left no room for negotiation. Unsurprisingly, Zinnia had never heard of it. Apparently she was now booking holidays to pre-existence.

"A sanctum between realms," Divina continued. "Angel-forged. Untouched by corruption. Shadow cannot persist there. Malice cannot pass through. You do not enter unless your intent is honourable."

Zinnia grimaced. "Guess that rules me out then."

"Intent, not attitude," Divina corrected. "You're messy, not malevolent."

Zinnia filed that under unexpected compliments from beings who could smite her. It didn't help with the worry or the guilt—but it felt good anyway.

Matthew, quiet until now, tasted the word Caethera in the back of his mind. It rang no bells, left no impression. That alone disturbed him.

He knew the Veil—its creases and predators. Knew what fed between dimensions and what whispered behind worn crossings.

But this was outside all of it.

Whatever Divina was talking about—it was more than hidden.

It was holy.

He didn't like what that meant.

"You're sure we can cross?"

Divina's attention zeroed in on him. "I can open the way. It is within my dominion." She tied her hair back with practiced ease. "You're Veil-touched, Matthew. That grants you passage—if your will remains coherent."

He nodded, his soul heavier than he wanted to admit.

Could he stay coherent?

Guess he was about to find out.

Divina turned.

And Zinnia felt the full impact of those intense blue eyes slam into her.

"But our girl here—"

"What about me?"

"You ripped a hole in the world less than twelve hours ago. That kind of power doesn't exactly say 'I come in peace.'"

Zinnia rolled her eyes. Hard. "What, you think I'm gonna set off security alarms?"

"I think the threshold may refuse you," Divina was more than a little concerned. "And refusal there is not gentle. This is our only option, and we don't know who—or what—is on our tail. I will not be left explaining to your mother why the daughter she just recovered was erased by sanctified design."

Zinnia winced despite herself. The image was harsher than she cared for.

"Yeah. Let's put that in the *avoid* column."

"The Caethera isn't built on power. It's built on alignment. You bring fear—it reflects it. You bring dominance—it rejects you. But if you bring protection..."

Her voice shifted. Calmer now. Almost gentle.

"That core part of you that exploded last night? It will know."

Zinnia considered that carefully.

Divina was right.

Under all the rage and nerve-splitting magic was a singular, electric drive to shield what mattered. Protection had been the centre of it.

If that was the key to getting through this next part, then fine.

She'd find it again—even if she had to dig past everything else to reach it.

Matthew crossed the cavern and crouched beside Lilly.

He gathered her gently, the way someone lifts an heirloom already cracked.

Zinnia met his eyes. No flirtation this time—just the thud of shared risk and the strange, temporary trust of people who had both seen each other nearly unravel.

"You drop her and I'll pry your soul apart with a dinner fork."

He chuckled. "I have no doubt ye will, lass."

Her threat didn't rattle him. It landed with the same impact as everything else about her—dangerous, real, impossible not to respect.

Lilly barely stirred in his arms, breath shallow but regular.

Matthew turned to Divina.

She had already begun.

Her left hand rose, fingers extended, and the entire chamber recognised her.

Sound poured in—high, harmonic, endless. A chorus with no mouths behind it. More than one tone. Less than a thousand. It filled his bones and rearranged his thoughts, each note peeling something personal back without apology.

Then came the light.

Blinding in its simplicity—a white so absolute it erased the outlines of everything he'd ever used to define himself.

His eyes watered. His grip tightened on Lilly, but he said nothing.

Stone turned translucent. Matter softened at the edges. Form bowed to will—and the will belonged to Divina.

She stood motionless, arm extended, face expressionless. A vast presence leaned forward through her skin, endless and precise. Her eyes gleamed, lit with judgement.

Not a single ounce of power moved with effort.

This was command. This was dominion.

Matthew exhaled slowly through his nose, adjusted his hold on Lilly, and stepped forward.

The Caethera combed his memory, touching places he hadn't. It measured not only action, but reason.

It registered the kill-count. The regrets. It found the love too—the one thing he'd never compromised.

He couldn't have resisted if he tried. There was nowhere to hide here. No tactic. No bluff.

Lilly escaped the full reckoning he endured; she was barely holding on, and mercy, apparently, counted for something in this place.

For a long moment, nothing happened.

Then something unseen clicked into place.

Passage granted.

Relief hit harder than a bull with a thorn in its arse.

He crossed.

Behind him, Zinnia stopped.

The light poured toward her, relentless in its clarity. It didn't burn. It didn't soothe. It exposed.

Her feet refused to move.

This place wasn't meant for her. Even brushing against it felt presumptuous. Her magic churned beneath her skin—unrepentant, still carrying the imprint of what she'd torn open.

She hadn't earned sanctity or forgiveness. She was held together by stubbornness, adrenaline, and a refusal to let go when everything in her history said she should.

The Caethera weighed her.

Zinnia swallowed. Her jaw locked so tight a dentist was in her imminent future.

Every instinct screamed: Run. Retreat to the comfort of being unwelcome. Of not having to prove she belonged.

But her legs stayed planted.

What was she doing?

She thought of Lilly—broken and unconscious, but breathing. She thought of the look Matthew had given her. No condemnation. Just belief. As if he didn't care what she'd done, only who she protected.

Something in her chest twisted.

Fine.

If this place wanted the truth, it could have it.

She stepped forward.

The pressure hit immediately. Memory poured through her in a ruthless cascade—every time she'd chosen force because it was faster, every time she'd struck first so she wouldn't have to wait for rejection.

The quiet, corrosive belief that love was temporary. Conditional. Always one misstep away from being revoked.

Protection was easier. Protection had rules.

The sound swelled around her in full resonance. Light threaded through her body and tugged her forward.

She crossed.

Relief wasn't an indulgence Divina typically allowed herself.

But it came anyway.

The Caethera had let Zinnia through. That volatile soul had been peeled open without mercy—and found aligned.

Divina lowered her arm and stepped after them.

The instant she crossed the threshold, the strain coiled into her since sentencing—since the clipping of her wings, the repurposing of her orders to suit a lesser war—unwound.

The light rose to meet her, acknowledging her not as soldier or servant, but as kin.

Sound unfolded through her in layered threads, harmonies she hadn't heard since before the fall—before function devoured feeling, before she'd been rewritten to obey.

The Caethera knew her essence.

Peace washed through her. She swayed.

Home.

For a moment.

Long enough to remember she had once been loved without condition. Without expectation. Simply for being.

The gate sealed behind them.

And Divina let the light carry her.

Sixteen

"All sanctuaries are mirrors. You do not rest inside them.
You face yourself."
— inscribed above the entrance to the Caethera

The moment they were admitted, the world reassembled itself around them into something too perfect to have evolved naturally.

The cave was gone.

Replaced by softness. Texture. Colour.

Beneath Zinnia's feet, grass bent but didn't break. Lush and cool, it bruised under her weight, releasing crushed wild thyme and a tangy citrus note that lingered at the back of her throat.

She crouched and dragged her fingers through the blades, half-expecting her hand to pass through them. But no—the grass was real. Damp with dew. Woven with pale, star-petalled flowers and herbs blooming outside any season she recognised. They were standing in the middle of a rolling, seemingly endless meadow.

Above them, the sky held a blue so deep it felt purposely designed. Clouds moved across it in slow, impossible spirals. Pearl-white, smoke-soft.

The air tasted of raw honey and sun-warmed fig.

Somewhere nearby, a bird was singing—high and unrestrained, full of the kind of joy that didn't need a reason to exist.

Zinnia stood rigid while the world around her kept revealing itself—vivid, surreal, colours so lush they felt almost indecent.

It was bloody hard to trust.

The meadow unfurled into long stretches of wheat, burnished gold in the light. Coppery hills rose beyond. Trees clustered in gentle thickets, none taller than they needed to be. Their branches curled in welcome.

Even the wind soothed.

And at the centre of it all, a dome.

Pale, seamless, curved in perfect equilibrium with the land around it. Sunlight touched its surface and it responded, shimmering with a quality quieter than reflection, deeper than shine.

There was no door, no threshold, but the invitation was unmistakable.

The grip of the past week—the grief, the constant edge of danger—began to soften.

She inhaled deeply—then caught herself, waiting for the axe to drop.

When she wasn't struck by lightning, or its metaphysical equivalent, she allowed her eyes to close.

Let the hush of the meadow and the living light of the dome move beneath her skin.

Let it soothe—unfamiliar, but honest in a way nothing else had been for days.

Behind her, Matthew resettled Lilly in his arms and knelt, lowering her onto the soft earth.

The ground gave slightly beneath his knees, reminding him what it felt like not to run.

He looked up at the sky and softened.

He hadn't seen real light since the Veil. Not true light. Not the kind that spoke to the part of him still untouched by shadow.

Oh, powers to be... I missed this beauty.

For a moment, he thought he might break under it.

But that wasn't the purpose of the Caethera.

It held them.

Without condition.

Letting each of them equalise to what it offered.

Zinnia took a step forward. The wind braided through her hair, warm and cool.

Her hands curled, then uncurled.

This peace—insane, impossible—was weaving through her soul like it belonged there.

For the first time since her magic exploded into existence, it was nothing more than a low hum in the background—content as a newborn.

Divina stayed where she was.

The others were absorbing the Caethera the way they needed to.

She didn't interrupt that.

The light here no longer startled her.

The calm didn't feel like relief anymore.

It just *was*.

She let her body calibrate.

The energy she'd given to save Lilly was already returning—measured and intact.

Her limbs rebalanced. Her spine realigned.

Her wings, retracted into their unseen span—completing the illusion she was whole. She knew better. But for the first time in a long time, the lie didn't hurt.

She wasn't sure what to do with that.

She flexed her fingers over and over.

Everything answered.

That shouldn't have felt strange.

But it did.

There had always been a cause. A consequence.

Even when she'd followed orders without question, she'd felt the pull of cost in her soul.

Here, there was no cost.

Only continuity.

She glanced toward Zinnia.

Operating on a hair trigger, even now.

Matthew was adjusting. He had a survivor's instincts—he'd bend with the terrain.

They would all have to move forward differently now.

The Caethera turned its attention to Lilly.

The light found her. Reached. Touched.

And loved.

It *wrapped* around her with the kind of tenderness that made the wind stop in reverence. Fine strands of gold rose from the ground, drawn to her skin. Where blood had dried, colour returned. Where pain had held fast, warmth unfurled.

The wound was erased—bone knitted, flesh restored, the story of violence undone without scar or residue.

She stirred, eyelashes fluttering. Her mouth parted on a breath that no longer hurt to take.

Zinnia was already moving. She dropped to her knees beside her, fingers shaking as they found her mother's face.

Oh, thank every fucking power—

"Mum."

Lilly opened her eyes.

And smiled.

Zinnia folded into her, arms tight, heart tighter. Maybe if she held hard enough, time would stop trying to steal things.

A breathless sound emerged between them.

"Okay, honey... you're squashing me."

Zinnia jolted upright, half-laughing, half-sobbing, her grin wide enough to split her face. Relief threatened to knock her flat. Every muscle shaking from the inside.

"Sorry."

Lilly sat up.

She pressed a hand to her side, to the spot that—last she checked—had been pitchfork swiss cheese.

Nothing was leaking.

Even the damn dress was intact. Not a rip. Not a bloodstain. Not a hint of murderous farm equipment.

She blinked, squinting. Every colour around her looked like it had been turned up to divine. Wildflowers, sky, grass—none of it subtle, none of it real in the way the world usually was.

Okay. So, this wasn't Ashwick Vale.

She looked over at Zinnia, whose whole face was still caught somewhere between disbelief and joy.

"Are we dead?"

Her voice came out normal, which was another surprise.

"Is this the other side?"

She continued looking around.

"If so—I gotta say, I kind of like it."

Lilly's eyes moved between them. The look said *please explain.*

"Well?"

Zinnia grimaced inwardly. *Okay. Minimise. Deflect. Avoid the lecture.*

"Nutshell version?" The words came out flippant. "You almost died. I may have… slightly torn a hole in reality. This place—" a vague sweep of sky and gold-edged grass, because how else did you point at something this big "—is where Divina hauled our sorry arses so you wouldn't bleed out. Also, the twats hunting us can't get in. We're in the Caethera."

"The what?"

Divina answered before Zinnia could. Her voice still carried the afterglow of something holy she hadn't quite come back from.

"It's a sanctum. It sits within the angelic realms. A place built for safety. It sees the soul and responds to need. Malice doesn't survive the crossing."

Lilly turned slowly, taking it in again with new understanding. "And what I needed was a miracle."

Divina's smile broke open into honest joy. A soft laugh escaped before she could stop it.

"Seems we all did. Come on. Shelter, food, rest is that way." She hooked a thumb toward the structure waiting patiently for them. "Let's take the gifts while they're offered."

***

They stepped through the veil of the dome.

And stopped short.

"Holy shit," Zinnia blurted. Her eyes didn't know what treasure to land on first.

"That about sums it up," Divina chuckled.

The interior was all clarity and geometry. Curved walls held a muted lustre, the colour of pearl under water. The floor beneath them gleamed smooth and cool—clear quartz shot through with silver filaments that reconfigured themselves according to some private logic.

Zinnia caught a ripple of herself reflected back—not her face. Her energy.

Because that's not confronting at all.

The kitchen to the left wasn't wood or stone. Its surfaces were sculpted from obsidian laced with malachite, black depth threaded with green veins that reacted to passing movement. The counters caught the sun and held it, bending it toward their centre. Shelves gleamed with a constant, inner fire. The basins—wide, polished, patient—looked built to hold more than water.

Maybe confession. Maybe memory. Maybe both.

The staircase in the middle curled upward in a graceful spiral—formed entirely from amethyst, soft violet and smoky plum streaked with gold. It radiated something—transparency, maybe. Knowing, either way it was disconcerting.

Each stair was solid beneath her feet, sending small electrical currents that spoke welcome.

Upstairs, the doors were different shades of rose quartz, set flush into the walls without seam or hinge. Smooth to the touch.

Zinnia stopped beside the nearest wall and let her fingers trail across it. Embedded deep in the curve were slivers of emerald, catching green light that hadn't come from any lamp.

Truth.

That was the word it offered.

The Caethera wasn't just showing them safety.

It was showing them who they were.

The dome wasn't architecture.

It was a resonance chamber.

A sanctuary built for the parts of a person no one else ever saw.

Well, hell.

This was going to be interesting.

Zinnia stood there a moment longer, hand still pressed to the wall, letting the emerald shimmer beneath her fingertips. It pulsed once, so faint she might have imagined it—but the warmth that travelled up her arm didn't feel imaginary. Neither did the loosening in her chest, the lifetime of emotional bullshit she hadn't realised she was carrying until the dome started peeling it back, layer by stubborn layer.

She wasn't ready to go into her room.

Her hand dropped, and she turned toward the staircase, half-expecting to still be alone.

Seventeen

"You don't stop lovin' 'em just 'cause they gone.
You just learn how to carry it."
— Pauline Broussard

Zinnia didn't mean to go outside.

She'd meant to sleep. Or pretend to.

But something kept tugging.

The more she ignored it, the stronger it pulled.

Another damn thing in the dark, dragging her where it wanted. Just like everything else lately.

She sighed, swung her legs out of bed, and followed it.

Barefoot, she slipped from her room, down the amethyst stairs, and through the dome. The air met her, cool and damp, fragrant with crushed green—mint, maybe, or lemon balm. She drew a breath and felt her shoulders loosen, which annoyed her. Nothing in her life right now had earned that kind of trust.

The moon sat high and full, washing the meadow in silver. Enough light to see without effort.

She didn't know where she was going. However, her body did. That was the unsettling part.

The ground beneath her feet felt awake—soft, responsive, guiding without urgency. Overhead, the stars weren't fixed. They shifted as

But footsteps found her.

Matthew crested the top first, his gaze sweeping the curve of the upper level before settling on her. He didn't say anything—just dipped his chin once in acknowledgment. His eyes were clearer. Not entirely unburdened, but steadier. The Veil still clung to his edges, but it didn't own him.

Behind him came Lilly and Divina. For a moment, Zinnia watched them—shoulders unbraced, steps unguarded. Nothing clinging to them. Nothing performing survival. Nothing hiding the unadulterated truth of who they were under everything else.

The dome didn't push them toward anything.

But each of them, without prompting, drifted to the doors that had been waiting.

There was no question of whose was whose.

Lilly brushed her hand over the nearest handle, the blush-pink surface responded instantly. Warm light flowed outward, soft and sure. She smiled under her breath.

Zinnia felt it move through her—that unmistakable ripple of awe, of tenderness, of gratitude. Her mother radiated love, not the performative kind, the genuine kind.

And right now, Zinnia couldn't think of anything more extraordinary than finally getting to know her.

Pride rose quickly in her chest. So did love. Big, bright, ridiculous love.

Lilly turned and caught her daughter's gaze.

The look they shared didn't need translating.

Matthew's door received him with a grounding thrum. As he stood on the threshold, something internal dismantled itself. What remained didn't feel fragile. It felt actual. The habit of moving between worlds without leaving footprints faltered—uncertain, briefly unmoored. He stood in it, heart thudding, unsure if this was the beginning of peace or the end of pretending.

Divina lingered in front of her own. The quartz whispered against her senses, tuned to places within her buried so long she'd forgotten they existed. Peace moved through her in careful increments.

Smiling gently, she turned to the others. "Anyone else hungry?"

Zinnia's stomach answered with a loud, undignified growl.

"I'll take that as a yes," Divina laughed.

They drifted back down to the kitchen.

Ingredients had already appeared across the counters: fresh bread, preserved lemons, roasted root vegetables still warm, salted cheese crumbling at the edges.

No one questioned it. They moved and began chopping, plating, stirring, assembling. Not like they'd done it forever, but without the awkward choreography of strangers.

They carried their meal into the library. No formal dining room here. Only low tables surrounded by cushions and shelves, the light between the stacks shifting to match the mood.

They sat.

For a few minutes, no one spoke. The food was simple. Perfect. Comforting in a way that eased more than appetite. The Caethera didn't just feed the body—it mended whatever else had gone neglected.

Zinnia broke the silence, because someone had to. "Alright. We can't stay here forever."

Lilly picked up a piece of cheese, considering. "You sure? Bit of me wants to see if it's got hot springs and a margarita tap." She grinned and popped it into her mouth.

Zinnia snorted. "Margaritas? Yep. We're definitely related. But reality's still out there trying to kill us. We need a plan."

Divina set her bowl down. "My thoughts? We go to the Enclave. Maison Bellarose, to be exact. That's the point of intersection and protection."

Matthew took that in, fingers tracing the rim of his glass. "So ye'll be draggin' this woodsman to the future, then?"

Zinnia met his look. "We all know you're more than a woodsman, Matthew. And there's no 'I' in team, so yeah. You're coming."

He didn't argue. In fact, he liked the idea immensely.

Lilly slapped her leg. "Oh my stars, I'm going home. And with my beautiful daughter. The 1600s really aren't what they're cracked up to be. My kingdom for indoor plumbing."

Matthew huffed through his nose. "Ye'll miss the bugs. I can feel it."

Zinnia didn't bother hiding the shudder that passed through her. "If I never see another outhouse, I'll die happy."

He looked like he wanted to debate the cultural merits of moss again. She shut him down with a single look.

Divina's attention lingered on the curvature of the shelves. She was already half upstairs in her mind. "Let's save the sanitation reviews for the morning."

Zinnia leaned back on her cushion. "Yeah. Plans can wait. For once, no one's bleeding. Let's not ruin the vibe."

No one disagreed.

Divina stretched her legs out, catlike, ankles crossing loosely. "The Caethera wants us here. Might as well soak up the hospitality."

Matthew gave a grunt in exhausted agreement. His shoulders had finally dropped, the constant edge of readiness melted down to something almost restful.

Lilly yawned, unapologetic. "Alright, you don't have to tell me twice."

They drifted back upstairs.

Zinnia stayed downstairs a little longer, fingers tracing the rim her empty bowl. Something about tonight felt like a *hinge*. A sr turning, before everything opened again.

She exhaled, stood, and followed the others up.

she walked, drifting in loose patterns that felt deliberate rather than decorative.

She crested a low rise and the land opened into a shallow dip. A narrow brook curved through it, water so clear it barely looked real. Moonlight threaded across the surface in long bands; the water bubbled softly beneath it.

A bridge arched over it—smooth and seamless, made from some luminous stone that glowed from within, warm-toned and immovable.

She stopped at the edge of it, hands planted firmly on her hips.

"I swear, if this is a trap…"

The bridge didn't react.

She crossed anyway, each step measured, half expecting proof that this place wasn't the safe haven it claimed to be.

On the far side, the pull let go.

Her lungs evicted the air she had been holding onto. The night stayed quiet. The water kept moving.

She folded her arms across her chest, more reflex than defence, and stared at the brook.

"Alright," she muttered to no one. "I'm here."

Woodsmoke reached her a heartbeat later, followed by the unmistakable scent of the Bayou.

That didn't make sense—she was a long way from home.

Her confusion increased as a harmonica cut through the night—the tune unmistakable. *You Are My Sunshine*, soft and familiar, the same way Mémère used to play when Zinnia wouldn't settle.

She turned.

The man stood a few steps back from the bridge.

Boots dark with creek water. Sleeves rolled to his elbows. Suspenders cutting across a white undershirt. Short black curls, sun-kissed skin.

Her eyes.

Zinnia shook her head. Blinked once. Twice. For a second she was sure she was stroking out. Nope—he was still there.

Recognition hit before thought had time to organise itself.

The last time she'd seen that face was in a picture frame hanging on Mémère's wall.

Her stomach did that weird swoop thing it used to do on roller-coasters, right before the drop.

The harmonica hung from a cord at his throat. He touched it once, thumb resting against the worn metal.

"Zin…" His voice cracked, thick with regret. "My bébé."

The sound of it split her clean through.

She sucked in a breath that didn't want to cooperate. Her hands curled into fists at her sides, nails biting skin.

"No." The word burst out.

He didn't move closer.

"I ain't here to hurt you, bébé."

"You don't get to stand there and talk like this is fine."

"I know."

"You left me."

His jaw tightened. He nodded once. "I did."

"You chose death." The words burned on their way out. "You chose that instead of trying."

He looked away, shoulders dipping slightly. Guilt riding him hard.

"I weren't built right fo' dat kinda emptiness, chèr. I thought dyin' would hurt less den livin' wit' a hole I couldn't fill."

Her throat closed. She hated how much truth lived there. Hated that she could relate.

"I didn't get that choice," she bit out.

"No, you din'. An' I'm so sorry, chèr. Every damn day, I'm sorry."

He lifted his eyes to her then, and there was nothing guarded in them. No defence. No justification. Just grief and love braided together.

"I'm here 'cause you growed up thinkin' mah leavin' meant you wasn't good 'nuff. But dat ain't de truth."

For a second she wasn't thirty-something being fine, being funny, being unbothered. She was eight, then ten, then thirteen—counting the ways she must have failed to be worth staying for, because kids always assume it's their fault when someone leaves.

"You ain't never been de reason, bébé," his voice gentle. "Not one time. I was already broke. You was de good thing I ain't had de strength to stay fo'. Dat's on me, not you."

Her vision blurred. She dragged the heel of her hand across her face, angry at the wet.

"Mais, you growed anyway," he went on. "Full'a fire an' grit. I see what you done become without me. An' I thank every damn star I ever fell under fo' Maman—'cause she loved you de way I shoulda."

Zinnia sniffed hard, wiping her face again. "Yeah, she did."

Then, because staying there hurt too much: "You look like the photos."

"Good 'uns, I hope."

She huffed a broken laugh. "Better."

He smiled then—wide, crooked, proud. A dimple cut into his left cheek.

Zinnia smiled back, the matching dimple in her right cheek falling into place.

Genetics didn't care who'd earned the right. They just showed up. Standing here, sharing a face with a man who had never been there, stirred a grief that hadn't ever gone away. The old wanting rose up fast, dangerous, already preparing for disappointment. This was the version of herself she'd never gotten to try on—daughter to a father.

They stayed like that, suspended between strangers and something more.

Behind her, footsteps slowed.

Zinnia tensed—every nerve on alert, caught somewhere between vulnerability and a punchline. The last thing she needed was an audience. Especially if it was Divina.

But it wasn't.

Lilly came into view—and stopped dead.

Her body reacted before her mind caught up. Breath stalled halfway in. Her balance turned unreliable.

She'd heard Zinnia leave. Told herself to give her space.

Then told herself not to panic.

But the worry had won out.

Of all the scenarios she'd played out in her head... this wasn't one.

The man by the brook turned.

Every part of her recognised him.

"Remy?"

His name left her mouth softly. It had been decades since she had spoken it aloud.

He didn't answer. He just looked at her.

The way he held himself undid her first—contained. He looked like a man who had learned to stand again after choosing not to. A man who had not expected to be found.

Her legs moved. One step. Then another. Her hands shook openly now, no effort made to hide it.

"I didn't know." The words tumbled out, clumsy and desperate. "I didn't know. I thought you'd be safe. I thought leaving was the only way to keep you breathing."

That fateful decision surged forward in full force. The night she'd walked away. The certainty she'd clung to because the alternative would have destroyed her.

"I thought I was doing what had to be done."

The rigidity left Remy. When he met her gaze, there was no accusation waiting there. No bitterness. Only a quiet grief that had already made peace with itself.

"You did, chèr." His voice carried no blame. "You did ya part." A breath passed through him. "I jus' didn't last long 'nough to see de other side of it."

The truth landed without cruelty.

Lilly's knees nearly buckled.

All that time, she'd believed leaving had helped.

It hadn't.

She reached for him without deciding to. Her fingers hovered inches from his chest, close enough to feel warmth, close enough to doubt it.

"Are you real?"

His answer came without hesitation. He caught her wrist gently and pressed her palm flat over his heart.

"I'm here," he murmured. "Das real 'nough fo' now."

The ache she'd been carrying since the day she turned her back finally broke.

She came undone. Years of restraint giving way all at once. No sound at first. Her fingers twisting into his shirt, as if letting go meant vanishing.

His arms closed around her, firm and familiar. He didn't rush her. Didn't try to fix it. He simply stayed and held through it, letting her grief soak the fabric between them.

She had missed this—his steadiness, the gentle humour that used to allay her fears, the safety of someone who knew her heart. Standing here now, the cost surfaced in full: leaving hadn't spared them. It had only rearranged the damage.

She had loved him. She loved her daughter. Completely.

And living without them had turned her into someone she'd spent years pretending she was ok with.

Zinnia stayed back, not because she didn't belong, but because this wasn't hers to interrupt.

She'd believed love disappeared when people did. But here they were, proving her wrong.

Whatever she was carrying forward would be different. She could feel that much, even if she didn't yet know how.

They stayed like that—no urgency, no demand to explain or fix or forgive faster than the moment allowed.

When Remy finally lifted his head, his eyes returned to Zinnia.

"Dat fire in you? Dat come from us. From her. From me." His mouth went soft. "But what you done with it—das yours. Das somethin' new."

He let go of Lilly and walked up to Zinnia.

He pulled a ring from his finger—a simple band, etched with looping script.

"Wear it," he told her. "Or give it to de one who kept you strong when you was ready to tear ya'self apart. Either way, let it remind you—

you ain't never carryin' it alone."

Zinnia closed her fingers around the ring.

It warmed against her skin.

Remy smiled once more. "I'm proud of you, bébé. Always been. Always will be."

He stepped back, his eyes moving between Lilly and Zinnia.

"Mah heart an' soul carry both of you. Dat ain't gonna change. But it's time fo' me to go."

His form receded until the night no longer contained him.

Zinnia slid her arm around Lilly's shoulders and held her there, the two of them watching until he was gone.

Maybe closure didn't need to be tidy.

Maybe all it needed was honesty.

Zinnia didn't move for a while after Remy was gone.

The night kept doing what nights did. The brook kept talking to itself. The stars kept drifting. None of it cared that her whole internal wiring had been rearranged.

Lilly's shoulder stayed under Zinnia's arm. She wasn't ready to loosen her hold.

Lilly's breath was still catching in odd places, caught between hurt and release.

"He's gone." Her voice was quiet.

"Yep." Zinnia didn't look away from the place Remy had been.

Lilly's exhale wobbled. She stared at the water.

Zinnia tightened her arm around her. "You good?"

Lilly made a sound that wasn't a laugh. "No."

"Me either."

They stood like that for another minute, then Lilly's hand rose and pressed at her own throat, fingers resting there.

"I didn't leave because I stopped loving him or you." Lilly confessed softly. "I left because I loved you both so much that I genuinely thought I was saving us."

Zinnia took that in—the faith behind the decision, the hope that had made it feel necessary at the time. It didn't change the damage, but it shifted how it sat in her mind. Love could be real and still fail. Wanting to protect someone didn't mean you knew how.

Her legs gave out and she sank to the ground. A moment later, her mother sat beside her.

Lilly blinked hard, then looked sideways at her daughter.

"You've got his eyes." Her mouth pulled into a small, wrecked smile. "And his mouth. That same look he had when he was trying to be brave without making a fuss about it."

"I wish I'd known him."

Lilly reached for her hand. "I wish you had too."

Zinnia stared at the ring, twirling it around on her finger. "He felt real."

Lilly's smile held. "He felt like the man I first met."

Zinnia turned her head, studying her mother.

This was a story she had waited her whole life to hear.

"Tell me." The request came out rougher than she intended.

Lilly's brows lifted slightly, she was surprised Zinnia wanted it. She'd assumed her daughter would only ever want the accounting of what went wrong.

Zinnia held her gaze. "I want to know mum, tell me who he was. Who you were."

Lilly's throat worked. She looked down at the brook, then up at the bridge, then back at the water again as if the direction might help her decide where to start.

"It wasn't dramatic. Not at first."

"Good," Zinnia replied. "I'm allergic to dramatic."

Lilly's mouth twitched.

"I was nineteen," Lilly laid back in the grass, losing herself in the memories. "I'd just left home. Not in a 'follow my dreams' way. In a 'I will die in that house if I stay' way."

Zinnia laid back, eyes on the stars and listened to her mother's words. She had no intention of interrupting.

"I ended up in Lafayette," Lilly continued. "I had a bag, a bad attitude, and enough spite to keep me upright. I slept on a couch in a flat that smelled like cigarettes and fried oil. I took shifts wherever I could. Diner, bar, anywhere that paid cash and didn't ask too many questions. I had only ever known the Enclave and family duty, yet all I craved was normal."

She paused. Zinnia looked over at her and met her eyes.

"I thought I was clever. Thought I'd outrun everything. Thought if I kept moving, none of it could catch me."

Zinnia knew that instinct. It lived in her own body.

"One night," Lilly went on, "I finished a shift and walked outside and there was this man leaning against my car like it belonged to him."

Zinnia's eyebrows shot up. "Excuse me?"

Lilly's eyes flashed with the ghost of that same outrage. "Exactly. I was ready to tear him apart."

"What did you do?"

"I told him to move before I moved him."

Zinnia grinned despite herself. "Exactly what I would've said."

Lilly laughed at that truth.

"He looked at me like I was the most interesting problem he'd ever seen. Not in a gross way. Not in a 'you're pretty' way." She shook her head once. "In a 'you're dangerous and I respect it' way."

Zinnia's grin faded. That sounded familiar. Her thoughts went straight to her woodsman. *Shit, when had she start thinking of him as hers?*

"And he said," Lilly continued, voice lowering, "'You can't keep drivin' dat thing like you hate it. She's gonna throw you in a ditch.'"

Zinnia laughed mainly at Lilly's impersonation of her father.

"He flirted by insulting your car?"

"It worked," Lilly admitted, then grimaced, clearly wishing she could interrogate the logic that had once felt so reasonable.

"What did you say?"

"I told him it was none of his damn business. And then I asked him what the hell he was doing leaning on it."

"And?"

"He said he was waiting for his cousin. He'd been told to meet him outside. But the cousin had gone back inside because he'd forgotten something." Lilly's eyes rolled. "Men."

Zinnia nodded solemnly. "Men."

Lilly glanced at her. "Then I asked how the hell he knew how I drove."

"Very fair question."

"He said," Lilly continued, "'I've seen you round town, *chèr*.'"

"I told him he was blocking my door," Lilly laughed at the memory. "And he stepped aside immediately. Waving his arm, like I was some sort of princess."

Zinnia could picture it. Too easily.

"And then," Lilly huffed, "he asked if I was always that angry."

Zinnia's laugh burst out. "The audacity."

"Oh, I wanted to break his nose," Lilly admitted. "But then he smiled—wide, crooked, completely unrepentant—and I knew I was in trouble."

Zinnia's fingers tightened around the ring again. Somehow it made her feel close to her father.

"What did he do next?" Zinnia asked.

Lilly's eyes lifted. "He asked if I'd share a meal with him."

"After you threatened him?"

"Yep," Lilly confirmed. "He never made me feel like I was too much. He made me feel seen."

Zinnia stared at her mother, trying to reconcile that. Lilly, nineteen, raw as a cut. Remy, young enough to still be half-bright. The two of them colliding in a parking lot with fries and stubbornness and no idea what would come later.

"You went?"

Lilly snorted. "I told him no. Obviously."

"Obviously."

"And then I followed him inside."

Zinnia laughed, a real laugh, the kind that untied a knot in her lungs she hadn't noticed was there.

Lilly's face softened at the sound. "He talked to everyone. He knew the cook. He knew the waitress. He knew the old man at the end booth."

Zinnia could see that too. She could see how someone like Remy would make you feel safe without trying.

"He kept stealing my food," Lilly continued, and her voice warmed into the memory. "Not because he was being rude. Because he assumed I wouldn't mind. And it hit me, right then, that I'd never let myself relax around anyone before."

Zinnia was clocking the similarities between herself and Lilly. She could count on one hand how many people she relaxed around.

"He asked me my name," Lilly blushed. "When I told him, he repeated it, telling me it was a pretty name for a prettier lady."

Zinnia raised a brow. "Wait, you had a man eating your food, but you didn't know each others names?"

Lilly laughed at the judgment swimming in Zinnia's voice. "In my defence, I was fresh out of the magical community and in the mundanni world. I didn't know how things worked."

Zinnia shook her head. "Clearly."

"Anyway, he told me his name was Remy. And I remember thinking that was the sexiest name I had ever heard, and it suited him."

"You fell fast, huh."

"Oh, I fought it," she turned to Zinnia with a wide grin. "But your father was persistent. I didn't trust it. I didn't trust him. I didn't trust me."

Zinnia nodded slowly. That she understood.

"But he kept showing up," Lilly continued. "Not every day. Not in a way that crowded me. Just… enough. He'd appear at the end of my shift. Or outside my building with a bag of beignets and a look that said don't argue woman."

Zinnia breathed out. "Whoa dad, stalker much."

"Patient," Lilly corrected, while chuckling. "He was patient with me in a way I needed."

Lilly's gaze dropped to the brook. "I started letting him in. And then one day I woke up realising I was in love."

"He made you softer?"

"He gave me space to be softer."

Zinnia's throat tightened again. She'd spent so long thinking of her parents as damage, as fallout, that she'd never let herself imagine what came before. Whatever had broken them hadn't been the beginning.

Lilly's eyes flicked to her. "You don't have to apologise for what you are, Zinnia."

Zinnia froze. "I didn't—"

"You didn't say it," Lilly cut in gently. "But you carry it. The idea that love is something you have to earn. Or tiptoe around."

Zinnia looked away, jaw grinding. *I guess mother's intuition never leaves. Let's change the subject.*

"What was he like, when it was good?"

Lilly's smile came slow. "He sang. All the time. Terrible voice. Big confidence. He'd sing while cooking, while fixing things, while driving. He'd sing at the most inappropriate moments just to make me roll my eyes."

Zinnia snorted. "That sounds kooky-fun."

"He danced," Lilly continued. "In the kitchen. Barefoot. No rhythm. He didn't care. He'd grab my hands and spin me until I got dizzy and swore I'd kill him."

"But you didn't."

"I considered it," Lilly managed a fake solemn look, then her mouth cracked into a grin. "But he'd kiss my forehead, tell me I was lyin' cos we loved each other more than that."

The picture formed without her trying, uninvited, vivid enough to hurt.

"He used to talk about having a kid. Like he was testing the idea out on me."

Zinnia stared at the water.

"He told me once, that if we ever had a child, he wanted her to know she was wanted every day of her life."

Zinnia's eyes burned. She didn't speak. If she spoke, whatever came out would betray her completely.

Lilly's hand found Zinnia's forearm. "He wanted you. He didn't fail to want you. He failed to stay."

Zinnia cleared her throat, but the lump didn't budge. "That's not… a small failure," she managed.

"No," Lilly agreed. "It's not."

Zinnia stared at the ring, took it off and turned it in her fingers. The etched script caught moonlight and held it.

"What does it say?" she asked.

Lilly leaned closer, squinting. "It's old French," she murmured. "Remy was always sentimental in his own way."

Zinnia waited.

Lilly's lips moved silently as she read. Then she exhaled. "It says: *Hold fast*."

Zinnia stared at the band.

The universe had a sense of humour she didn't appreciate.

Lilly's shoulders sagged slightly, telling the story was both freeing and heartbreaking.

Zinnia glanced at her mother. "Did you ever…" She stopped. The rest of the question sat on her tongue like poison.

Did you ever regret me?

Did you ever wish you'd never had me if it meant you could have kept him alive?

Zinnia swallowed it back down hard.

Lilly watched her and knew what she was struggling with. Her eyes softened. She took both Zinnia's hands.

"The only regret I have, baby girl, is not finding another way to stay."

"You sure?"

Lilly willed Zinnia to see the truth in her yes. "I've never been surer."

Zinnia looked away, but not before tears escaped down her cheeks. "OK."

Lilly drew in a slow breath. Rubbing her daughters arm.

"We should go back." She rose, stretching her arms to the sky. "Before you start making jokes about being lured into a fairy tale."

Zinnia huffed. "Already did."

"I know." Lilly's mouth twitched. "I heard it from inside. Very subtle."

Zinnia's cheeks warmed. "Subtle's my middle name."

Lilly chuckled, she held her hand out to Zinnia and pulled her upright.

They started back across the field.

Zinnia kept her pace matched to her mother's without thinking about it.

Halfway back, Lilly spoke again.

"He loved us both you know and he still does."

"Yeah, I get that now."

"That's good."

Zinnia didn't know what to say to that, so she didn't try. Instead, she reached out and threaded her fingers through Lilly's for a moment.

Lilly's hand squeezed back.

When the dome came into view, the illusion of reprieve disappeared. Returning to the shelter meant returning to reality. And she still had no idea what the hell she was doing.

Lilly noticed. "Hey."

Zinnia glanced over.

Lilly's expression held no judgement. "You don't have to always be the strong one, we got you. Even that cantankerous angel."

"Easier said than done, mother dearest."

Lilly hid the quiet joy the endearment sparked.

"I know, but it's important you know you are not alone in this. You got some serious arse kicking mojo surrounding you kiddo."

"Wait til you meet the rest of the crew."

"From the present?"

"Yep."

"I look forward to it. I have a feeling we'll need all the help we can get."

They stepped through the dome.

Straight into a warm welcome. The pearl curves gleamed. The quartz floor hummed underfoot, faint and grounding.

Upstairs, the doors waited.

Zinnia stopped at hers, fingers resting on the surface without opening it. Her body was lead, exhaustion catching up in a wave now that her system had stopped running on adrenaline and rage.

Lilly paused beside her.

Zinnia turned, and for a moment her throat clenched hard enough she couldn't speak. All the years without this. All the nights she'd gone to bed pretending she didn't care. All the mornings she'd woken up and decided she was fine because being anything else was inconvenient.

Lilly opened her arms.

Zinnia hesitated exactly one second, then stepped into it.

The hug wasn't delicate. It wasn't careful. It was real.

Lilly's arms locked around her. She'd been waiting decades to be allowed to do it.

Zinnia's face pressed into her mother's shoulder. The smell of her was witch and earth and coffee and fight.

"I'm tired," Zinnia muttered, voice muffled.

"I know," Lilly replied, her hand gliding up Zinnia's back, firm and reassuring. "Sleep well."

Zinnia pulled away.

Lilly's eyes were red-rimmed.

"You ok?" Zinnia asked, because that question lived in her mouth now.

Lilly placed both her hands on Zinnia's face. "Better than I have been in years."

She leaned forward and pressed a kiss to Zinnia's forehead.

Zinnia blinked in surprise, then yanked her in for another hug, tighter this time.

"Night, Mum," Zinnia said into her shoulder, the word still strange and still right.

Lilly's arms tightened. "Night, love."

Zinnia stepped back, opened her door, and slipped inside.

The room greeted her with peace. Rose quartz light, soft and forgiving.

She closed the door behind her and stood there for a long moment, hand resting flat against it.

She walked to the bed and sat down. Zinnia stared at her hand, watching the ring catch the low light.

Hold fast.

He wasn't wrong. Whatever this life was turning into, it would take exactly that.

Her brain tried to do what it always did: catalogue threats, map exits, build a plan, keep everyone breathing.

But the Caethera refused to play along. It didn't escalate, didn't provoke, didn't give her anything to push against.

Zinnia threw herself onto the bed without undressing.

She didn't know what to do with all this bloody zen.

Peace required trust.

Trust had a history of walking out.

She stared at the ceiling as it played patterns in all colours of the rainbow.

She watched them dance around each other.

Remy's voice played over and over in her head.

My bébé.

The words carried wanting, grief. They carried an entire life she'd been denied.

She rolled onto her side and pressed her forehead into the pillow to muffle the sound of everything she'd been holding back. She didn't want to wake anyone.

You're never carryin' it alone.

She believed those words now.

Zinnia wiped her wet face with the edge of the sheet. She stared at the wall.

I weren't built right fo' dat kinda emptiness

She swallowed hard as the words bounced around inside her skull.

She understood him in a way she didn't want to.

Because she'd been building her whole personality around not needing anyone for so long that she'd forgotten it was a tactic, not a truth.

In this place, her magic didn't flare.

It rested.

She felt that reprieve right down to her soul.

Zinnia stared into the dim and let a thought rise without pushing it away.

I miss him.

Not the man she'd never had.

The idea.

The version of childhood where there was a father who stayed.

The version of herself who might not have needed to armour up so early.

A week ago, she'd been an orphan.

Now she had a living, breathing mother down the hall and her late father showing up with apologies and gifts.

Zinnia lay there, staring at the ceiling, and let herself hold those facts without turning it into a joke.

A minute passed. Maybe five. Time behaved differently here.

"Okay," she told herself. "We'll hold fast."

Her eyes closed.

Sleep took her the way exhaustion always did when the body finally believed it was safe enough to stop—fast and deep.

Eighteen

Present day

Maison Bellarose hadn't slept.

The scriptorium vibrated with managed urgency—chalk sigils half-erased and redrawn, vellum pinned beneath weighted stones, crystal arrays humming under layered wards that had been reinforced twice already.

Killian dragged a hand through his already ruined hair.

"Alright. That confirms it. We're not using the portal in the keep."

Samthrax had claimed coffee duty with religious intensity. He nodded once.

"Smart call, bossman. That thing sends souls where it wants, depending on how vindictive it's feeling. Let's not roll that dice."

A low sound of agreement moved through the room.

Pauline paced, instincts prickling. Something had changed but she didn't know what. "Last thing we need is to follow her trail and come out wrong."

Samthrax snorted. "Or inside-out. Seen that once. Didn't improve morale."

Seraphina lifted a mug from the table where Samthrax had stacked an alarming number of cups. She raised a brow at him—he shrugged. One sip, and her eyes closed briefly. The demon did make a mean brew.

"I agree. We don't trust our fates to the keep and its toys." Her attention turned. "Mum. Do we have a spell for a time-linked portal?"

Saffron stood near the central lectern, fingers tapping lightly against her lips.

"As a matter of fact…" She drifted toward the far shelves, where the oldest tomes resided. "This section tends to be avoided. Family consensus labelled it 'taboo.'" A faint smile. "My mother used one once. Tried to stop an ancestor from being killed. The Council was furious. History wasn't favourably impressed either."

She moved upward without effort, gliding past shelves that would've required ladders in life. At the highest corner, she paused, glanced at Killian, grinned, and flicked her fingers.

The book launched free.

"Catch."

Killian crossed the room in three strides and caught it against his chest.

Sage shook her head, laughing. "Nice parlour trick grams. Good reflexes dad."

Saffron winked. "Death has its perks."

Killian grinned back at her as he carried the tome to the table and laid it down.

The group closed in. Seraphina passed her hand over the cover.

The grimoire responded instantly.

The lock clicked. The pages turned. The spell revealed itself.

Sebastian leaned in, brow furrowed.

The symbols wouldn't stay put. He focused on one and it slid away, rearranging itself the moment he tried to understand it.

Unease crept along his nerves. This magic stuff was really messing with his head.

"Anyone else feel dat?" Pauline looked around the room.

Saffron's expression tightened. "The tether's weakening. And… it isn't pointing forward."

Killian looked at her. "Explain."

Before Saffron could answer, Sebastian made a sound that cut straight through the room.

His chair scraped hard against the floor.

He folded over the table, one hand braced against the wood, the other clutching at his chest like he was trying to grab something already gone. Ink spilled. A crystal tipped and shattered.

"Sebastian."

Seraphina was there instantly, her hand on his shoulder.

She realised he was in the grip of tether magic.

She still hadn't adjusted to this—her children grown into full witches. And her son, brilliant, reckless and smack bang in the middle of hormonal teenage angst, was the one most likely to lose himself.

It scared the living crap out of her.

She didn't let it show. Fear was useless here. Panic even worse.

So she stayed exactly where she was, hand firm on his shoulder, grounding him the only way she knew how—by refusing to move, refusing to let him face it alone.

Sebastian didn't respond.

No wards flared. No alarms screamed.

This wasn't external.

He sucked in a breath that didn't seem to reach his lungs.

His fingers dug into the table edge until the wood groaned.

Sebastian's eyes lifted.

The pupils rolled back until there was nothing left but white.

His hands rose, palms open, fingers spreading with mechanical precision.

The air above his hands thickened, lines resolving out of nothing—a geometrically flawless dome emerged.

Samthrax set his mug down with deliberate care. "That can't be good."

Sage moved without thinking, dropping to the floor beside her brother. She felt it immediately—Sebastian shoved to the edge of himself, locked out, panicked. She sat close, rested a hand against his leg, and let her light slip inward. She found him there and stayed.

Sebastian's mouth opened.

The voice that came out was not his.

It carried weight without volume. Authority without warmth. Language stripped to function.

"The subject no longer occupies the temporal lattice."

That caught everyone's attention.

Pauline tilted her head.

"Translate."

Sebastian's jaw worked, resisting.

"The anchor persists. The location does not."

His hands lifted higher. The image clear and concise above his palms.

Saffron moved closer to the projection.

Angelic realms were not unknown to her. She had brushed them since crossing over—felt their boundaries in passing, the way a shoreline announces itself long before water touches skin.

This place did not acknowledge shadow.

Did not accommodate compromise.

"Is that The Caethera?"

The voice answered her without looking.

"Sanctum confirmed."

The projection shifted. Land unfurled beneath the dome—meadow, river, boundary markers glowing with sigils older than recorded dominion law.

Pauline stepped closer, loa stirring low.

"Dat place sits outside time?"

Sebastian's head tilted at an angle that made Seraphina's stomach turn.

"Correct. The subject has been removed from sequence."

Killian's fingers curled at his sides. Well, there goes the original plan.

"Removed how."

The pause that followed felt deliberate.

"The timeline no longer recognises her as available."

The room digested that piece of information.

Seraphina closed her eyes and sighed so deeply it felt structural. Seriously, did the universe have some kind of loyalty card for unnecessary complications?

"Okay, bottom line. Can we get to her and bring her home."

The dome flared.

"Threshold access is contingent upon alignment."

Irritation tightened Killian's gut. He knew where this was going and he didn't like it.

"And alignment means."

Sebastian's mouth curved.

"No shadow. No coercion. No false intent."

Pauline let out a soft, humourless laugh.

"Well, that rules out half this room."

The projection ended suddenly.

Sebastian crumpled forward, out cold.

Samthrax moved first, pulling the chair back and lifting him with surprising gentleness. He laid him on the couch.

Seraphina followed, guiding Sebastian's head into her lap. The skin on his face was chalk white, but his breathing was strong. She placed her hand on his chest, trying not to give in to the worry eating away at her.

Sage sat on the floor beside them; fingers laced through her brother's and felt the weight of the prophecy becoming real.

She didn't know how this ended yet—only that she would spend every breath she had making sure it didn't end the way it was supposed to.

***

The Council sat assembled in the side chamber, unrest winding between them.

Yvane stood at the head.

She had not slept, but she did not require the appearance of rest. Fatigue was for people who doubted their authority. She did not.

The extraction team waited along the lower tier. Blood still traced their boots from the failed sweep in 1695. They had gone exactly where the records said the girl should have been.

She wasn't.

Yvane did not allow the irritation to reach her face. Irritation suggested uncertainty, and uncertainty was contagious.

"The site was empty," the team lead reported, spine straight, voice precise. "No residual heat. No active concealment. Whatever removed her did not leave a trail we could follow."

A murmur moved the table.

"Moved to another time?" Maltren ventured, hopeful.

"No," Yvane answered. She had already ruled that out. "If she were moved forward or backward, we would see the residue."

Her gaze swept everyone at the table.

"There's none."

Rowena sat two seats down, hands folded, posture immaculate.

Inside, every instinct she possessed was screaming.

The girl was more than hidden.

She was gone in a way they didn't yet understand.

Yvane stepped away from the table towards the ancient glass clouded with dormant light.

"There is one way we can find her."

No one protested as she whispered words no ears could hear. The looking dome responded with a low resonance as layers of concealment peeled back under force.

An image appeared.

A meadow.

A river.

A building nested into the land itself, seamless, luminous.

Several councillors inhaled quickly, caught off guard by what they were seeing.

Yvane was not.

Recognition landed with professional satisfaction.

"The Caethera."

A few heads turned. A few brows furrowed.

"That place is myth." Varas objected.

"No," Yvane replied. "It's not."

Her fingers traced a control spell in the air. The image magnified.

Rowena's stomach dropped.

The Caethera did not appear on extraction maps because it had specific entry rules few could pass.

Yvane smiled faintly.

"So," Maltren drawled, leaning back. "The girl ran to an angelic cradle."

"A sanctuary." Salen added. "How very strategic."

Yvane's satisfaction went up a notch.

"Sanctuaries are designed for protection, not permanence."

Rowena felt cold gather between her shoulders.

That assumption would kill people.

"The Caethera reads intent," Rowena cut in before she could stop herself. "It doesn't respond to command structures."

Several eyes slid toward her.

Yvane turned slowly.

"Are you suggesting," she asked, voice measured, "that an ancient holding space can override Dominion authority, my authority?"

Rowena met her gaze.

"I'm suggesting it doesn't recognise it."

Yvane laughed—soft, indulgent.

"Everything recognises authority when pressed correctly."

She turned back to the chamber.

"The extraction proceeds immediately."

The team straightened, saluting as one.

Rowena's heart pounded.

"That place assesses worth and alignment. You're sending them to their deaths."

Yvane shot Rowena a withering look.

"You misunderstand the nature of barriers. They can be broken."

New coordinates locked in.

Orders rippled outward.

The extraction team moved.

Rowena stayed seated, perfectly still, watching the image of the Caethera glow with serene indifference.

It knew they were coming, and it was already judging them.

***

Brinnan watched from the Between.

This certainly merited his attention.

Three currents moved at once.

The hybrid was ensconced in a sanctum that he could not pass.

Her friends from the present were preparing entry which, considering the Graves shadow ties, was going to be entertaining.

Perhaps a few would be eliminated.

As for the demon, he would be sent back to where he came. Bound or not.

And the Council—fractured, arrogant, still mistaking force for inevitability.

Fools.

Brinnan's focus moved back to the Caethera.

He tested the perimeter out of habit.

It pushed back, the intention clear.

Access denied.

That amused him.

The extraction team reached the threshold.

Six of them.

Saturated in warding, souls weighed down by ritual permissions they believed counted as virtue.

The first crossed the marker.

The Caethera read him.

Brinnan felt the assessment ripple outward.

The man froze mid-step.

His wards peeled away in layers, completely stripped and rejected. His body remained intact long enough for the truth to register.

Every act. Every compromise. Every cruelty justified as necessity.

The soul beneath it all stood naked.

Blackened and dense.

Corruption outweighed potential. Disposal followed.

The ground beneath him fell inward, not down but through.

Gone.

The second tried to pull back.

Too late.

Judgement did not require proximity.

His retreat ended mid-motion. The lower half of him remained long enough to fall.

The third attempted a counter-spell, hands already shaping coercion.

That earned speed.

His body collapsed inward, ribs cracking, breath crushed out of him as the sanctum denied his form the right to remain coherent.

The fourth never made a sound.

The fifth lasted long enough to understand.

The sixth wept.

Six assessments. Six refusals.

Each soul routed cleanly into the understructure that fed the Caethera.

Much like a mail sorting room.

Efficiency always impressed him.

He watched in amusement as the horror of the scene landed in the council chamber.

Several councillors recoiled as the viewing surface continued to display the aftermath with clinical indifference.

Anger cut through Yvane.

She stepped forward and layered spell over spell, authority braided into every command.

The barrier flexed.

It lasted for a fraction of a second.

Then the Caethera corrected the imbalance.

The spells dismissed.

The viewing dome cracked down the centre, the image fracturing into static light before going dark.

Silence slammed into the chamber.

Yvane stood rigid, hands clenched, jaw clamped so tight she felt a tooth crack.

She refused to accept this as defeat.

It was nothing more than a delay.

She turned and left without acknowledgment, already calculating a different angle.

Brinnan watched her go.

Patience had taught him what arrogance never could.

Force failed where inevitability succeeded.

The girl remained untouched.

The Graves/Bellarose line adapted.

The Council exposed itself.

Brinnan settled back into the Between, satisfied.

Let them struggle.

He had time.

And time, when wielded correctly, always bled the loudest players first.

***

Sebastian sat hunched on the couch, colour returning in uneven patches. His eyes were unfocused, but he was there.

Whatever had spoken through him was gone.

Killian watched him carefully. It had let go too easily.

That never meant anything good.

A shrill sound echoed through his head, the unmistakable tone of Alaric's ring.

Twice in two days, he was starting to feel special.

He cut the air.

The stone wall split cleanly.

Rowena stepped through without hesitation, hair in disarray, expression brittle with restraint. The portal sealed behind her.

Her voice didn't waver—but her hands did.

"They're dead."

Killian had seen Rowena walk out of massacres looking cleaner than this.

Whatever she'd witnessed had left its mark.

Seraphina moved without a word, one hand at Rowena's elbow, the other guiding her to a chair.

Samthrax followed with a coffee, pushing it into her hands.

His answer to every catastrophe. And maybe the only one that made sense right now.

"Who's dead Rowie?" The nickname Killian had called her when he was a child slipped out.

She looked at Killian. Horror lingered in her eyes.

"The entire extraction team."

No one spoke. Not even Samthrax.

Killian closed his eyes.

They'd trained together for years.

They were tight. Efficient. Loyal.

But they also followed orders.

Rowena wrapped her hands around the warm mug to compose herself. "Do you know where Zinnia currently is?"

Seraphina was starting to think maybe their rescue wasn't going to be a quick in and out. "Yes, we traced her to a place called The Caethera."

"Are you aware of the unique entry requirements?"

Pauline nodded, "We are, chèr."

"Well, they didn't pass the test." Rowena took a sip, setting the mug on the coffee table. "The Council was gathered to watch the extraction, we saw everything."

Shadows crept up from Killian's boots. He forced them back down.

"I don't know what to be more annoyed at—the continued machinations behind my back, or the fact that Yvane has just killed six of my people."

Seraphina's mouth twisted. "Bet that set the cat amongst the pigeons."

"It certainly has," Rowena replied. "Yvane's overplayed her hand. They're starting to realise she's using them as insulation."

"And they also know they can't get to Zinnia."

"Yes."

That earned a small smile. "Good."

"Yvane's not going to retreat. She'll pivot."

"She can pivot all she bloody wants, I have a plan for the entire council once we get Zinnia back. The bastards will rue the day they went behind my back."

Rowena looked at him.

And thanked whatever gods still bothered listening that she'd chosen his side early. There were people you opposed, and there were people you survived. Killian Graves belonged firmly in the latter category.

Killian turned back to the table, the spellwork was assembled. "We were about to attempt entry."

Rowena didn't bother disguising her reaction. "You absolutely are not."

Her attention cut to Killian, then Sage, then Sebastian.

"The Graves blood disqualifies you. All three of you."

Sebastian stiffened. "We didn't do anything."

"I know," Rowena replied evenly. "But that's not how the Caethera works."

"And you." She looked at Samthrax. "I don't even need to explain."

Samthrax raised both hands. "Listen. I respect boundaries. Especially holy ones that would fry me from the inside."

Saffron snorted. "Interesting image." She turned to Rowena. "So, who in your opinion will pass through unscathed."

"You. You're already on the other side of judgement."

Saffron's mouth twitched. "Death does simplify things."

"Seraphina you too will be welcomed."

Seraphina frowned. "What part of me screams 'sanctified'?"

"You don't want anything from your friend. You carry love, nothing else."

The humour drained from Seraphina's face. "I do."

Her gaze moved to Pauline. "You protect her without trying to own her. That'll be enough."

Pauline inclined her head.

Killian paced. This wasn't the plan. They moved together. That was the point.

Now half of them were staying behind. Including him.

He didn't argue. He could see the logic. That wasn't the problem. It just didn't sit right.

Letting others take the risk while he stayed clear of the blast? That was someone else's strategy. Not his.

And Seraphina—

No. He wasn't going to let that thought finish.

"We better get this done before Yvane finds a way to break in."

Seraphina walked over and kissed Killian. Long enough that no one interrupted.

"Try not to start a war while we're gone, babe."

She tapped his chin.

"No promises." He smacked her backside, already planning to make good on it.

Groans followed from the others—exaggerated gagging, eyes covered.

The three women moved to stand together.

Killian traced the final symbol into place.

The table lit from beneath—a pulse of raw force.

The walls shivered. The roof shook.

Then the threshold opened—white and blinding.

Saffron floated to the edge.

"I'll go first. If we're going to be smote, I'll feel it less."

She went through. Seraphina and Pauline followed.

For one heartbeat, the sanctum and the witches saw each other clearly.

The rest waited in the dark.

Nineteen

"The crossing succeeds only when no single soul claims the journey."
— From the Apocrypha of Shared Passage

The light stretched ahead of them.

Then the veil dropped.

Seraphina had no idea what to expect—but stumbling waist-deep into a freezing brook wasn't on the bingo card. She gasped, scrambled to the bank, and hauled herself out, already imagining eels, crocodiles, or some sentient Caethera-style river beast slithering up for a snack.

Holy shit.

She flopped onto her back, breath sawing in and out, the sky above so clear it looked manufactured. Not combusting from latent darkness? Great. Not eaten? Even better. Now if her heart could stop trying to jackhammer through her ribs, that'd be ideal.

Come to rescue Zin—die of cardiac arrest. Ironic.

Saffron drifted to her side, arms out like some theatrical angel descending from glory.

"How was the water, dear?" Not even trying to hide her smirk.

"Wet." Sarcasm helped more than the breathing exercises.

Pauline stepped through last.

The threshold skimmed her skin—hesitating, reading her power, her intent. It opened.

She landed with both feet solid on the ground, then knelt—hands flat to the earth.

"Thank you," she murmured. "For lettin' us in."

She stayed there a moment longer, letting it adjust. Letting it know she wasn't here to take anything that wasn't offered.

Then she rose, brushing her palms clean, and turned to the others with a grin that was more relief than bravado.

"Well. We made it. And I gotta say—it don't suck."

Ahead of them, the dome waited. It winked in the morning light, aware of their approach.

Pauline nodded toward it.

"That's where she is."

Her voice didn't shake. But her loa sure did.

***

Zinnia drifted up through the last threads of sleep, reluctant to leave.

Matthew had pulled her into his arms. He was kissing her thoroughly, like he didn't plan to stop.

She would've liked to stay in that dream.

But voices were breaking through—

Familiar ones.

Her feet hit the floor. She didn't bother with shoes. Body tight with anticipation, heart already moving ahead of her.

Zinnia took the stairs two at a time, barely touching the rail, skidding to a halt as three women crossed the threshold.

Seraphina. Saffron.

And—

Her breath caught.

Mémère.

No one spoke.

Her grandmother crossed the floor, tears on her cheeks and arms already open.

Zinnia flew into them. A guttural sound broke loose as she clung back, fists bunched in her grandmother's shirt like she was ten years old again and her world had come apart.

Pauline pressed a kiss to her hair.

"Mais bébé, it do dis heart good to be settin' eyes on you, yeah."

Zinnia shook her head, words tumbling out between sobs she couldn't hold back.

"Everything's a mess. I tried to hold it, but I—"

Pauline cupped her face, gentle but sure.

"You done held more'n most ever could, bébé. An' you still here."

Behind them, Seraphina cleared her throat. Her eyes were glassy, her arms open.

"I'd like my emotional breakdown now, if no one minds."

Zinnia launched at her—or maybe they both moved at once. The hug was fierce and undignified, full of laughter punched through with too much feeling.

"God, your hair's a mess," Seraphina muttered, voice thick.

Zinnia sniffed. "So's your face."

"You're glowing like a damn saint. I'm offended."

"You're offended? I ripped a hole in the world."

"Yeah, yeah. We'll unpack that after a stiff drink and collective therapy."

Both women were laughing and crying at once.

They stepped back.

Zinnia moved to her grandmother, slinging an arm around her shoulders. Pauline squeezed her waist in return.

Zinnia turned to Saffron.

"Thank you for coming, Saffy. I'd hug you, but the whole death thing still weirds me out."

Saffron beamed. "You and me both, my dear."

Zinnia exhaled, still trying to catch up with herself.

"Seb let me know you'd found me. Then we had to escape to this place, and I was worried you wouldn't be able to track the tether."

She kept the shadow riding him to herself—for now.

"So much has happened I don't even know where to start—probably somewhere between divine interventions, hunky woodsman, and weaponised pitchforks."Top of Form

Seraphina raised a brow. "Oh, colour me interested. Point me to the nearest coffee pot, so we can do this story right."

Pauline slapped her arm gently. "Zinnia Maisie Hart, a woodsman? Dis be no time t' be lookin' at dat, bébé."

Zinnia winked. "Always time, Mémère."

They drifted toward the kitchen, the quiet shuffle of feet against the flooring grounding them. On the sideboard, a tray waited—coffee, mugs, creamer, sweetener. Exactly what they needed, exactly when they needed it.

Seraphina let out a low whistle. "Okay. This place reads your cravings? Dangerous. I may never leave."

She poured two mugs, passed one off, then paused—her expression shifted. Still teasing but laced with concern.

"Okay, real talk. You good? Because you look like someone rewired your soul with jumper cables."

Zinnia managed half a shrug. "Define good."

The others trailed after her into the seating alcove. Pauline lowered herself, with the ease of someone saving energy for later. Seraphina carried the tray, setting it down with enough care to hint her hands weren't as rock-solid as usual.

Zinnia stayed standing.

"Okay. So. You know where I landed—after Brinnan yeeted me through a portal like a discarded sock. Since then… it's been pretty bloody hectic."

She rubbed her arms, suddenly aware of how much tension hadn't left her body.

"My power's jacked to full voltage. I tore a hole in the Veil. Accidentally. Witchhunters showed up. Tried to skewer Mum. It didn't go well for them."

Pauline, mid-honey stir, looked up slowly. "Didn't go well how?"

Zinnia hesitated. "Let's say I exploded and leave it at that."

Pauline returned to her stirring. "You always had a flair for da dramatic."

Seraphina held up a hand, as if stopping traffic. "Wait—Mum? As in your actual, biological, pushed-you-out-the-loin-mother?"

Zinnia nodded toward the upstairs area.

"Sleeping. Along with a literal angel. And the woodsman."

She rubbed the back of her neck, suddenly aware of how insane this all sounded out loud.

"Who, as it turns out, is not actually a woodsman."

Seraphina stretched her legs out, crossing them at the ankles.

"So. Angel upstairs. Veil ripped open. Woodsman who isn't. Actual mother in the flesh. And you exploded. That about cover it?"

Zinnia nodded slowly. "Give or take a divine intervention."

Saffron saluted. "To divine interventions."

Pauline's eyes stayed on her granddaughter, full of knowing.

"Bébé, you talkin' fast, but your heart still catchin' up."

Zinnia exhaled hard. "Yeah. It does that."

She didn't know where to start. Half the shit still didn't feel real. There was blood on her boots and power clawing through her—and here she was, drinking coffee with her family and friends, feeling nowhere near normal but wishing she did.

Seraphina tilted her head.

"So, what's the deal with the 'not-a-woodsman'? He got a secret stash of holy relics, or is he just here as your eye candy?"

Zinnia's lips quirked. Trust Seraphina to spot her attraction with sniper-level precision.

"Turns out he's a Veil-walker. Not much more I know, because chatty Cathy is not his style. I do know he has way too much honour and a disturbingly solid jawline."

Pauline grunted. "Sounds like trouble."

Saffron grinned. "Sounds like your type."

Zinnia couldn't disagree with that.

The silence that followed wasn't awkward. It was the kind that emerged when everyone in the room was holding something fragile and knew better than to rush it.

Footsteps came from the stairs.

All eyes turned as Lilly walked into the room.

She'd heard voices and followed them down. She knew Pauline on sight—there was no mistaking that line, that presence. And the two Bellarose witches were obvious even without the matching hair and eyes.

Her daughter had powerful allies.

She cleared her throat.

"Morning, ladies."

Her eyes flicked to Zinnia, uncertain where she fit in this moment.

Zinnia stood and crossed to her mother. She felt Lilly's nerves tapping under her skin—so she wrapped her into a quick hug.

"Morning, Mum. Let me introduce you."

She gestured to Pauline.

"This here is Mémère. Pretty sure you can tell—she looks like Dad."

Pauline rested her hands on her knees, fingers moving over her joints in an old, familiar rhythm. Her eyes on the woman her son had loved. The aura was bright, greener than spring shoots—healing, open. She could see why Remy had fallen.

Her smile came easy.

Lilly managed a small one in return. Her chest was a hive of agitation, buzzing too loud to ignore. She'd never met her mother-in-law, and gods help her, she wanted to make a good impression. She wasn't sure why that mattered so much—but it did.

Zinnia lifted a hand toward the cushions.

"This is Seraphina. She's literally my ride or die."

Seraphina offered a soft nod and a cheeky grin.

"Morning Zinnia's mum."

"And this is Saffy," Zinnia continued. "Seraphina's mother. She's, well—"

"Dead," Saffron supplied cheerfully. "Is the word I believe Zin is looking for. Lovely to meet you, Lilly."

Lilly's shoulders dropped as she relaxed into the moment. Her entire body tingled in relief at being accepted.

Zinnia nudged her gently toward the cushions. "I was filling them in. Broad strokes. We need to talk logistics, but it can wait 'til the rest show their faces."

She didn't even finish the sentence before the sound of bickering floated down from the landing.

"Divina, for Pete's sake, lass—let them catch up before ye start throwin' strategy at their heads."

Matthew was clearly exasperated.

"We don't have that luxury." Divina hissed back. "Time's not on our side."

Zinnia stepped into the archway, arms folding, one brow already raised. "You two are about as subtle as stepping on a rake in the dark. If you're done eavesdropping, come join us."

Matthew nudged Divina with his elbow, she shoved him back then gave Zinnia a wide smile.

"Don't mind if we do."

Divina made her way down the stairs, Matthew trailing behind, shaking his head.

Zinnia angled a thumb toward the group still seated—three of them full of curiosity. Lilly… not so much.

"Everybody—this is Divina. She's the actual angel. She grows on you. Kinda like mould."

Divina lifted her chin in greeting—then surprised both herself and Zinnia by sticking out her tongue in a childlike flip-off.

Matthew inclined his head. "I'm Matthew. Pleased to be meetin' ye."

Zinnia turned toward the others, hand gesturing lazily.

"Seraphina, Saffron, and Mémère—otherwise known as Pauline."

Seraphina gave Matthew a slow once-over, then tipped her head toward Zinnia.

"So this is the honourable jawline you were gushing about."

Zinnia groaned, heat rushing up her neck. "I was not gushing."

"You kinda were," Saffron chimed in, grinning. "We were all very polite about it."

Matthew's brows shot up. Apparently that part of the conversation hadn't carried upstairs.

"Happy t' be useful," he chuckled.

Pauline was still watching him—curious. Her loa were dancing all over the place. This man mattered.

"You from one o' dem old lines, ain't ya?"

Matthew shrugged. "Somethin' like that."

Not the time or place to unpack his history. But he knew he'd have to, eventually.

Zinnia noted how her Mémère's question hit him—her own power picking up the defensiveness, the evasiveness.

She let it slide. For now.

"He's saved our lives more than once, so let's all try to be suitably impressed."

Pauline gave a soft grunt.

Then she looked to Divina. "An' you, angel—dat glow always dat bright, or jus' when somebody get you good an' irritated?"

Divina's expression didn't change, but her eyes flashed with dry humour.

"Depends on the level of irritation."

Saffron let out a low whistle. "She's terrifying. I like her."

Lilly had sat back—watching, absorbing—but now she gave a heartfelt smile.

"Well, I for one am glad you're all here."

Zinnia nodded vigorously. She sank down onto the cushions. "Me too."

Divina and Matthew took their seats.

Small talk bubbled up while hands reached for coffee, buttered the fresh pastries that had appeared, or swiped pieces of fruit.

The laughter was real. The calm? Brief. But welcome.

It didn't take long however for the bigger questions to press in.

Seraphina set her mug down, eyeing the group.

"Okay, as lovely as this reprieve is, we need to get down to business… I've been thinking. We came through a portal that should still be open. Couldn't've been more than a couple hours ago from our end."

She looked to Pauline and Saffron for confirmation.

Her mother nodded. "Should still be there."

Pauline just shrugged.

Divina savoured the last mouthful of her very creamy, sweet beverage. You couldn't die of heart disease or diabetes when you were an angel. She loved that perk. She shook her head.

"Unfortunately, it's not."

That statement pulled every eye to her.

"The Caethera shut it the moment you crossed. It let you in—but it was a one-way deal."

A flicker of alarm touched Seraphina's face. "So… what? We're stuck here?"

Saffron raised a brow. "I quite like it here. Fresh pastries, bottomless coffee—what's not to love?"

Zinnia didn't smile. "Saffy, I love you. But I'm beyond ready to go home."

Divina held up her hand. "Don't get your panties in a twist. I know a way back."

Matthew leaned forward slightly. "What kind o' way we talkin'?"

"A slide," Divina answered. "Through the Veil. Not a door—that's too unstable. But if you and Zinnia work together, we can ride the Veil's current back to the moment you left. Or close enough."

Pauline tilted her head. "Soundin' a lot like stitchin' a hole in a boat… while it's still sinkin'."

"It's risky," Divina agreed. "But it's the only path guaranteed to drop us exactly where we need to be. The Veil remembers your timeline. We can use that."

Zinnia looked at Matthew, who was already watching her.

Their connection pulsed—shared power.

Shared risk.

He nodded.

She prayed she wasn't going to live to regret this.

"Tell us what to do."

Lilly crossed her arms, mind ticking too fast to ignore.

She wasn't about to jump onto this escape hatch without a little more information.

"Hold on." Her voice was even, but every word carried. "Let's not forget—I'm Gateborn. I know the Veil. And I'm telling you now, it's not exactly known for generosity. Especially not for one hybrid, one runaway—me—and a Veilwalker who, unless I'm mistaken, left without permission. Add an entourage of powerful witches and this starts to feel less like a journey and more like a provocation."

The others didn't speak, but their silence tilted toward agreement.

Divina had expected it. Lilly never accepted the surface level—she examined, she questioned, she considered what was being asked.

"You're right," she agreed. "I may have… skipped a few of the finer points. The Caethera has told me our time here is done. This is the only way back."

She looked around the circle. "There is no plan B."

Divina pushed on.

"Yes, it's a risk. But it's not reckless. We have two Gateborns, one Veilwalker. That's a combination strong enough to cut a path—and hold it. And the rest of us aren't exactly fragile."

Her voice softened. Not pleading, but clear.

"We can do this. But we do it together. With trust. And precision. Because that's what it's going to take."

Zinnia snagged a piece of melon and bit down with zero ceremony. "Well, hell. At this point, we're not exactly strangers to risk."

The juice ran down her thumb, but she didn't care. Small pleasures. Last ones, maybe.

Lilly gave a tight nod. Apprehensive didn't cover it, but in a no-other-option scenario, peace was something she'd have to fake until she found it. Her daughter was about to walk headfirst into danger—for the umpteenth time in as many hours.

She'd thought absentee mothering was hard. Turned out being present came with higher stress levels.

Pauline patted the table softly. "Well, bébé, if da path's there, den we walk it. Ain't never been a Broussard born who ran from hard ground."

Saffron arched an eyebrow. "I second that. I didn't cross realms just to float around waiting for the next apocalypse."

Seraphina shot her mother a long-suffering look. "Technically, you're already dead."

"Details," Saffron replied breezily.

Matthew leaned forward, elbows braced on his knees.

"It's got t' be clean. No second guessin', no hesitation. The Veil don't play soft—step wrong, and it'll turn on ye quicker'n breath."

Everyone felt the gravity.

Divina stood, brushing invisible dust from her palms. "Alright then. No time like the present."

Zinnia looked over. "So, how exactly are we doing this?"

Divina gave a sheepish cough. "The Caethera provided me with an exact map to follow. Albeit… in a rather unconventional format."

She turned and extended her wings fully for the first time.

Emblazoned across the span of her feathers were glowing orange runes, twisted vines, and unfamiliar symbols, as if someone had graffiti-tagged the angel in the name of navigation.

Zinnia couldn't hide her amusement. "Geezus. That's… not your colour."

Divina flipped her off without heat. "Apparently this is so we don't lose it. Short of someone cutting off my wings, the map stays intact." She hesitated. "Also… I can't actually read it. One of you will need to navigate."

Pauline stood, stepping toward her. Her loa stirred beneath her skin, rising to meet the energy laced in the runes. She lifted a hand and traced one of the vine-marked paths with a fingertip.

The glowing strand straightened, responding instantly.

Divina twitched. A laugh burst out of her, startled and unguarded. "Sorry—apparently I'm ticklish."

Pauline's smile pulled gently. She'd never stood this close to a being like this—celestial, radiant in a way no human ever could be. The feathers beneath her fingers were soft as breath.

She let the sensation pass through her before speaking.

"I can see de path," she followed it with her eyes. "Entrance, direction, an' where we land. Das doable, sure."

Pauline lowered her hand from Divina's wing, the markings still humming faintly in her vision.

She turned to Zinnia.

"Once we step off, bébé, ain't no turnin' back."

Zinnia met her eyes. Whatever fear had been there earlier had burned out, leaving only resolve.

"Yeah, I know Mémère. We got this."

Matthew rose, bracing himself. The Veil didn't offer second chances. If he got this wrong, prison would be a mercy. But failure wasn't on the table—not with Zinnia in the picture. Not when he had plans that involved freedom, a real bed, and her in it.

"Then we best get t' movin'."

Divina folded her wings, light dimming to a contained glow.

"The Caethera can't hold the path open for long."

Zinnia's eyes lingered on each of them in turn—every face, every choice that had led them here. The thought of losing even one surfaced, she stamped it back down where it couldn't interfere.

"Alright then, let's go home."

Seraphina stood and came over to Zinnia, she gave her a hug. She knew her moods, could see the stress-cloud hanging over her.

"You're not alone, Zin. You got us. We got you. Yeah?"

Zinnia sighed. Appreciative that this shitshow wasn't hers alone.

"Yeah."

One by one, they stood.

The Caethera listened.

And the Veil began to stir.

Twenty

Maison Bellarose

The early morning light filtering through the stained-glass windows of the Scriptorium was soft—too soft for Killian's current temperament.

He stalked the length of the room, boots clipping against the polished flooring, agitation visible in every movement. He was worried about the women. Sitting idle wasn't in his nature—and with the Caethera sealed, updates weren't an option.

Behind him, Samthrax sprawled across an overstuffed chesterfield. Feet up. Scowl locked in place.

"This waiting shit is bad for morale," the demon muttered, flicking a glowing coin between his fingers.

Killian didn't answer.

He paused by the window, eyes fixed on the shimmer of the Crescent's protective dome. From here, the Enclave looked peaceful. As always. But beneath the glamour, fractures were showing. The Council had overreached with the extraction stunt—Yvane especially. And he was beyond pissed.

235

The familiar shrill of Alaric's ring split his already aching head. He answered instantly.

The portal opened.

Rowena stepped through swiftly, taking in Killian's dishevelled state and the demon's deceptive calm. Her eyes moved over the room.

"Where are the twins?"

"Bed. Bit early for teens," Killian replied dryly.

"Good, because the news I bring is not for their ears."

That got their attention.

"Yvane's circling the drain. That failed extraction cost her more support than she expected."

Killian moved to the bar, pouring three whiskeys. He handed one to Rowena, the other to Samthrax. This conversation needed fortification.

"She's overplayed her hand. Who's turned?"

Rowena knocked back the glass and passed it back for a refill. He obliged.

"She's lost three allies. Oltren screamed at her across the chamber. Miri refused to vote with her. And Salen—well, he's already busy covering his own arse. She's bleeding support."

Samthrax unfolded from the couch and wandered over, loose-limbed as always.

"Might be time for a teachable moment, bossman. Council kiddies need a lesson."

He poured himself another generous shot.

Rowena paced toward the fireplace, lips set tight. "I agree with the demon. If you're making a move, it has to be soon. Once they see she's losing control, they'll either circle the wagons—or throw her to the wolves."

Killian was already there.

No way in hell was he letting someone else take out that viper.

Annihilation was too easy.

He had something far more unpleasant in mind.

"We take her off the board. Who else needs to go with her?"

Samthrax clapped his claws together, eyes lighting with glee. He'd been bored out of his ever-loving mind waiting on the others—this was exactly the kind of distraction he craved.

Rowena glanced sideways at Samthrax. He was still an unknown—and a little *too* thrilled at the thought of subduing Council members. She shelved the worry and focused on Killian's question.

"We can't martyr her." Rowena set down her glass. "So, my vote—she stays breathing. But Varas and Maltren? They're hers to the bone. They'll sink with her if they think there's power in the wreckage."

"They'll all live."

Killian moved to the side table, tracing a sigil into the wood with a fingertip.

"They just won't be going anywhere."

Samthrax chuckled darkly. "Oh, we're going subtle. I love subtle. How subtle?"

Shadows curled up Killian's boots. He didn't push them back.

"Think: vault-level magical hold, anchored beneath the Crescent. Null field. Sigil-locked. Not even light gets in."

Rowena folded her arms. "They'll scream politics."

"They can scream whatever they want," Killian replied. "No one'll hear them."

Samthrax perked up, fully alert now. "Want me to corrupt her mirror network? Slow her messages down? Make her think she's still in control of the others?"

"Do it." Killian didn't even look at him. His focus had already shifted, calculating the chain reaction this move would set off. "I'll get to the other members and feel out who can be trusted—and who's going into the vault. It's time to clean house."

Samthrax let out a whoop, half-standing—then groaned and dropped back onto the couch. "Shit, bossman. I'm tethered to Seraphina—I can't leave the damn house without her." He lifted his glowing wrists in proof. "Turns out demon leash magic? Highly effective."

"Shit indeed. I need you to get into Yvane's quarters to do this. I can't undo the spell—but if Sage and Sebastian go with you, it shouldn't strangle you. Might twist a little, though."

Samthrax paused long enough for it to count as consideration—then tore off at a sprint, vanishing toward the twins' rooms.

Rowena followed his exit with narrowed eyes. "You trust him with this?"

Killian laughed, catching the horror etched across her face. "Believe it or not—I actually do."

Her lips parted for a reply, then closed again. Best not to chase that thread. "Alright. Where do you need me?"

He turned back to the table, the answer already waiting on his tongue. "Here. The four of us will handle the takedown. But if the girls come back and we're not—"

His glance cut toward the hall, toward the world outside. "They'll need someone to bring them up to speed. Someone I trust."

Relief threatened to show, but Rowena kept her face neutral. She wasn't a fighter—never had been. She was a strategist, a diplomat. Corruption was bad enough. Violence made her skin crawl.

She gave a single nod. "Then I'll hold the line."

Killian turned from the window, strategy stacked up in his head.

"Make yourself comfortable, Rowena—we've got work to do."

***

They stood at the bridge. The brook lay clear as glass—no ripple, no sound.

The Caethera had opened a way forward. Across the other side:

nothing but heat-haze.

Pauline didn't trust it. Neither did her loa.

Divina's wings spread beside her, the map moving across them. Orange runes shifted over white feathers. Pauline let her hand drift along one mark, watching the path adjust under her touch.

It leaned toward her.

She moved, the bridge accepted her weight without a creak.

Her loa drew close, whispering caution in a language older than the Bayou.

Each step took more effort than it should.

"Dis place we steppin' into? It lie pretty. Y'all keep ya wits 'bout ya," she called back.

The others followed, single file.

Matthew brought up the rear—his protective instinct running hot.

Leaving the Caethera had his teeth set on edge. Each footfall toward the Veil was a return to a battlefield he once guarded blind.

He scanned the opening ahead and felt it clean through to his soul.

This was a place he'd escaped. A place that had hunted him for decades.

And now he was walking straight back in—offering himself up on a silver platter.

He counted the ways this could go bad. Stopped at thirty-seven.

Knew he'd missed at least a hundred more.

Pauline crossed into the haze, she felt a dry flick against every part of her skin, quick as a lizard's tongue. Was this place *tastin'* her?

Every hair on her body rose.

"Bon Dieu," she muttered. "I'm gon' need a scaldin' hot bath an' a handful o' sage jus' t' scrub dis filth off my bones."

She kept moving forward, ignoring the insidious whispers that were now reaching her ears.

Her loa bucked wildly, desperate to leave. She started humming low under her breath, a cradle song passed down from swamp mothers. It calmed the spirit enough to hold.

This was gonna be a damn treacherous road.

She glanced back.

Divina staggered as she crossed. A violent tremor ripped through her frame.

Something scraped against her grace—deep, invasive. Her wings snapped in, reaction honed by centuries overtaking reason. The glow of her power dimmed, drawn tight to avoid attention.

The Caethera had warned her the Veil was sentient. It hadn't warned her it *disliked* her kind. She didn't belong here—and the Veil didn't pretend otherwise.

Zinnia came behind Divina.

And walked smack into a brick wall, not literally but that was the effect on her body.

Her vision whited out for half a heartbeat, lungs catching mid-breath. Her mouth dried.

She yelped, stumbling.

What the fuck?

Recognition sparked.

Of her. Of what she was.

The Veil reached for her.

Her throat clenched. Power reared high and fast, trying to tear its way out. Her fists pushed into her sternum as if she could stop it by touch alone.

No.

She gritted her teeth, dragging it back down before it erupted out of her.

If she cracked now, she wouldn't be Zinnia anymore—she'd be a breach.

An opening.

Something they could crawl through.

Voices bled into her head.

Welcome home, Gateborn. You carry the keys. Free us.

Her legs obeyed only because she forced them to. One step. Then another.

Her back went clammy.

This is not my home, dirtbags.

And freedom's not on the damn menu.

The Veil hissed.

Seraphina stepped off the bridge and through the opening.

Her witchy senses caught the tilt—like the whole world had slanted off-axis and hoped she wouldn't notice.

She knew glamour when she saw it. Illusion was second nature to a Bellarose.

But this?

This wasn't illusion.

This was *bait*.

And the Veil? It knew how to fish.

It draped the path ahead in beauty—sunlight slanting through trees, petals drifting, the scent of citrus and lavender.

The kind of scene that invited your guard to drop.

The kind you didn't question until it swallowed you whole.

Seraphina wasn't dropping a bloody thing.

She let her senses stretch—just enough to feel the hooks hiding in all that sugar.

Nice try, arsehole.

She didn't bother shielding. Shields made a statement. A big one.

Instead, she moved light, loose, eyes wide.

It would think she was compliant.

Let it.

And if the Veil reached for her?

It'd learn quick, compliance was not part of her makeup.

Saffron drifted through the threshold.

She hovered for a moment. Where it struck at the living, it simply… missed her. Passed right through like she wasn't there.

Because to the Veil—she wasn't.

She turned, expression unreadable as she took in the others.

How anti-climactic.

Pauline was humming softly. Distraction was Saffron's bet.

Divina moved stiffly; her glow dialled back to almost nothing.

Zinnia looked ready to combust.

Seraphina's movements were controlled in a way that meant *she felt it too.*

But what?

Saffron frowned. She didn't see the threat. Couldn't feel it. Just the heavy churn of their energy, the fight they were locked in.

She said nothing. Just kept moving, drifting ahead—while the others choked on phantoms.

Whatever the Veil was doing—she was outside it.

And that, she thought, could be useful.

Lilly followed apprehensively.

The moment her foot crossed the boundary, the recognition struck hard and fast.

There was no gentleness or grace, just a bodyslam of claim.

Gateborn. The true one. The lost one.

She crushed the sound between her teeth, her body going rigid as the Veil surged to meet her. The whispering didn't stop.

You are a key.

A pull took hold and spread outward. A compulsion guiding her toward something just beyond reach.

She resisted. Hard.

"I am not your key," Lilly was not giving into the perceived sweetness.

"And I am not here to release you."

The Veil took offence.

She couldn't care less.

Voices tangled. Promises slithered.

We will take the other. But you are the first. You are the root. Let us through.

Lilly lifted her chin. The voices crowded her mind, but her thoughts stayed fixed.

Not on herself.

On the others.

Zinnia. Barely holding it together.

Matthew. Already shielding the rear.

Divina. Radiance dimmed.

Pauline. Seraphina. Saffron.

All of them in her charge. That's what it felt like. A strange, maternal knowing. A burden she didn't resent—only feared she'd fail.

Hands clenched, she pushed forward. Step by step. The pull tried to splinter her focus. The voices turned to pleas. Then threats.

She didn't answer.

The Veil pressed tighter.

But she held.

Not because she was the strongest. Or the most magical.

Because she was *needed*.

And the one thing Lilly Les Revenantes had never walked away from—was being needed.

Matthew forced himself to cross after Lilly.

His gut churned every which way. He knew he was staring down a fate worse than death if it got its hooks in.

The Veil basically slapped him as soon as he entered.

He staggered one step, then another, boots dragging as if the ground was made of quicksand.

It remembered.

Not who he'd been.

Who he'd belonged to.

A veil-walker. A jailor. A traitor.

He'd walked this place as enforcer once. The Veil knew that scent. It didn't forget.

Mores the damn pity.

It closed around his ribs like shackles, breathing him in.

Property. Returned.

A rupture burst open behind his eyes—one he hadn't felt in years.

His knees threatened to give. He didn't let them.

Not with the others watching.

He knew this wasn't personal.

The Veil didn't hate.

It owned.

Or tried to.

He forced his lungs to expand as he inhaled, eyes fixed on Pauline's shape ahead.

Focus. Anchor. Get to the other side.

But the path blurred, appearing to melt around him.

From the corners of his vision, things crawled and writhed.

Hungry. Desperate.

He ignored them, he would deal with them only if they attacked.

He kept walking.

One foot.

Then another.

And every step cost more.

The Veil didn't care about pain. Only submission.

But Matthew Thorne had escaped this place once already.

And nothing—nothing—would drag him back.

Twenty One

"Every empire is only five lies away from collapse."
— From the sealed archives of the 2nd Council

Maison Bellarose

Samthrax bounded down the stairs, tail twitching with purpose. He hit the Scriptorium with all the subtlety of a stage cue, spinning into the room with unnecessary flair.

Behind him, the twins trudged in—the world's most unimpressed cavalry.

Sebastian's hair was halfway to feral. His hoodie sleeves swallowed his hands, hiding the burns from last night. He hadn't slept—hadn't even tried after the Caethera kicked him out when he tried to trace Zinnia's tether to find his mum. It hadn't played nice.

He didn't say a word, just collapsed into his favourite chair and glared at the floor.

Sage followed, blinking blearily. At least her clothes matched. Her brother looked like he'd dressed in the dark during an exorcism.

She took one look at the lineup and groaned. "We're doing something stupid, aren't we?"

Killian offered a lopsided smile. "Morning to you too. And no—it's strategic."

Samthrax whipped up a latte without breaking stride, setting it in front of Sebastian with unexpected grace. It was the closest thing the demon offered to an apology. The kid looked wrecked.

Sebastian accepted it with the enthusiasm of someone who needed caffeine more than oxygen. He didn't speak until the second sip. "Where are we going?"

"Yvane's quarters," Killian replied. His gaze lingered on his son's face—still startled by how much of himself he saw there. "Samthrax is going to corrupt her mirror network. Delay her messages. Make her believe she still has allies."

Sebastian stirred his drink. "And we're going because he's chained to Mum?"

"Bingo." Samthrax chimed in. "You two are the only Bellarose blood in the house. My spell leash says stay close or combust. I've seen combustion. It's messy."

Sebastian's lip curled. "You sure this is smart? Last time I played conduit, I nearly exploded."

Killian's expression didn't soften. "There'll be no need to call on your magic. You're supervising. You're there for the bloodline, not the talent."

"So, babysitting," Sebastian cast Samthrax an amused look.

Samthrax turned, scandalised. "Do I look like I need adult supervision?"

Sebastian looked at him wryly. "You're wearing hellhound slippers. You need *something*."

Rowena snorted, the laugh catching her off guard. She hadn't expected this casual defiance. There was no fear in the boy, only razor-sharp sarcasm, barely held worry, and the kind of edge that came from watching too much fall apart too fast.

Samthrax was completely unbothered. "For the record, this is a top-tier infiltration mission. Not babysitting. Try to show some respect."

He handed Sage her coffee, then flopped into a chair—crossing his legs theatrically, slippers on full display.

Killian didn't quite smile, but the corner of his mouth twitched. Samthrax's attire made it hard to take the threat level seriously—but the demon knew exactly what he was doing.

Sage sipped her drink, fingers white around the mug. Her nerves were showing. She hadn't heard from her mother, hadn't dreamt of her either. It was like a light had gone dim, completely out of reach.

"Still nothing from Mum?"

Killian understood her unease. That's part of the reason he was sorting this council nonsense out now.

To get his mind off the incommunicado.

"No."

She nodded slowly, concern ratcheting up yet another notch. Not knowing was next level torture.

Sebastian stared at his father. "Do you think they're okay?"

Killian crossed the room and laid a hand on his son's shoulder. "Yes. I'd feel it if they weren't. So would you."

Sebastian didn't quite believe that. He wasn't sure what he'd feel anymore.

Samthrax stood and clapped his claws together. "Alright. Bellarose bellhops, time to take your favourite demon on a field trip."

Sage groaned. "Dear God."

Sebastian got to his feet, draining the rest of his drink. "Is this a magical road trip or are we stealing Gram's car again?"

"Alas, no Gran Turismo, young Seb. This mission requires stealth." Samthrax pressed a claw to his chest. "We'll travel by demon chariot—don't you fear."

Sage didn't look convinced. "That sounds traumatising."

Samthrax waggled his eyebrows with far too much enthusiasm. The twins shook their heads in synchronised dismay.

Killian's voice cut through. "Keep them safe."

Samthrax saluted with mock solemnity. "I'll guard these little treasures with my life, bossman."

"Be sure that you do." Killian crossed to Rowena passing her a warded scroll.

"If I'm not back in two hours, you trigger this. And for the love of all that's holy, don't open it until then."

She accepted it with outward calm, but her organs shuddered. This was a fail-safe—a contingency if he didn't return. And gods help them all if that scroll was ever needed.

She didn't want to imagine a Council without Killian at the helm. No one else had his integrity. Or his get-shit-done-no-matter-the-cost resolve.

Rowena tucked the scroll into her sleeve.

"Understood."

Killian's attention flicked once to the window. The Crescent enclave sat peacefully on the horizon.

But peace was a lie.

"Let's move."

***

Satisfaction moved through Brinnan, subtle as vapor.

The kind the preceded ignition.

Three threads spun beneath his gaze—tangled, tightening by the moment, poised to snap.

Killian was building a coup beneath the Crescent's glass smile.

He observed Yvane from the outer seam of time. Watched as she bled allies, clinging to the illusion of control with white-knuckled delusion.

The Council would not mourn her.

Power loved a vacancy and Killian was about to create a few.

Let them eat their own.

His attention drifted outward, farther, into the churning dark.

The Veil boiled.

Seven lights now moved within it.

Six breathing. One not.

The ghost glided untouched—an anomaly within the field.

The hybrid flared brightest.

His gaze slid to the Gateborn who had defected.

Lilly.

No hybrid fire in her, but powerful nonetheless.

She hadn't opened a door in decades—but the locks still knew her.

The Veil whispered to her.

She remained aloof and deaf to the insistence.

That… interested him.

But not as much as Zinnia.

His eyes found her again, cataloguing her.

Her magic was erratic. Her bloodline was mud-thick with complications.

She was the one the Veil wanted most—and the one it would never fully hold.

He watched her struggle. Felt her resistance. Her determination.

He touched the boundary of the Veil.

A brush, nothing more.

It shuddered in defence.

Shadow Ascendant was not a title—it was a state of being.

A resonance that the Veil could not unsee.

He did not interfere.

Why waste energy when arrogance and loyalty would finish the job for him?

Let them destroy themselves.

Then—when the strongest stood bleeding, and the weakest lay twitching—

He would walk through the smoke.

And claim her.

***

The portal opened with a reluctant hiss and the ungodly stench of sulphur.

Samthrax stepped through first, claws flexing, eyes glowing that low red that meant mischief was coming whether the world liked it or not.

"Alright, sugarbabies," he threw over his shoulder. "All aboard the Demon Chariot. Keep all limbs inside at all times—unless you're ready to part with one."

Sage winced as she followed. Crime-scene wrongness hit her square in the face. She pinched her nose. "This place needs an air-freshener. Industrial strength."

The chariot was... surprisingly luxurious. Polished onyx walls. Velvet seats. A dim amber glow that felt indulgent.

Sebastian slid in beside her. His shadows had stirred the second he'd entered. They slipped through his thoughts, murmuring encouragement, nudging for attention.

He ignored them.

Killian entered last, settling beside Samthrax, who was already flipping switches at the helm.

"Nothing'll bite while I'm driving," the demon assured him. "Demon highways are clean in, clean out. Unless something nasty's waiting at the exit."

Killian grunted. "I choose to remain vigilant."

"And I choose to remain awesome."

The chariot launched. Speed slammed them back into the seats.

Samthrax turned briefly. "Where do you want to be dropped, bossman?"

"Courtyard entrance. I've got council members to visit."

Sebastian kept his death grip on the seat. "Let me guess. They're not getting gift baskets."

"No. Some will be getting unemployment with new living arrangements."

The chariot screeched to a halt.

The twins yelped, arms flinging out to stabilise themselves.

Sebastian gagged. "Do you even have a license? You drive like you're racing yourself to hell."

"Correction." Samthrax tapped a button and seatbelts snapped into place, yanking them upright. "I drive like I own hell. Safety first."

Killian reached for the door. "You've got twenty minutes. Take the kids back when you're done. I'll meet you at the manor."

"Copy that." Samthrax rubbed his hands together. "Time to break the pretty lady's toys."

Killian gave one last look to the twins. "Be careful. I'll see you soon."

"You too Dad." Sage bit the inside of her lip, nerves firing on the same channel as every horror movie victim she'd ever watched.

Killian nodded. Then he was gone, disappearing into the corridor nexus beyond the courtyard.

The chariot reversed fast.

A map appeared mid-air. Samthrax tapped a bright red flare. "That's her."

A second later, the chariot slammed to a halt again—this time in front of what looked like a solid stone wall.

"And this." Samthrax leapt out all barely leashed excitement. "Is us."

The belts vanished. The twins got out on shaky legs, adrenaline peaking—dreading the return trip.

They stepped through into Yvane's private wing.

Samthrax pressed a clawed finger into the threshold of the room's magic, drawing a flicker of red light that slithered toward the nearest wall rune.

It fizzled.

He hissed between his teeth. "Right. These run hot."

Yvane's wing felt… alert. The kind of charged atmosphere that preceded detonation. The sigils weren't decoration. They were a language—one Sage had seen during her reading of the forbidden tomes in the scriptorium.

A binding script.

Sebastian moved toward a side table. "You sure we shouldn't just torch the whole place and call it sabotage?"

Samthrax grinned. "Tempting. But alas this is a *disruption mission*, not a declaration of war."

Sage glanced over her shoulder again. Her instincts were screaming at her.

The door remained closed. There were no sounds to indicate someone was approaching. But something was off.

She pressed two fingers to her temple, calling up the little shield her mother had taught her. Not a full one—just enough to blur their forms. If Yvane's systems were intelligent, she didn't want them logging their signature.

Samthrax crouched by the mirror console dominating the far wall. Seven nested panes of smoky glass shimmered with waiting glyphs.

"She's hooked into half the Crescent's communications through this. Her personal uplink's piggybacked onto the Council core. Which makes this… fun."

He reached into his coat and pulled out what looked like a silver marble. It pulsed faintly red.

"What is that?" Sebastian was genuinely intrigued, Samthrax had the most fascinating gadgets.

"A listener. I plant it in the spellroot of her mirror network—it hijacks signal flow, duplicates her permissions, and pings me anytime she thinks a thought too loudly."

"Subtle."

"Delicious," Samthrax corrected.

He pulled back a panel at the console's base and delicately inserted the device. Sparks danced.

For a heartbeat, the mirror fought him. Light fractured across the surface. One of the nested panes darkened. Then another. Then the whole structure dimmed to idle grey.

Samthrax sat back on his heels, satisfied. "She won't notice a thing. Every message she sends will still look delivered. But will actually bounce to me."

Sage let out a relieved breath, great now they could haul arse. Her sense of unease was growing, fast.

Sebastian frowned. "What about countermeasures?"

Samthrax stood and dusted his hands. "Already accounted for. I laced the relay with a hex shell. If she tries to purge the network, she'll purge the wrong half."

"Won't that tip her off?"

"Oh, eventually." He grinned. "But by then she'll be too busy trying to salvage her reputation to worry about her Wi-Fi."

A soft tone rang out.

Glyphs flared on every wall.

Sage spun toward the source. "That wasn't you, was it?"

Samthrax's eyes narrowed. "Nope. That's the security grid shifting. Which means someone's moving toward this wing."

Sebastian swore under his breath.

Samthrax reached for them both. "Time to go."

He used one claw to slice open the portal.

"Back to the chariot. Chop chop."

They slipped through.

The far wall rippled open behind them. Yvane stepped into the space they'd vacated with seconds to spare.

Twenty Two

"First it peels the skin. Then the name. Then the memory.
What's left still walks, but it's not you."
— Veil Survivor's Account, Sealed by Crescent Order

Pauline was halfway through tracing the path on Divina's wings when the map jumped.

She stopped; fingers suspended in the air. The glowing runes—so precise a moment ago—skipped, one symbol landing where another had been.

Her loa lit under her sternum with a snarl, kicking hard enough to blur her vision. Pauline reeled.

"Somethin' shiftin', an' it ain't takin' its time. Divina—don't you move, chére."

The runes began rewriting themselves outright—strokes reversing direction mid-curve, as if something unseen had taken control of the script.

Pauline squinted. Realisation hit, hard and fast.

"Da Veil's reworkin' the damn road right out from under our feet."

Confusion wrapped around Seraphina, with a healthy dose of 'oh shit'.

"How's that possible? We're following a locked path—"

"It ain't locked no more." Pauline pulled her hand back.

Zinnia scanned the fog rolling in, up to this point it had been all blue skies, fluffy clouds and lush meadows. She had even spotted a deer running in the distance, their feet following an actual yellow brick road.

Fairy-tale perfect. Which meant one thing—bullshit.

Underneath it reeked of danger. Her power had been bristling for release since they had crossed through.

"We need to keep going." But there was no ahead anymore— only ever-increasing white-out. At this rate, they'd lose visibility in seconds.

They were being tracked, actively.

Pauline felt it drag across her skin. A breath that didn't belong to anything with lungs. Her loa shoved closer, whispering in an ancient tongue, warning loud and clear. She held up her hand.

"No sudden steps. Y'all feel that?" Her palm hovered inches above the dirt. "It's under us."

The map flickered again—the glyphs dropped one by one. No longer a guide.

Saffron didn't feel any of it. She could see it, but she couldn't feel what they were standing in—and yet everything in her said run.

Saffron moved closer to Matthew, enough for the dead cold of her presence to register.

"This is your playground, Veilwalker. Tell me you have a way out."

Matthew didn't answer. Not because he didn't hear her. Because he did.

He was busy listening—to the rattle in the ground. The static in his teeth. The quiet before slaughter.

"Circle." Matthew snapped. Veil-born symbols appeared beneath his boots. "Backs together. Close as ye can."

They moved.

Zinnia on his left. Lilly on his right. It wanted *them*. One opened gates. The other *was* one. And him—he was the one who broke the leash.

He didn't bother sugar-coating it.

"It's fixed on th' three of us. Zinnia, Lilly, me. Th' rest o' ye—it don't care. We're th' ones it wants."

Saffron huffed. "Hard to damage someone already detached from the mortal coil."

Lilly's hands curled. Fear itched inside her body—old fear. The kind that had driven her to leave everything behind. She could feel the pull again. The whisper of thresholds calling to her.

"This is exactly why I ran."

Zinnia could feel it building. Her mark throbbed at the base of her neck, ready to explode, to shield, to consume. She didn't care which.

"It's here."

The fog stopped dead.

Pauline staggered. Her loa shrieked.

"This ain't natural."

The ground beneath them heaved.

Something climbed up.

Multiple somethings.

The mist congealed into form.

Limbs stacked where they shouldn't be.

Joints kept rotating long after they should have locked. Skin that didn't fit slouched over bones that didn't belong. Something crawled forward on four arms, dragging a torso that convulsed with every step.

The features drooped where muscle was supposed to hold firm— one eye intact, the other twitching.

A smile split across its skull, far too wide, as if the flesh had torn to make room.

It looked at them.

And grinned.

It careened toward Divina.

She moved fast.

Her wings erupted into their full span, a thunderous whoosh rolling outward.

Incandescence drove from her centre—sacred and vicious.

It cleaved the creature from crown to spine.

It keened. Not in agony.

In *delight*.

It tasted her divinity and wanted more.

Pauline threw a word into the dirt that split the glyphs wide. Her loa lunged. Another creature caught fire—then kept coming, wrapped in flame.

Zinnia's hands turned lethal. "What the hell *are* these?"

"Constructs," Matthew growled. "This place eats souls an' spits out weapons. They're made from everythin' th' Veil's swallowed down."

Lilly stepped in beside him, already summoning a spell between her palms.

"Tell me what to do."

"Anchor me."

"Left or right?"

"Both."

Zinnia nodded. "I'm in."

They locked formation.

The Veil *howled*.

Matthew crouched.

"Right," Matthew's eyes darkened with Veil magic. "We'll bring th' entrance down behind us. We don't run."

He drove his palm into the dead ground with the kind of force that came from old obedience.

Veinwork glyphs tore outward from the impact point, bleeding silver through the black soil.

The creatures *screamed*.

They remembered who he was.

The enforcer. The one who dragged them back in pieces.

Matthew's mouth curved into something that didn't qualify as a smile.

"Let's see how ye like bleedin', then."

The first row of constructs took it full force.

One exploded in a spasm of brittle calcification and bile-slick tissue, shrieking as splinters knifed outward.

Another convulsed and vomited light—the sound of a child laughing echoed from its throat, the tone fractured, curdling before it cut off mid-spasm.

The third didn't die at all.

It collapsed—then began to reassemble.

New limbs punched through the mist, stolen from something else. Its mass doubled. Mouths multiplied. Bones cracked and reset into unnatural symmetry.

Matthew felt the change beneath the surface. The Veil wasn't resisting.

It was adjusting.

It had been years since his sphincter had puckered this tight. But it did so now.

The Veil was just getting started.

Lilly dropped to one knee beside Matthew.

The spellwork was driving outward, uncontrolled. It would eat itself soon if they didn't pin it.

She felt it trying to climb her skin, desperate to break through flesh.

Only one thing came to mind.

She reached into her coat, pulled a curved ritual blade, and scored a clean line across her palm.

Her blood hit the soil.

The casting field drew in the red. Drinking greedily.

She pressed her hand flat to the dirt, fingers splayed, drowning out the chaos, and whispered the root-word that fused divides.

"Sta."

The wailing arcs stabilised, veins sliding into place. The ripple no longer lashed—it flowed.

Contained.

Channelled.

Matthew felt it the moment it clicked.

He caught her eyes—gave a nod.

Smart lass. Without her, the glyphwork would've punched through his lungs and kept going.

Now he could aim it.

Matthew zeroed in. He freed his magic—sending it through the field in bursts that didn't shake the earth so much as threaten its integrity.

And Zinnia let go of the leash.

Her power launched, raw and ravenous. It scraped heat from her lungs and reason from her mind. It didn't ask—it demanded release.

Zinnia doubled down, planting her stance. Her hands flew outward.

Brute-force destruction detonated from her core.

It met the nearest construct head-on—one of the tall ones, stitched together with half a dozen torsos and a head that didn't fit any of them. The thing exploded in every direction.

Something came with it.

A sound—high, endless. It scraped behind her eyes, wrapped around her ears. She staggered, blinked hard, tried to shake it off.

But it clung.

Zinnia's hands lowered slightly, breath caught in her throat. *Man, this job really needed better warning labels.*

Her magic wasn't satisfied.

It wanted to *devour* now.

The fog pulled inward.

Swirling faster and faster, until the mist went dense as cloth, then denser still.

And from that mass—

Something stepped out.

Every sense rebelled.

It didn't glitch or drag like the others. It didn't sway or stagger.

It stood. Steady. Balanced.

Engineered.

The Veil had assembled it with purpose. A bounty hunter. A lure.

Its torso ran too long, the joints stiff, layered beneath near-human skin that twitched as if remembering the person it once was. The face was a blank sheet—no mouth, no eyes, no promise of expression—

Until it found her.

Then it rearranged.

A mouth opened where there hadn't been one. Wet and waiting. Teeth pushed through like a secret breaking the surface. Sockets appeared and *watched* her.

Her gut somersaulted.

There was no question this thing was here for her.

Matthew saw exactly what was about to happen.

"Zinnia. Shield *now*."

Shield?

Her brain stalled. She hadn't even got to that chapter yet, in fact she hadn't even opened the bloody book.

But her power knew. Knew better than she did. Knew what it was *meant* for.

Her hands moved—the spell flared into action as the thing launched.

It didn't glide.

It didn't fly.

It *vanished*—

—then reappeared in front of her.

Zinnia barely had time to brace before impact.

The ward took the brunt, but the force was savage. Zinnia flew backward, boots carving trenches in the dirt, ribs jarred, arms locked against the pressure screaming through the barrier.

Pain rang through her arms. Her chest. Her mouth, she had bitten her tongue.

The construct didn't follow.

It stood there.

Head cocked. Studying. Measuring.

This thing wasn't mindless.

It had *orders*.

And she was the box it had come to check.

Fuck that.

She spat the blood out of her mouth, wiped her chin with the back of one shaking hand, and pushed to standing. "You want me?" Her voice came out feral. "Come earn it."

Lilly's protective instincts fired.

The way that thing hit Zinnia—no one else was a target anymore. The Veil had chosen.

Chosen her daughter.

Unacceptable.

Pauline's fingers plunged into the soil, knuckles grinding deep, drawing on her loa so fast it made her head spin. The spirits answered in a rush—with breathless warnings crackling behind her ears.

"It's fixed on her," she grit out. "Da others were bait. Dis one's collectin'."

Matthew's jaw clamped so tight he'd need a crowbar to prise it open later.

"Zinnia—don't let it lay a hand on ye."

He looked at Divina.

"You—amplify Lilly. If we blend all three channels, we can create a counter-resonance. A triad. Go."

Lilly didn't need to be told twice.

Her eyes shut. She raised her hands—and sent Gateborn energy flying. She felt it attach to Zinnia's aura.

Zinnia's magic surged. Lilly felt it punch through her. Her boots left the dirt—held in the grip of something much older than either of them.

Divina felt the clarity.

This was war.

And she was *built* for it.

Wings blazed to full span. She moved beneath Lilly and let herself shine.

A divine current coursed through the channel, and for one breathless instant—

The three of them *linked*.

Zinnia. Lilly. Divina.

The circuit closed, and magic thundered through it.

"For your sake, Matt," Divina hissed, eyes glowing, "this better work."

Matthew didn't answer.

Because in that moment, they all felt it.

This wasn't about eliminating Zinnia.

It was about retrieving her.

The construct opened its mouth—

And released a pulse. Low and guttural—like vertebrae grinding in a jar.

It didn't hit the ears.

It hit the bloodstream.

Zinnia buckled. Lilly arched mid-air as the drain yanked hard at her centre.

Divina opened her mouth—and what came out was a *choir*.

Full-throated, celestial, *mesmerising*.

They all understood in the same second:

If they didn't succeed here—

the world was lost.

And then—Zinnia's magic betrayed her.

It pitched forward, unbidden, drawn to the construct like floodwater to a fracture.

Trying to fill it.

Match it.

Merge.

She shoved it down with a growl, nearly gagging on the force clawing up her throat.

What the fuck is happening—

She turned, caught the others in her line of sight. Her voice came cracked.

"Someone wanna tell me what the hell that is?"

Matthew's face drained of colour. His eyes stuck on the thing like it had come back from his worst nightmares.

"Shite. It's baitin' the bond."

"The Veil knows yer blood—it's calling ye forward."

Pauline's body jerked into motion, scrambling for the edge of the circle.

"No no no—nononon," she gasped. "She touch that thing, her whole damn gate system's gonna flare like Mardi Gras. It'll drag us *all* in."

Saffron turned, eyes sharp as scythes.

"Then stop her."

Pauline didn't answer.

She was running.

Zinnia didn't hear the shouting.

She couldn't hear *anything*.

The pulse from the creature was still vibrating inside her, worming deeper—past power, past will, into every cell.

Her magic surged again, more violent this time.

Her hands went slick with energy.

Every part of her screamed to let go.

To *match* the thing in front of her.

To surrender.

And it knew her.

The part she'd buried under chains and dead days.

The part that didn't speak in human tongue.

The part that remembered what she'd been born for.

She took a step.

Another.

A puppet on a string.

"Zinnia," Matthew barked. "Don't ye bloody move."

It didn't reach her.

But the glyph Divina hurled beneath her boots did.

Silver veins flared up through the ground—threading through her soles, reaching into her legs, trying to *hook her back into herself.*

A hiss broke through her teeth. A tremor through her jaw.

She grabbed her own wrist, jerking it back—muscle fighting muscle—physically stopping the next spell from launching.

The construct tilted its head again, as if amused.

Like it already knew how this would end.

Zinnia lifted her chin, eyes burning.

Her power still boiled, fed by Lilly and Divina's open current.

But if she gave in—

They were all gone.

Zinnia's grip on her own wrist wouldn't loosen. Her whole body trembled from the inside out, magic straining, begging to finish what it started.

The construct gave one last lopsided grin as the fog peeled away from its body, unravelling until the creature was gone.

The mist disappeared along with it, like it had never been there and once again they were in the picture-perfect realm they had arrived in.

And wasn't that a huge arse lie.

For a heartbeat, no one moved or spoke. The danger had passed. But the dread stayed.

Matthew staggered, knees catching ground. His hands braced in the fading ash of the glyph field, heart thudding loud enough to drown out thought. It didn't feel like a win. It felt like being spared.

For what?

Seraphina's adrenaline hadn't gone anywhere. It still sat hot and restless under her skin, a side effect from having her life turned into a travelling horror show. *Her kingdom for a single, boring day.*

She glanced at Saffron—who, for someone technically dead, looked like she'd commit minor crimes for a stiff drink.

Pauline sucked in a lungful of much needed air. "Well," she wheezed. "We ain't dead."

Her loa purred inside her now, all sugar and smirk. "Y'all feel that? It let us go."

Divina turned slowly, wings half-furled. Runes burst back into place across the feathers. The road returned—highlighting a path through the maze.

Relief at not dying tragically was unfortunately becoming her new normal.

"I vote we get the hell out of dodge before it comes knocking again."

Saffron ghosted forward, her voice soft as embalming cloth. "I second the motion."

Lilly agreed wholeheartedly. She dropped beside Zinnia, hand out. "Hey. Still with us?"

Zinnia stared at her. She coughed as she tried to speak, her throat was full of dust. "Did we just get ghosted by a fog demon?"

Lilly grinned despite herself. "That's one way to put it."

She pulled Zinnia up—giving her a hug. "You did so well honey, I'm so proud of you."

"Thanks mum." Zinnia sagged into the hug for half a second longer than she meant to. Her body hadn't caught up to safety. Maybe it never would.

Matthew swore under his breath. "Divina's right—this ain't no victory. Jus' a breather. We need t' be gone."

Pauline was already packing up her talismans, half-muttering to them. "Dis road's like a jealous lover—don't look back, don't pause, don't even think about runnin'."

Zinnia laughed, "You're not wrong Mémère, I'm so grateful you're all here with me, but man I wanna go home."

Divina flew up to scout. Her voice rang down from above. "It's clear. But we better run like we owe it money."

Matthew helped Zinnia into the lead. "How's the grid lass?"

She flexed her fingers, sparks running from wrist to knuckle. "Stablish."

"Good," he kept his head on a swivel. "'Cause if this thing tries again, I'm none too sure we've got another round in us."

"You and me both." Zinnia had no doubt she didn't. Right now, she felt like curling up to sleep for a month.

Pauline assessed the map, got their bearings and the group started off quickly.

The sooner they got to the other side the better.

The Veil didn't speak again.

But it didn't need to.

It had seen her.

It had picked her.

And it wasn't finished.

Twenty Three

Killian marched into Oltren's office without knocking.

It smelled of steam and old parchment—maps draped across every flat surface, some curling at the corners from heat. Miri was perched cross-legged on the low bench near the back, sleeves rolled, ink on her hands.

Excellent. Two for one.

Oltren sat back in his chair, one hand resting on a carved armrest, the other gesturing to the seat across from him.

Killian took it.

These two had always held the line, even when politics got messy. But he wasn't here to test old loyalties. He was here to see if they still meant something.

"I need your voices, and I need them fast."

Oltren inclined his head. The man was as unreadable as always, but tiredness sat behind his eyes.

"How much do you know?"

"Enough."

Miri glanced between them. "Thank the stars." Her voice fell somewhere between relief and guilt. "I'm sorry, Killian. For not coming forward sooner. We didn't know who to trust—not even each other. But if you're making a move…"

She clasped her hands together.

"We're with you."

Killian held her eyes. Miri never apologised unless she meant it. A knot eased in his chest. He hadn't realised how tightly he was wound until right this second.

"I'm calling a council meeting. Yvane isn't invited."

Oltren steepled his fingers, nodding slow. This was no surprise—he'd seen this storm coming.

Killian leaned forward, elbows on knees.

"There's been planning. Behind closed doors. Actions that go against everything the Enclave is meant to stand for." He let the words sink in. "That ends today."

Miri stood. Ink smudged across her hip where she'd rested her hand. "Tell us when."

"Soon." He rose, eyes on both of them. "Stay alert. And keep your comms close. I've got a few more stops to make."

Killian left Oltren's office and headed for Salen's quarters.

Most of the council preferred to live on-site, buried in their sanctums and politics.

Killian never had. He liked to keep distance between himself and the madness.

Salen answered on the second pound—robes skewed, belt loose. His mouth was pressed into the kind of line that tried to pass for composure. Eyes rimmed red. Sleepless, but not from guilt—Killian recognised the fatigue that came from waiting to see which side would win before picking one.

"You redeemable?" Killian asked without preamble as he stepped past Salen into the room.

Salen had been waiting for this moment. Now doubt flew out the window—crossing Killian was a death warrant. He sighed, shut the door, and let his back meet it hard.

"Is that rhetorical?"

"I don't need the run around, Salen. I need the fucking truth."

He rubbed his hand down his face. "If you came here to arrest me, just do it."

"I came to offer you the choice. You don't get another."

Salen's eyes flicked toward the window. A new day rising, but it didn't cleanse a damn thing.

He swallowed. Meeting Killian's bullshit-me-and-you-will-die gaze. "You always were the better king."

Killian looked at him properly then. Gods help him—he'd trusted this man once. Worn the cost of that mistake ever since.

"I never wanted the throne."

"That's precisely why you should have it."

Killian felt no pity. Let the bastard sweat—agents had died, and they had come after his family. Unforgivable. For a heartbeat the room felt too small, shadows leaked from his boots as anger started to rise. He clamped it down.

Salen wiped his hands down the front of his robes. His breath shuddered out, a resignation more than surrender. "I won't shield them. Not anymore. I'll stand down."

"That'll do."

Salen moved aside as Killian walked to the door. He left as quickly as he had come and didn't look back. Salen's usefulness was over, and to his credit, he knew it.

By mid-morning, he'd visited everyone else on his list.

Doors opened. Conversations stayed short. No arguments.

He could feel the fear curdling in corners, eyes tracking his coat down the hall. But no one stopped him.

He didn't need a sword.

He was the sword.

By the time he was done, only three names remained.

Maltren. Varas. Yvane.

And he was out of mercy.

***

The chamber doors closed behind Killian. He took his place at the head of the table.

"I thank you all for coming. Yvane won't be joining us at this time."

He took his time to assess the assembled councillors. Most looked chagrined and somewhat terrified. Some fidgeted with robes, pens—most unable to meet his eyes.

Rowena looked up at him. He'd called her back for this meeting once Samthrax and the twins were safely back from their mission—he needed her here, visible, so no one suspected she'd been the informant.

Maltren and Varas, however, who Killian had not included in his visit, were all about confidence and swagger.

He almost laughed imagining their faces when they realised they were solidly screwed.

Your time is near, you treacherous pricks.

He held the thought long enough to stop his jaw from ticking. He couldn't afford to show his hand—yet.

"I won't keep you all long. It has come to my attention that meetings have been called without my knowledge to plot. Specifically, to obtain the Gateborn. In doing so, lives were lost—and by my tracking, this amounts to treason."

Varas tapped her bright red nails on the table. "If you're accusing members of this Council of treason, I suggest you present your evidence."

Killian loved nothing more than to take down those who had their heads shoved so far up their own arse they couldn't genuinely tell when they were in the shit.

He waved his hand, pinning Varas with lasered focus. "Will this suffice?"

The recordings that Rowena had taken of every underground meeting started to play in the looking dome. The voices echoed against the glassy black walls. Rowena winced at the sound of her own, barely audible in the background, but there.

Maltren broke into bluster. "Surely you don't expect us to believe this nonsense. This is a fabrication. We haven't attended any such meetings."

Miri slapped both her hands down on the cold obsidian. "Enough lies, Maltren. You know damn well this is all true." She looked at every face in the room. "We are all guilty, and we were all complicit. Yvane does not have the Enclave's best interests at heart, and she would dispose of us as quickly as she did the blighted one and the extraction team. This was never about what's right. It's always been about power—and we let it happen."

Miri leaned back in her chair, feeling flushed. She rarely spoke up—never like this. Her voice had come out louder than she meant. Eyes were still on her. She hated that: being exposed. But worse than fear was silence.

All she wanted was to have policies that were fair and just, and good people around her.

Rowena cleared her throat while standing up. She looked directly at Maltren and Varas. "I'm the one who recorded the sessions."

Her confession shocked Killian—he had wanted to ensure her safety by not revealing his sources. Brave, he thought. Or reckless. Maybe both. But the look in her eyes wasn't regret. It was defiance.

"You traitorous bitch." Varas launched for Rowena across the table.

Killian snapped a shadow leash toward her, binding her to the chair. Another lashed out, wrapping Maltren before he could rise. Their mouths kept moving, but no sound emerged.

He looked at the rest of the council members.

"I've spoken with you all individually this morning, and I trust that your allegiance will remain with me—that any further manipulation will cease immediately. Three will be taken into custody. Where they go is my concern, not yours. Is anyone here opposed to this verdict?"

Oltren stood. "You have my vote, Killian."

Miri's voice followed. "Seconded."

Salen lifted his hand in agreement. "Aye."

One by one, the heads around the table nodded. But it wasn't relief on their faces—it was fear. Not just of Killian. Of what they'd almost become.

Killian turned to Maltren and Varas, watching them twist in their binds. Their faces rippled with anger, mixed with horror, as dawned.

Their time in power was over.

"Very well, you are all dismissed." He glanced toward Rowena. "Except you."

Chairs scraped against stone as the councillors rose, robes rustling. None of them looked at Maltren or Varas as they filed out.

Killian waited until the chamber was empty. Only four remained.

Rowena. Maltren. Varas. Himself.

He moved toward the wall behind the high table, palm out. The glyphs carved there weren't decorative. They were old—older than the Enclave, older than most remembered magic. With a whisper of will, he activated the seal.

The wall shuddered.

Stone groaned as a passageway revealed itself—narrow, arched, heavy with the dry reek of old dust. A hall that hadn't seen footsteps in decades.

Varas stiffened.

She'd been in the Enclave her entire adult life and hadn't known this corridor existed. That alone was terrifying. But worse was the certainty that this place was for traitors—and for those meant to be forgotten.

Maltren's expression fractured, confusion starting to give way to fear.

He'd known Killian would move. He'd accounted for that. What he hadn't accounted for was *this*—the scale of it.

Yvane had promised leverage. Protection. A longer game.

The shadows at his spine tightened, and for the first time, Maltren understood he'd overestimated her—and fatally underestimated the man in front of him.

And for one brutal heartbeat, he had no idea what to do next.

Killian spoke without turning.

"Get up and walk."

He could've killed them. A dozen times over. But this—this would last longer. This they'd feel every second of. And that, at least, satisfied him.

They obeyed, herded silently by the shadow-tethers trailing from his boots.

Rowena followed, eyes flicking across the ancient walls as they passed—watching the sigils shift in response to their presence.

She'd studied Enclave architecture for years. This corridor wasn't in any archive, which meant it was hidden for a reason.

She wasn't afraid, but she felt the significance of it—the intent etched into every surface. This was more than exile.

It was straight up containment for when execution wasn't an option.

At the end of the hall: a black iron gate.

Behind it, the elevator.

It wasn't made of metal or wood, but petrified shadow—a cage of bound magic bolted into the bones of the Enclave. No buttons. No gears. Just a central seal, waiting for command.

Rowena's voice was a whisper. "This place… doesn't exist in the records."

"I'm aware, I'm also trusting it stays that way." His meaning was loud and clear.

He touched the seal.

The gate opened.

The elevator didn't hum. It thudded—deep magic pulling it downward through layers of unmarked design.

Killian stood with arms crossed, coat rippling at the edges, shadows tugging toward the stone.

This place remembered what it had been built for.

So did he.

The vault beneath the Crescent wasn't designed for comfort.

It was built for permanence.

Maltren and Varas stood behind him, restrained and muted by magic.

Their bodies twisted uselessly against the binds. The peacocking they displayed earlier long gone.

The lift stopped.

The vault door opened with a slow, grinding pull.

Light didn't greet them. The walls inside absorbed it, every flicker of torch or spell swallowed by the etched obsidian.

It wasn't dark—it was *null*.

The kind of absence that made you twitch.

"Welcome home," Killian ushered the prisoners forward with a grin that had no warmth to it.

Rowena followed behind.

Two containment cells cut directly into the walls, identical in every way except one had claw marks carved into the floor from its last occupant.

Varas screamed soundlessly as she was pulled involuntarily into the left cell.

Maltren snarled, baring his teeth in rage—Killian tightened the shadow leash and threw him into his cell.

He held his hands high chanting to lock the field in place. No doors were needed here.

Killian let the muzzle spells fall, calling his shadows back.

These two were going nowhere.

He waited for the yelling.

It didn't take long.

"You have no authority to do this!" Maltren's voice cracked on the edge of hysteria. "This is illegal imprisonment—you'll be tried for this, Killian."

"Not likely."

Varas slapped her hands against the wall of the containment spell—veins lit faintly beneath her skin. "Yvane will gut you for this."

Killian approached slowly, his eyes so cold, frostbite was imminent. "She's next."

Varas faltered. Her bravado vanishing under the stark realisation that no brigade was coming.

"I'm going to make one thing crystal clear: this isn't a negotiation. You're both done. For good."

Maltren lunged. The sigils flared. He hit the barrier like he'd tried to punch through glass and got his soul slapped instead.

He crumpled, groaning.

Killian didn't even blink.

"I'm not going to torture you. I'm not going to monologue. I'm not even going to ask for your side of the story. You made your choices."

He looked between them—his voice level, even bored.

"Now live with them."

He turned toward the vault door.

Varas spoke again, voice lower this time. "She will come for us."

Killian paused.

"No, she won't."

He turned from them, stepping back into the elevator. He waited for Rowena to join him before sending them hurtling back towards the surface.

The screams faded before the gate sealed fully.

Killian had been right—no one would hear them now.

Rowena glanced at his shadows, watching them curl close again—no longer weapons but companions, familiar and loyal.

They stepped out of the elevator and made their way down the corridor, emerging once more into the council chamber. Behind them, the entrance sealed shut—stone sliding back into place until the wall was smooth and featureless, as if it had never opened at all.

"I need to get back to the manor. Are you comfortable coming with me to continue with this until we have Yvane in custody?"

"Of course. Frankly, I'd rather be at your side than in her crosshairs."

"Agreed."

He flicked his hand, summoning the portal.

He stepped through with Rowena close behind—returning to the Scriptorium, to the waiting maps, the whispering wards, and the war table that would chart Yvane's downfall.

The next move would not be quiet.

Twenty Four

"The Veil always offers a way forward.
It just doesn't promise what you'll become when you take it."
— Divination Fragment, author unknown

The Veil

They walked fast. At this point they all knew better than to linger.

Pauline traced the map on Divina's wing periodically to keep the path alive beneath their feet.

Each time her fingers passed over the feathers, the runes adjusted. Not chaotically—but not cleanly either.

She didn't show her unease, but the delay in response told her plenty. The veil was still testing.

Divina's stride never faltered. Their exit was written across her bloody body—and the Veil was reading it, too.

No wonder they'd needed Gateborns and Veilwalkers.

This place was beyond dangerous.

And coming from a literal war angel, that meant something.

Zinnia moved up beside Pauline. "Mémère, how much further?"

Pauline didn't answer right away. Her fingers paused over a cluster of shifting glyphs. "Don't know yet. Da road's reworkin' itself each time we pass a marker."

Seraphina was about two minutes away from declaring herself

legally dead just to cop a break.

Her hair felt like it had been steam-cleaned in a bog, her boots were sticking to things she didn't want to identify, and she was starting to itch.

She sighed.

"So—no ETA, and our last welcoming party had extra heads sprouting from its shoulder."

Zinnia scratched her leg, giving a shudder of revulsion. "And eyes in its neck. Don't forget that charming detail."

"Someone needed a makeover for sure." Seraphina glanced sideways. "You okay?"

Nope. Not even close. But throwing a full-blown tantie wouldn't change a damn thing.

Zinnia gave a small shrug. "Define okay."

"Conscious, sarcastic, still walking."

Zinnia cracked a smile. "Then sure. Let's go with that."

Pauline gave a small grunt. "Could be worse, bébé."

Zinnia snorted. "Yeah. Brinnan could've shown up to kick us all in the teeth for good measure."

No one rushed to fill the gap—and that was telling.

Saffron mulled it over. One thing was certain—he wouldn't be far behind.

"He can't get in here without you. But my brother's cunning, he'll have a plan."

Lilly kept her arms swinging loose, more habit than ease. Her stomach hadn't unclenched since the attack.

"So… he's playing the long game?"

"Essentially, yes."

Matthew finally spoke from the rear of the group.

"He ain't a man. Not no more. He's a Shadow Ascendant—made so by Umbral rites."

They all turned toward him.

He shrugged.

"Brinnan don't move how we do. He don't think in hours nor days. He walks the in-Between. He's formidable."

What he wouldn't say was how he knew.

He'd seen it when he'd linked with Zinnia back in the cave, he hadn't meant to pry.

But when their minds brushed, the trauma of her being thrown through the portal was still live. He'd seen the whole thing unfold.

Later, while the others slept, he'd opened a careful mind-to-mind contact with an old wizard he trusted. One who knew the rites, the costs, the aftermath.

The man hadn't asked why Matthew wanted to know. Merely confirmed what Brinnan had become—and told him to keep his wits sharp if he was running with the likes of an Ascendant.

Wise words.

Matthew kept walking, eyes forward, pace unchanged.

Some things were better carried alone.

Saffron couldn't say the news surprised her; the man had sacrificed his only child for power. "That explains a lot. How do you know this exactly?"

"Contacts."

Saffron narrowed her eyes but didn't press.

Everyone had ghosts. Some talked to theirs; she was a glowing example.

Matthew however, seemed the type to keep his buried with a shovel and salt.

Seraphina kneaded her shoulder muscle, rotating her arm as she walked. She was stiff all over.

Trust Uncle Brinnan to turn himself into the actual boogey man.

"Let's unpack that disaster later."

Zinnia made a sound halfway between a laugh and a sigh. "Amen to that. My brain stopped braining hours ago."

They continued walking along the polished cobbles winding through fields of lush green—grass so even it could've been combed. Flowers leaned toward them in a cute Disney way. It was more terrifying than what they had just experienced.

Seraphina caught a whiff of something that smelled suspiciously like lemon cake. Her stomach perked up, clearly it had no sense of self-preservation.

"Alright, is anyone else getting serial killer bake sale sniffs, or is that just me?"

"Yeah, I clocked the bake smell too." Zinnia side-eyed a daisy the size of a dinner plate. It fluttered its petals in greeting. "Geezus, that thing is waving at me."

Lilly stepped carefully around a puddle of what looked like caramel but smelled like bleach. "This is the most aggressively cheerful nightmare I've ever been in. If a bunny offers me a massage, I'm punching it."

"Speak for yourself," Seraphina chimed in. "I'll take the massage. But not from a squirrel. I don't trust anything that hides their food in dark places."

Zinnia's laugh slipped out before she could stop it.

She needed that.

She needed this dumb conversation before the knots in her chest strangled her lungs. The moment she stopped moving, she'd spiral. So walking, talking—it helped.

Divina stretched one wing, wincing as something popped near the base. "Remind me—why I'm here again?"

Matthew gave her a wry look. "Yer here cos ye couldn't keep yer mouth shut."

Divina answered by lifting one finger without breaking stride.

Zinnia smiled to herself. It was comforting, in a strange way, to see something celestial so thoroughly irritated.

"Right, so you got stuck babysitting me. Are you trying to tell me you're not enthralled?"

Divina's wings twitched. "I am. I was promised smiting and righteous glory. Instead, I get mud in places that should never see mud."

"Ye also promised obedience."

Divina cocked her head, giving him the side-eye. "Careful, Veil-walker. I've still got one smite left in me—and you're overdue."

Saffron made a quiet sound of amusement. "You two need a chaperone."

Matthew didn't deny it. "We've had worse. Remember the gremlin in the archives?"

Divina rolled her eyes. "You mean the one that stole your trousers?"

"Borrowed. Temporarily."

She gave him a long, unimpressed look. "Yeah, that's definitely how theft works."

Pauline chuckled, not even glancing up from the runes on Divina's wing. "Y'all sound like a pair of pigeons fightin' over breadcrumbs."

Divina shot her a look. "Are you calling me a pigeon?"

"If the squawkin' fits, bébé." Her tone was light, teasing, soaked in fondness. "And if one of y'all don't slow down that mouth, I'm fixin' to stick a honey spell on it. Keep it sweet or keep it shut."

Zinnia loved it when her grandmother got all motherly. "Mémère, that's actually terrifying."

"Good. Means it gon' work."

Matthew coughed, clearly trying to stifle something. Zinnia caught it—and saw the way he rubbed the back of his neck. She looked away before he caught her looking.

Seraphina groaned. "Alright, raise your hand if you'd sell your soul for a cup of coffee and a shower."

"Shower? Depends on da soap," Pauline mused. "Coffee—only if dat demon y'got leashed be brewin' it."

Saffron floated past, one brow arched. "Samthrax does have his uses."

"Wait," Divina muttered darkly. "You have a demon who makes coffee?"

Zinnia rolled her neck, then waggled her brows. "Oh yeah. You two will get on famously. What could possibly go wrong with a demon and an angel in the same room?"

The laughter came easily after that. Which, considering their luck, probably meant something awful was about to happen.

***

Yvane's Private Quarters – Moments After the Council Collapse

The door sealed behind her with a muted hiss as the wards locked into place.

Irritation prickled under her skin. If the whispers drifting through the upper halls held any truth, then everything she'd orchestrated— every careful, strategic move—had been dismantled.

She'd given those feckless twits structure. Purpose. She'd led them while they clawed at power like children.

And now they wanted to bury her?

She stood where she was, spine straight, chin lifted. Refusal rising in her like bile.

Her mind moved quickly, sorting through contingency lines, burn routes, coded failsafes. Most were useless now.

She needed confirmation.

Her cloak unfastened with a single flick. It hit the floor in a heap. She didn't look back. Let the fabric wrinkle. Let it lie where it dropped.

She had more important things to correct.

She crossed to the control array and set her palm to the surface.

The panel stayed inert.

Yvane frowned, a shallow crease formed between her brows.

She pressed harder, intent bleeding into the interface the way it always had.

The array remained dark.

Her fingers tightened.

That was incorrect.

This wasn't a communal system or some half-trained relic she'd inherited from a predecessor. She had built this network herself—safeguard by safeguard. Every failure point anticipated. Every override calibrated to her authority. Nothing *ever* failed to respond unless she permitted it.

She drew her hand back and forced her breathing into compliance.

A fault, then. Temporary interference.

Killian didn't make careless moves. This wasn't his style. Someone had helped him. Someone clever enough to find a way in.

Let them think they'd found a weakness and won.

She would make a lesson of them.

Yvane set her palm down once more. This time, the array responded—hesitant at first, then bending to her will.

She reached for Maltren's tether.

The space where his glyph should have registered sat blank.

Her thoughts clipped mid-stride.

Maltren didn't disappear. He endured. He adapted. He obeyed.

She had mapped every flaw in him. Fear, pride, purpose—she'd weaved them all into loyalty.

He wasn't built to unravel.

And yet—

The tether was gone.

She reached for Varas.

Another void.

Yvane's vision narrowed behind a wall of black. Rage reared—violent, insistent. She crushed it. There were still pieces to reposition. Still ground she could take back.

She stared at the space a moment longer, then keyed a private line.

One of the retired councillors, who understood how power moved beneath the surface.

The projection flickered into view, half-formed behind a screen of static. Wards strained to hold the contact.

He looked haggard. Exhaustion leaking through the glamour.

"You need to go."

Yvane's gut twisted enough that she had to straighten her shoulders against it.

"Explain yourself."

"Killian's consolidated the chamber. They're not hedging anymore. Maltren and Varas are gone—as in no one knows what happened to them, and Killian made it clear we weren't to ask."

"He can't do that."

"He can. And he has."

The confirmation struck cold.

"They won't protect you now," the elder continued. "You misjudged how much they were willing to tolerate."

Misjudged.

The word landed like a hooked nail, dragging through everything she'd built.

"They wouldn't dare." She heard the doubt as it left her mouth.

"They already did."

The connection blinked out.

Yvane remained frozen, haloed in the flicker of the afterimage. The sanctum felt small. Like a death chamber waiting for its occupant to realise there was no escape.

No.

This wasn't how it ended.

She hadn't spent decades cultivating loyalty, buying silence, reshaping resistance bit by bit—only to be undone by Killian Graves and a few scattered reformists with guilt complexes.

A tremor started at her knuckles. She locked her grip and killed it.

She would not feed fear. She would not give panic a foothold.

Those were tools. And tools were meant to be wielded—not worn.

But beneath the control—beneath the certainty she gripped with white-knuckled delusion—understanding arrived with the subtlety of a sledgehammer.

She'd been outsmarted.

Outmaneuvered.

A laugh climbed her throat, bitter and reflexive. She swallowed it back.

There would be no record of this moment. No fissure to examine.

Fine.

If the board had changed, she would change with it.

Let Killian have his chamber.

She would take the war somewhere else.

***

Maison Bellarose

The portal opened in the main rotunda. Killian stepped through first. Rowena followed.

They didn't pause as they crossed into the Scriptorium.

Samthrax was already draped across a velvet chaise he had absolutely no right to occupy with that much satisfaction. He raised one brow as Killian entered, his fanged smile gleaming.

"Welcome back, bossman. How goes the takedown?"

Killian dropped into the nearest chair, tired in a way that had nothing to do with his body. "Easier than I expected. How did you go?"

"All wired up. Contacts on the outer ring confirm she's active—too many pulse echoes near dead gates. Chatter's picking up around Maltren and Varas."

Killian pinched the bridge of his nose. "Good."

Rowena moved to the worktable, eyes scanning the layout with a tactician's precision. "Yvane won't wait long. She'll pivot to her own networks and independent gates. We need every record that even smells like a backdoor."

Sage was already reaching for the register logs. "Do we have clearance for the restricted layers?"

"You do now." Killian moved to the central table. "Start with anything stamped with her old sigil. If it flickers, tag it. If it fights back, flag it."

Sebastian lingered outside the main cluster of activity, hands hovering over the manifest scrolls, unsure whether to touch or pull back. Power stirred under his skin at the thought—restless, reactive, too eager to misbehave.

He hated how he felt in here.

His father moved with total conviction, certainty hard-coded into every decision. Rowena tracked patterns with ruthless efficiency. Samthrax operated by some private system of mayhem and mirth.

And Sage—

Sage slipped into the work as if the magic had been waiting for her specifically, answering sweetly and graciously.

Sebastian felt the weight of his own inheritance instead. The darker current. The part of the prophecy they couldn't decipher yet.

Learning it meant restraint, not flow. Control, not confidence.

And he hadn't mastered either.

He forced his hand down onto a nearby log, feeling the texture of the page. "What exactly am I looking for? Besides the obvious 'doom port' label?"

Rowena didn't look up. "Cross-referenced gate keys. Anything that shows reuse without standard trace—think of it like a re-summoned thread."

Sage's sleeves were rolled to her elbows, sigils climbing her forearms as she worked. She glanced over once. "Ghost steps. You'll feel it when you hit one."

Sebastian tried not to bristle. She wasn't showing off—she was being helpful. Still, every word from her mouth widened the canyon between where she stood and where he was still trying to get.

He tapped the scroll's surface. It opened; resistance prickled along his fingers.

"Whoa, I think I got one, feels… weird. Like two different threads crammed into one."

Samthrax leaned over from his perch, eyebrow raised. "Yep, she's cross-hitching. Makes tracking a bloody nightmare."

Killian leaned forward, scanning the disrupted layer. "Well done son. Flag it. Add it to the override runes."

Sebastian paused. The approval was unexpected. He wasn't good at this yet. But maybe he wasn't hopeless, either.

Rowena scraped her hair back and twisted it into a knot. "She's already shifted to contingency plays."

She met Killian's eye.

"We will have to be quick to catch her."

***

Yvane didn't run. She walked with purpose, cloak snapping at her heels.

Only fools sprinted when the floor fell out from beneath them.

Real power moved on a different tempo.

The upper halls carried an expectant kind of quiet—eerie, watchful. The hairs at her nape lifted.

Her steps didn't slow.

She took the east passage, shoes clipping against polished stone.

Every turn, every junction had been chosen long before this moment. Contingency was a language she spoke fluently—and she had prepared for disloyalty long before Killian had risen to power.

She reached the threshold behind the scribe's alcove. It was a blind spot in the building's structural glyphwork—her own design. One that no one had thought to question because no one else had been capable of drafting it.

She pressed her palm flat to the false panel.

A slit of air sighed outward as the stone receded.

She stepped into the dark and let the wall close behind her.

"Illumina."

The light obeyed.

The enchantments here hadn't been touched in decades—not since she'd buried the escape protocols under six layers of plausible deniability.

It was time to unearth them.

She crossed to the secondary array and activated the private channel. Not a Council line. Not even a domestic one. This route bled straight through the ley-thread to the Old World Enclave—somewhere near Lake Ohrid, Northern Macedonia.

A piercing tone vibrated through the vault's bones.

Then he appeared.

Maelen of the Third Vault.

White gloves. Silver cuffs. Black robes with no markings. A face too still to belong to anything mortal. Hair too long to be decent. He had always kept his own counsel. Even now, she couldn't decide if he was bored, brilliant, or here for the entertainment.

Behind him: a library chiselled into the mountain, every wall alive with whispering glyphs.

"Yvane," he greeted smoothly. "You look like someone discovering gravity."

She didn't indulge him. "Killian has the Council. My channels are compromised."

"Mm." He clucked his tongue. "You overestimated your pawns. And underestimated the ones willing to cut them free."

The truth of it scraped. She ignored it.

"I need an extraction route."

"Of course you do."

His tone carried amusement and mockery. He moved with the ease of someone who'd already anticipated the request.

"I assume you want no fuss. No signature, no trail?"

"Obviously."

His fingers traced a pattern in the air. A series of coordinates appeared faintly beneath the surface of the projection.

"Vault passage beneath the ruined Septry of Kael. Still intact. If you move now, you'll make the drop before they triangulate your flare signature."

Yvane's gaze narrowed. "Why help me?"

"Because I like balance," he replied. "And right now, the scales are tipping too cleanly in Killian's direction. Messiness is… informative."

"I won't be a pawn."

"You never were." He smiled faintly. "That's why you're still useful."

He ended the call without further word.

The channel severed.

She left the vault and began the descent—each step calculated, every breath spent designing her next move.

She hadn't fallen.

She was repositioning.

Twenty Five

"You can cross any road if you bind right.
But only the living know where home is."
— Bayou Root Proverb

The Veil

The banter had tapered off, worn down by miles and near-misses. Everyone walked now with their attention turned inward. No one wasted energy they couldn't afford to lose.

Exhaustion sat heavy in Zinnia's limbs, not the kind sleep fixed. This ran deeper—bone-tired, nerve-frayed, the aftermath of being hunted and held together by a wing and a prayer.

Still, she kept moving.

They all did.

Because stopping meant thinking. And thinking meant fear had room to speak.

One thought kept looping, blunt and unhelpful.

How much further to the friggin' exit door.

Zinnia eased back, letting the others pull ahead. She needed some time out. The Veil kept brushing too close, its constant, needling intrusions grinding at her focus.

Matthew matched her pace almost immediately.

His presence cut through the mess in her head in a way nothing else

290

had managed since the constructs.

The quiet between them fit easily.

She liked that about him. Liked how he didn't crowd her. Liked that she felt protected without being diminished. In the short time she'd known him, he'd stepped in—again and again—without spectacle, without expectation.

It rattled her more than the Veil did.

"Lass. I want t' speak with ye about what's simmerin' between us."

Zinnia's foot caught. She recovered before she stumbled, but not before he noticed.

Matthew's hand came out on instinct, fingers closing around her elbow.

Her body reacted before her brain caught up—heat, awareness, a sharp pull low in her gut that had no business choosing *now* of all times. She drew in a breath and focused hard on putting one foot in front of the other.

"This isn't the time," she murmured, keeping her voice tight. "Or the place."

"I ken that," he replied. His grip eased but didn't fall away. "And I wouldn't bring it up if I could leave it be. I just can't walk beside ye and keep pretendin' this is nothin'."

That stopped her properly.

She angled her head, to catch his face in profile.

"Ok, what would you say it is then?"

Matthew's mouth pulled at the corner, not quite a smile. "Somethin' that's been on slow boil since the moment ye squared off with me."

That earned him a look. One that said she was tired of games. Hers or anyone else's.

"Look, I'm not denying the attraction. It stands out like dog's balls."

Matthew raised a brow, half a breath from laughing. The lass did have a funny way with words.

"I just don't know if I trust it," she added.

"Why is that lass?"

Zinnia looked ahead and started walking. Matthew's hand slipped from her elbow, but he stayed beside her.

"A lot of reasons, Matt. The big ones? We've only known each other in extreme danger. What if that's all this is? A survival bond. What if once things calm down, we decide we despise each other?"

"Everythin' ye're sayin' is fair, lass. But what ye're missin'? Most folk live their whole lives and never feel the kind of pull ye and I have. That's worth explorin'."

He looked at her long and hard without breaking pace.

"Fear's no excuse to leave somethin' real undone. And fair warnin'—once we get where we're goin', I fully intend to woo ye proper."

Matthew winked at her, all mischief, as if the Veil wasn't curling at their heels.

That cracked a breath of laughter out of her.

"You're romantic under all that brooding."

"Don't know about that, lass. Just statin' my plans so ye're aware."

Zinnia couldn't stop the rush that moved through her. She could easily picture exploring the physical side of it. That part didn't scare her.

But anything deeper?

Letting someone *see* her, hoping her softness wouldn't be weaponised?

She hadn't done that in years.

Still… Matthew wasn't wrong. If she kept the gates locked, she might miss something good.

Something real.

And that would leave a what if.

"Noted. I look forward to the wooing. Should we ever get out of this bloody mess."

Matthew didn't speak again right away. His eyes stayed forward, but something in the set of his mouth said the conversation wasn't over.

Another twenty paces passed before he spoke.

"When we linked back in the cave…"

His voice carried a caution she hadn't heard before.

"I saw some things, lass."

Zinnia rolled her suddenly tight shoulders.

Yep. This was about to get very uncomfortable.

"What did you see?"

"What ye've been through. At the hands of other men."

Zinnia's throat turned into the Sahara Desert. She wanted the Veil to swallow her whole.

Her past was a graveyard of red flags she'd ignored. One abusive arsehole after another, until she'd stopped trying. Since then, she'd built herself into pure bad arsery—capable, contained, and untouchable.

Now here he was.

The one man who'd managed to get under her skin in every way—

Knowing *exactly* how broken she really was.

"I want ye to know—you never deserved that. Not any of it. And I swear to ye, I'm a man of honour. Even if we disagree—and we will—I'll never treat ye with anything but respect. Ye ken?"

Zinnia nodded. She didn't trust her voice not to betray the level of emotion running through her.

They kept walking. Boots pressing into the cobblestone that shimmered faintly with each step.

"Lass, I'm not askin' for a future ye can't promise. I'm not askin' for anythin' beyond what ye've got to give. I just want to walk beside ye while ye figure out how to come home to yerself."

Tears welled, sudden and unwanted. Zinnia blinked hard to force them back.

No man had ever spoken to her like that—calm, sure, with care that asked for nothing in return.

She didn't know what to do with it.

So, she did what she always did when feelings came too close—she deflected.

"You realise you're laying it on thick enough to qualify for a proposal," she muttered.

Matthew grinned. "If I were proposin', there'd be whiskey and a view. And maybe a horse."

"What, so I can ride away halfway through?"

"I'd tie ye down. But only gentle like."

Her laugh slipped out before she could stop it.

She glanced sideways. "You're dangerous, Matt."

"Aye," he nodded. "But only to the parts of ye that don't believe ye deserve more."

Zinnia's smile faltered. How was it possible a man she had known for the shortest time knew her better than most people who had known her, her whole damn life?

At this rate, she'd be joining that annoying demon in personal growth.

Before she could come up with a reply, Divina's voice echoed from up ahead.

"Houston, we gotta problem."

Divina stopped—abruptly enough that Seraphina nearly walked into her.

Zinnia strained her neck, trying to see what said problem was. "When don't we?"

Matthew's grin lingered. "Aye, ye're not wrong about that lass."

They bunched with the rest of the group. Matthew beside her, his hand brushing close. The familiarity felt right.

Zinnia watched as her grandmother looked intently at Divina's wings.

They flexed, feathers twitching as if disturbed by a draft that wasn't there.

"What's going on?"

"Map's done gone."

Divina spread her wings wide and turned so the group could see.

It was like someone had wiped a cloth clean across them—nothing but blinding white remained.

Ahead, the path simply… stopped.

The road that had been folding itself into existence with every step now cut off. In its place: nothing.

Behind them, the continued illusion of a Disney movie, unnaturally pristine. The Veil openly mocking the idea of escape.

Matthew scuffed his boot against the stone. "This'll be one o' two things, then—either that's the door… or we're about to be devoured."

Divina rolled her eyes, wings flaring in frustration.

"Oh, that's morale-boosting."

She turned slightly toward Pauline. "Well, oracle? Got any divine breadcrumbs left, or are we winging it blind? Pun fully intended."

Pauline clucked her tongue at the angel. She didn't answer straight away. Instead, she stepped to the very edge of the path, shoulders tipped forward, gaze tilted not at the nothing ahead—but *through* it.

Zinnia recognised that look. Mémère had stopped listening with her ears and started listening with her loa.

"Map's not needed no more," she murmured. "It's waitin' on us."

Seraphina leaned out, staring hard at the abrupt end of the road. "Define waiting. Like 'please proceed,' or like 'step here and die'?"

Saffron hovered close behind Pauline, her ghostlight flickering at the seams. "It's definitely a gateway," she confirmed. "I can feel the hinge point. But it's… fuzzy. Beyond that I got nothing."

Lilly crossed her arms, tight across her chest. "I'd prefer a labelled exit, maybe with a glowing arrow and a welcome mat."

Zinnia's gut turned, low and mean. If she'd eaten anything in the last twelve hours, it'd be on someone's boots by now.

She was so damn tired of choices that were nothing but loaded weapons. Pick a door, pull the pin, hope your insides stay inside.

She dragged in a breath, counted to ten, then let it go.

"Alright. Here's where we're at. We can't go back—the map's gone and the Caethera's not opening again. We can't stay put unless we fancy becoming Veil leftovers. Which leaves us with whatever that is." She tipped her chin toward the nothing ahead. "And if we jump in—we might be stepping straight into death. That about sum it up?"

Pauline didn't miss a beat. "Sums it up just fine, bébé."

Matthew crouched at the edge of the empty span, one hand dragging across the stone. What he was about to do was a bad idea. He knew it. But options had once again become extremely limited.

"Only one way to find out."

He tipped his head forward and opened himself.

The Veil rushed him.

It didn't arrive gently. It poured into him, thick and invasive, crawling through muscle and nerve. His breath punched out of him as heat detonated under his skin, veins standing out dark and violent along his arms and throat. Pressure built fast—too fast—his body reacting before his mind could organise the assault.

Hissing fractured the air around him.

His vision blew out to white, then nothing.

Hundreds of threads snapped into awareness all at once, crossing and knotting and tearing past him in every direction. Timelines. Places. Doors layered over doors.

His body convulsed as the Veil shoved him forward, trying to prise him loose from himself and throw him into the crossing whole.

Someone shouted his name.

Then again.

Zinnia.

Her hand slammed onto his shoulder, solid and real, fingers digging in hard enough to bruise. The contact cut through the chaos like a blade. He clung to it, dragging himself back along that single point of contact, hauling his consciousness into his body by sheer refusal.

The Veil fought him.

Then spat him out.

Matthew collapsed flat on his back. Breath tore in and out of his chest, sweat slicking his skin. The hissing faded. Whatever had him pinned relented enough for the world to reassemble.

"It's a crossin'," he rasped, voice shredded. "Not a trap."

He lifted his head, eyes burning as the afterimages faded.

"But it's busy. Routes piled atop one another. If we go in loose—" He shook his head once. "We'll break apart. Different exits. Different whens."

Zinnia held out her hand.

"Then we don't go in separately."

Matthew swallowed, took her hand. She helped pull him to his feet, his legs wobbled, refusing to remember their job. "We need to be bound to each other."

Pauline nodded and stretched slowly, joints popping in quiet protest. She reached into the deep pocket of her skirt and drew out a length of cord—dark, soft with age.

"This ain't a spell," she rolled the cord between her fingers. "Ain't no chant neither. It's a bind."

A solid reassurance filled Zinnia's chest. Of everyone in her life, Mémère was the one she trusted without question. She'd follow Pauline's judgement to the end of the earth if it came to that. Ironically—this moment qualified.

Pauline's gaze moved over the group, reading faces instead of futures.

"Dat crossin' Matthew touched?" She tipped her chin toward the blank ahead. "It scatter anythin' that ain't fixed proper. Mind. Body. Soul, if dey sloppy. An' trust me—we don't wanna step in sloppy."

Divina angled her head. "Fixed?"

"Mean when one o' y'all stumble, the rest gon' feel it. Mean if the Veil pull, it gotta pull all of us at once." She lifted the cord a fraction. "Dis keep us headin' the same way."

Pauline paused, giving the words time to digest.

"It ain't permanent. Soon as we through, I unwind it. Ain't gon' leave no hooks in nobody." Her eyes met each of theirs in turn. "But while it on us, it gon' carry every last one o' us to the right side—together."

She tilted her head slightly.

"If y'all got somethin' better, I'm listenin'."

No one spoke at first.

Zinnia grinned at her grandmother.

She lifted her hand, palm out. "I'm in."

Pauline moved with quiet efficiency, looping the cord once around Zinnia's wrist.

Warmth spread up her arm—a hum of awareness rooted deep that was not entirely unpleasant. Reminding her that she, too, was Hoodoo. The recognition settled her clear to the soul.

Pauline tugged once, testing. Satisfied.

"Alright, who next?"

Divina stepped in, wings folding close to her back to make space. "Do angels complicate this?"

Pauline snorted softly. "Chèr, everythin' complicate angels. Hold still."

The cord circled Divina's wrist. The hairs along her arms shivered, reacting to something they didn't quite recognise but didn't reject either. Earthbound magic was far denser than angelic. She actually liked the earthy feel.

Lilly made the sign of the cross, then stepped forward. "Fine. If we're landing somewhere horrible, I want company."

Zinnia grinned at that. "Seems to be a family tradition."

The cord touched Lilly's wrist and her magic bristled, flaring on instinct. It pressed back, tight and restless, before settling under the hoodoo's weight.

If this binding was what it took to get home with Zinnia—then her magic could behave.

She'd lost years. Lost chances. Lost her place beside her own child. She wasn't losing anymore.

Seraphina offered her hand next. "I know less than nothing about Bayou magic, but I do know I'd rather not be the idiot who gets left behind because I lacked faith."

The cord closed around her wrist, gentle but firm. It reminded her, unexpectedly, of holding her mother's hand as a child—of being steadied without being dragged.

She swallowed around the tightness in her throat.

Saffron drifted closer to her daughter. "I'm already bound to Seraphina whether I like it or not. Might as well make it official."

Pauline chuckled. "Ain't wrong Saffy."

The cord passed through her without resistance, then tightened all the same.

"That's… strange," she murmured. "But not unpleasant."

Pauline looked at Matthew.

Her heart softened. This one was good for Zinnia—but she needed to know he was ready to be torn from his time and dropped into a strange new world.

"You sure, chèr?"

He knew what Pauline was really asking him. He held out his hand in response. "Aye. Never been more sure of where I belong."

When the cord closed around his wrist, it hit hard.

Zinnia felt it immediately.

A connection aligned between them—powerful, undeniable.

Matthew sucked in a breath through his teeth. "Bloody hell."

They both dropped to their knees, looking at each other.

Pauline gave a quiet hum. "Yeah. Dat's da Veil expressing her displeasure dat you two be bound in more ways den one."

Pauline tied the final knot around her own wrist, fingers sure, movements economical.

"There." She tapped the cord, sealing it. "We're all linked."

Zinnia became acutely aware of everyone at once.

Not their thoughts or their memories.

A shared balance. A shared direction.

Matthew flexed his fingers. "I can feel where ye are."

"Good," Pauline replied. "Means it workin'."

Divina hopped from one leg to the other. "And if one of us panics?"

Pauline met her eyes evenly. "Then the rest o' y'all gon' feel it and pull 'em back."

Zinnia laughed at Divina's clear agitation. "Look—the kick-arse tough angel is all nervous. Wouldn't have believed it if I wasn't looking at it."

Divina flipped Zinnia off. "I said one of us, not me specifically. But you know what? Nerves are like a warning sign to stop before you do something dumbarse that will get you killed. I may be immortal, but I can still die and come back. I feel it before I don't."

Seraphina clapped her hands. "Alright ladies, let's just get this over with. I for one am rooting for a positive outcome, because I have children I need to traumatise for a few more years yet and a man who loves me."

That earned a round of snickers.

"Alright, chèr," Pauline drawled softly. "We goin' home."

She touched her gris gris, murmured a prayer to soothe her loa, and stepped forward.

The others followed.

The path released them.

Zinnia's stomach lurched as direction lost authority.

The cord snapped tight, asserting togetherness.

Her body protested immediately. Heat surged, then dropped away. Her ears rang with overlapping noise that wasn't sound so much as *options*. Her vision fractured into brief impressions that vanished before meaning could form.

This wasn't the Veil.

This was where exits competed.

Zinnia felt her magic flare, instinctive and defensive, shoving outward into resistance that didn't care who she was. It wasn't hostile. It was busy. Impersonal. Brutally efficient.

Pauline's voice cut through it.

"Don' fight it, bébé. Let it carry."

She loosened her hold on control. The bind responded instantly, warmth evening out, the pull smoothing into something directional.

Divina swore from somewhere behind her, wings snapping tight as something clipped the edge of her span.

Seraphina barked a breathless laugh. "Does anyone else feel like they're getting a facelift? I swear I'm going to look twenty years younger when we get out of here."

"My face feels like it's stuck in a wind tunnel," Saffron came back, her voice stretching oddly as the crossing tugged at her form. "I'll be impressed if I still have one."

Behind Zinnia, Lilly's magic flared against the hoodoo bind, met opposition, rebounded. Grudgingly, accepting it as the cord held firm.

The strain rattled straight through her joints. It reminded her of that old beat-up car she'd driven as a teen—with worn shocks, every pothole had made her teeth clack.

"I'm still here," Lilly managed, the words more for herself than anyone else.

Zinnia answered without turning. "I know, Mum."

The pull intensified without warning.

Walking stopped being a choice and became velocity.

The bind yanked them onto a blazing current. Sound flattening into force. Fragments streaking past too fast to register before the next replaced them.

"I'm gonna throw up—"

Divina bent at the waist, dignity abandoned as the contents of her stomach vanished the instant they left her.

No splatter. Just gone.

Time lost all structure.

It felt like every sci-fi fever dream Zinnia had ever watched had been stripped down to sensation alone—colour without boundary, speed without distance, space without mercy. Terror threaded through it, vivid and relentless.

And underneath it all, the sickening, helpless rush of the fastest, longest slippery slide imaginable—no rails, no friction, nowhere to brace.

Pauline gasped as the force slammed through her wrist.

The cord burned hotter now, vibrating with too much information forced through too narrow a channel. Every soul tugged at once, every direction insisting.

She locked down on it anyway.

White-knuckled. Stubborn. Unyielding.

She would not lose a single one of them here.

Zinnia felt Matthew falter at the far end of the line.

The crossing hit him harder than the rest. He was built to walk the

Veil, not this—this churn of intersecting routes where time stacked on itself and exits jostled for claim. He felt them crowding him, overlapping pressures trying to hook in, to convince him they were the correct way through.

His body struggled under it.

Breath came ragged. Muscles went rigid as if holding himself together by will alone. He swallowed a sound he refused to give voice to.

She reached for the bind.

Poured herself into it. The direction Pauline had set. The promise they'd made to land together.

The cord vibrated hard, heat spiking as it carried too much strain.

At the far end, Matthew latched on.

Desperation bled straight through the link as his body fought to stay whole, to stay *here*.

Zinnia held.

So did Pauline.

So did all of them.

Then the crossing released them.

Momentum shattered. Bodies slammed together. The cord pulled tight one last time—

—and the world let go.

Pauline came through first.

Her boots met the floor with a familiar thud, knees bending to absorb the last of the crossing's bite. Wood creaked beneath her weight—old planks, stubborn ones. She knew that sound. Had trusted it for decades.

She drew in a breath and felt the answer come back right.

Humidity wrapped around her lungs, heavy with green life and standing water and smoke that had sunk into the walls long ago. Cicadas tore into the night outside, loud and shameless. A frog croaked somewhere close, opinionated as ever.

Pauline lifted her hand and unwound the cord in a single smooth motion. The binding let go immediately, warmth receding as each soul slipped back into its own skin.

"We through."

Zinnia hit the floor a heartbeat later, knees taking the impact, palms slapping against warped boards that were solid in a way nothing in the Veil had ever been.

She stayed down a moment longer, breath still chasing itself. Her fingers traced the floorboards without thinking—scratches, dents, the soft give of old wood that had weathered floods and feet and time.

Then she looked up.

A photograph watched her from the wall. Crooked in its frame. Sun-faded. Remy's grin frozen mid-laugh.

Her throat closed.

She shut her eyes, and let it sink in.

They'd made it.

They were home.

Halle-fuckin'-leujah.

The cabin gathered them in. Low ceilings. Corners that leaned. Shelves crowded with jars, bones, candles.

Wind chimes clicked near the door, each note deliberate, warded within an inch of its life.

Divina turned slowly, wings half-spread as if the room itself might demand clearance. "This is... aggressively homey."

Pauline shot her a look designed to cut through angelic ego. "Mind that tongue, chèr. Dis place been standin' since before half o' your wars learned how to start."

Seraphina hauled herself upright, swiping hair out of her eyes, grin already breaking through the wreckage. "I have never been so glad to smell swamp in my entire life."

Lilly's laugh slipped out. She pulled Zinnia into a hug that didn't ask permission and didn't linger too long. Just enough to prove they were actually here.

"We made it," Lilly breathed.

Zinnia nodded against her shoulder. "Yeah. We did."

Matthew found the doorframe and leaned into it, chest still working too hard. His eyes stayed on Zinnia, tracking her in a way that wasn't about protection now—more a need to know she was okay.

When she glanced his way, he nodded and smiled. She smiled back.

Saffron drifted nearer to Seraphina. She took in the cabin slowly, expression thoughtful rather than sentimental. She'd only been here once—but this place didn't need repetition to be recognised.

"It's good to be back," she murmured.

Pauline's hands came to rest on her hips, satisfaction cutting clean through the exhaustion.

"Welcome home, chérs. Now go on—sit y'selves down. Get somethin' to drink. Let yer insides settle fall back into place. Trouble still out dere… but it ain't for tonight."

Outside, the bayou answered. Frogs tuned up. Cicadas took over the dark. Water shifted against roots that had learned patience the hard way.

And far off—far enough not to matter yet—Brinnan took note with a great deal of interest.

Twenty Six

*"Relief is not the absence of threat.
It is the decision to stand down—for now."*
— *Veil Response Protocol*

The Bayou

They crowded into the skiff, knees knocking, movements careful as the hull dipped lower than anyone liked. No one wanted to be the one who sent them all into the drink.

Seraphina reinforced it with a controlled line of magic. The hull complied, slicing forward instead of wobbling, the murk parting around them.

No one mentioned using a portal.

The boat creaked as it moved. The air smelled of wet earth, engine oil, and things that had been alive here longer than any of them.

They rounded the bend and Maison Bellarose came into view.

The house filled Seraphina's vision and the running inventory in her head stopped.

Funny how easily she slipped back into a life she'd sworn she was finished with.

"I'll never get sick of the sight of this place."

Saffron looked at the manor the way only someone who had lived there and ended there could.

Seraphina smiled at her mother. Her death was the reason this moment existed. The knowledge hurt, but it didn't cancel the warmth of standing here with her.

Divina let out a low whistle.

"This place is impressive. And the magical pushback?" She rubbed at her arms. "That's not subtle."

Matthew watched more of the place emerge, his eyes tracking stone, windows, the excess of it all. He'd spent his life with trees and hand-built walls. This was something else.

He turned to Zinnia.

"Ye live here, lass?"

She nodded. The first time she'd seen it; she'd been convinced she'd stepped into an alternative universe.

"It's a new arrangement, but yes, I now live here."

Pauline hmphed in the back of the skiff. "Don' be forgettin' your roots."

Zinnia shot her grandmother a 'duh' look. "That will never happen, grandmère. I've got too much of you in me."

Pauline gave her a wink. "Dat you do, bébé."

Lilly only half followed the conversation. Her attention kept tugging forward, toward the place she'd spent a good portion of her life. The Enclave had been all she'd known until she'd decided not to accept what it wanted from her.

She'd passed this house a thousand times, spinning private stories about it—herself inside, chosen, powerful, married to someone dangerous and devoted. Stupid fantasies. Now she was minutes away from walking straight into the reality.

The realisation made her giddy. She didn't bother pretending otherwise. Some dreams didn't fade because you grew up.

Seraphina eased the skiff the last few feet. Wood met wood with a soft, hollow knock.

Matthew didn't wait. He rose, stepped onto the dock, and took hold of the rope, securing the boat with practiced efficiency.

Then he turned back and offered his hand. Zinnia took it, letting him pull her up and out. She stayed close—close enough that it stopped being accidental. Their faces ended up a hair-breadth away, neither of them in a hurry to move.

Divina made a pointed sound behind them.

Zinnia jumped back, heat flashing across her face, with the distinct sensation of being caught with her hand in the cookie jar.

Divina said nothing as she unloaded herself from the skiff with obvious care, wings tucked.

Saffron floated up beside her, translucent form brightening. "There's no place like home."

Lilly stepped onto the dock next; tears close to falling. Home. She hadn't believed she'd ever walk the Enclave again—let alone here.

"It's so beautiful."

Seraphina climbed up alongside Pauline, the boards familiar beneath her.

"She can be, she can also be terrifying."

The back doors opened before anyone reached them.

Killian stood framed in the doorway, sleeves rolled, stress riding him hard enough to be visible. He took them in at a glance—heads counted, bodies scanned, magic assessed.

Only once he'd finished did the line of his shoulders ease.

"You lot took your sweet arse time," he remarked, dry as dust.

Seraphina broke into a grin and bolted for him, skidding the last foot before colliding with his chest. He caught her without effort, arms locking around her back as if he'd already decided she wasn't going anywhere.

She kissed him fiercely, to hell with the audience. Alone couldn't come fast enough.

"Alright, you two," Zinnia cut in, already shoving past them. "Out of the doorway. A girl needs to pee."

Killian didn't let go of Seraphina when Zinnia barrelled through. If anything, he held more firmly, palm spread at the small of her back. The contact was one hundred percent necessary. Touching her told him she was real. She was here.

"Let's head indoors." He took stock of the new faces. "We'll do introductions there."

Seraphina stayed tucked against his side as they moved, her body adjusting to his without thought, his hand sliding to her hip and staying there. She matched him, step for step. Neither of them broke contact.

The others followed without comment.

The Scriptorium opened around them.

Lilly was caught between curiosity and restraint. Tables bore the marks of use. Shelves were crowded with books and instruments that assumed competence rather than admiration. It was grander than she had imagined.

Divina stepped in, already cataloguing exits, sightlines, the way power sat without display. It was rather unnerving.

Matthew hovered near the threshold, hat in his hands, the room pressing in from all sides. He didn't intimidate easily—but nothing in here had been built for someone like him.

Seraphina pulled free of Killian barely in time to brace herself.

Sage and Sebastian launched from their seats with zero warning and no concern for her balance, colliding with her hard enough to knock the breath from her lungs. She caught them, relishing having her children back in her arms.

"Mum, you look like hell," Sage's voice wobbled despite the attempt at humour.

"You smell like it too," Sebastian added, nose wrinkling even as he grinned like he'd won something just by touching her.

She laughed, the sound breaking loose before she could stop it, and swatted Sebastian's butt on instinct. "Missed you too."

Zinnia wandered back in, hair wet, black cargos and a halter top clinging in places that made Matthew forget how his mouth worked.

She caught it immediately, sending him a come-hither smile. She sashayed across the room, dropped onto one of the couches, then patted the space beside her.

"Take a load off, Matt."

Matthew's body betrayed him before his head caught up. One step, then another, and suddenly he was sitting beside her.

She smelled clean. Soap and water and something faintly floral. The thought that followed was immediate and wildly inappropriate. He shut it down fast.

Behave.

Killian noticed.

One brow lifted as he looked at Seraphina, a silent question. She answered with the barest nod and a slow, knowing smirk.

Wait until Samthrax realised his crush had a crush on someone that was not him.

Oh, this was going to be entertaining.

"Grab a seat. Our home is your home."

That broke the tension better than politeness would have.

He tipped his chin toward the twins. "Sage. Sebastian."

They grinned at the attention, identical and unrepentant.

"And Rowena." His focus flicked to her briefly. "Explanations later."

Rowena lifted a hand in a small, uncertain wave.

Killian glanced around, frowning when one presence failed to register.

He brought two fingers to his mouth and let out a shrill whistle, loud enough to wake the dead.

Seconds later, Samthrax slid to a stop in the doorway, barefoot, shirt hanging open, expression smug enough to start fights.

Killian gestured at him with a thumb.

"And that's our demon."

Samthrax took in the room in a single, lazy sweep, the way he always did when deciding where the trouble would start.

His eyes landed on Zinnia first. The destruction he'd been carrying finally stood down. She was seated beside an unfamiliar male, close enough to suggest comfort, familiarity, and a complete misunderstanding of personal safety. Samthrax clocked that immediately and filed it under *urgent correction required*.

Seraphina was alive too, currently absorbed by the twins, all attention and hands and warmth. Pauline hovered nearby, completely at home.

Saffy perched in her favourite chair, relaxed.

Then Samthrax caught the scent.

Was that the stench of celestial?

His eyes shifted, crimson glistening as they landed on Divina near the window. Light clung to her in a way that felt provocative and defensive.

Samthrax grinned.

Ooohhhhh, they'd brought an Angel home.

"Charmed."

Angel energy always did something to him. They were dares wrapped in radiance, and this one didn't bother hiding it.

Samthrax's attention slid back to the man beside Zinnia. Too fucking close. Barbecue sprung to mind.

"And you are?"

Matthew didn't miss the threat. He knew demons. Knew the look that meant interest had turned predatory. Shite. That slimmed his options.

"Matthew."

Samthrax tasted the air, tongue flicking out, Veil magic snapping sharp and tangy at the back of his throat.

Veilwalker.

His kind survived by being smarter than the things hunting them.

Samthrax could solve that problem quickly. Painfully. Definitely creatively.

Divina had been around demons long enough to recognise the moment curiosity tipped into intent.

Oh no you don't.

There were lines that didn't get crossed under her watch. This was one of them.

If the demon tested that assumption, he'd regret it.

Samthrax glanced back at Divina. By the hellhounds, she was stunning. Oh yes this was going to be fun.

"Knock off the bullshit theatrics, Samthrax," Zinnia called out. "Sit down. Or better yet—make coffee."

"I'll take one too, chèr."

Samthrax ignored Pauline and the murmurs of agreement.

He wasn't done yet.

He crossed the room in three lazy strides, scooped Zinnia up without warning, and spun her until she was laughing despite herself.

"Put me down, you bloody idiot," she protested, swatting at his arm.

He set her back on her feet and kept his hands at her shoulders, eyes searching her face without humour now.

"You alright?"

Zinnia's power reached without permission. He didn't stop it.

What came through was persistent blame, circling the same fact: she'd been gone, and he'd believed that was on him.

Holy shit.

"Yeah, big fella." She patted his chest, gentler now. "I'm good. I'm really glad to be home. And… yeah. Kinda glad to see you too."

That was all he needed.

Samthrax pulled her into a quick hug, released her just as fast, then turned on his heel and snagged his apron from its hook.

"Coffee it is," already firing up his beloved machine.

"Wow. Okay—my name's Lilly." She stepped forward and offered Samthrax her hand. "I'm Zinnia's mother. You're not what I expected."

Samthrax took her hand and smiled, showing far too much fang. "I get that a lot. Welcome to the circus." He tipped his head toward the coffee machine. "Drink?"

"Yes, please." Lilly moved toward the fire and claimed a chair nearby, easing into the warmth.

Killian looked at Lilly and Matthew. "It's a pleasure to meet you both." He turned to the angel currently glowing in the sunlight she was standing in. "And your name?"

"Divina."

She caught Killian's eyes briefly, then looked straight back at the demon.

She didn't trust the hellspawn for a second. No matter how much charm he deployed—or how unfairly well he wore an apron.

Twenty Seven

"Celebration does not dissolve danger.
It merely lowers its voice."
— Veil Response Protocol, Addendum VII

Rowena held back and watched.

People had started talking over one another, laughing too loudly, filling the silence because they could. It felt good to see, even if she didn't join in. Good in a way that lingered longer than she expected before she pushed it aside.

Samthrax was in his element, whipping up latte after latte, taking requests, thriving on being needed and indulged in equal measure.

Seraphina had conjured a table full of food. Everyone jostled one another good-naturedly, hands slapping as they reached for the same dishes. Plates filled. People sank into couches and lounge chairs; food balanced on knees and armrests.

Rowena wanted to give them more time. Unfortunately, the problem waiting on them didn't care.

She took another gulp of her coffee and looked to Killian. This wasn't going to resolve itself.

"Killian."

She widened her eyes slightly, tipping her head.

He popped a mini quiche into his mouth and chewed thoroughly, determined to finish it before engaging. Rowena was right.

Time to rip the band-aid off.

He squeezed Seraphina's knee.

"While you lot were off saving Zin and co, we imprisoned a few Council members and diverted a coup."

Saffron sounded like she coughed up a furball. "You did what?"

Rowena winced. Killian was not a diplomat.

"And mum, we took a demon chariot straight through demon territory to screw up Yvane's comms. Samthrax sucks as a driver, FYI." Sage rubbed the back of her neck. "Pretty sure I have whiplash."

Seraphina's head was on a swivel between her two grinning twins, Samthrax whistling dixie at the ceiling, and Killian looking uncharacteristically sheepish.

Sheesh, she couldn't leave them alone for five freak'n minutes.

She fixed on Killian.

"Start talking buddy, fast."

Pauline couldn't contain herself. She started chortling at Killian being taken to task by the diminutive redhead, slapping her leg as all eyes turned her way.

"Ah, sorry, chèr. Go on, bébé. You just went and tickled mah funny bone, is all."

Pauline waved a hand, laughter subsiding, signalling for them to continue.

Lilly snorted. She'd never trusted the Council, bunch of pompous gits.

"I'd be interested in hearing which ones were incarcerated," she added. "Pretty damn sure I might dance a jig."

Rowena looked at her properly then. The missing Gateborn. Gone for decades. Sitting right there. She couldn't fault her for running. The Veil broke so many.

"Varas and Maltren."

Lilly whooped, on her feet instantly, dancing exactly as promised. Samthrax bounced up and joined her, limbs flying with more enthusiasm than skill.

Rowena stared. She had absolutely no idea what she was watching.

"Alright." Killian clapped his hands, cutting through the bedlam. "I'll fill you in on the highlights. Then Rowena's got an update on Yvane."

He leaned forward, elbows on his knees.

"Varas and Maltren are locked up. There's no access. No exits. And no one's getting clever on their behalf."

Seraphina was sitting cross legged beside him. "And the rest of the Council?"

"I paid each of them a visit," Killian replied. "They swore allegiance. Salen included."

Matthew shifted deeper into the sofa, listening closely. Power always reshuffled itself the same way, no matter the place or the century. He respected how Killian handled it with authority backed by follow-through. That kind of integrity was rare.

The twins kept drawing his eye. One more than the other. Sebastian carried something that didn't sit right, something that moved where it shouldn't. Veilwalker instinct. He kept the thought to himself.

Saffron snorted, not impressed. "Salen always knows when to duck."

"Smart, if nothin' else," Pauline added.

"And Yvane?" Lilly had history with her in particular. She was smart, ambitious and emotionless. Deadly combination.

Killian turned slightly, giving the floor over. "Rowena."

She set her mug aside.

"I tracked her to an old underground portal. Supposedly decommissioned decades ago." She dragged a hand down her face, displeased with the news she had to impart. "She didn't do it alone. Someone helped her—someone strong enough to shield her and hold that portal open long enough for her to cross."

She turned her palm up. A crystal shard rested there, light spilling outward as an image formed in the middle of the room.

A long cavern. Stone walls slick with age. At the far end, a violet oval shivered in place.

"This sits well beneath the Enclave," Rowena continued. "Close to the Mundanni border."

In the projection, Yvane moved fast. She glanced back once. Then again. She didn't slow when she reached the portal—just stepped through and vanished.

The image faded.

"That portal branches to multiple Enclaves worldwide. Which means she could be anywhere by now." Rowena didn't pause long enough for that to sink in. "However—she once studied under a mentor in one of the European branches. I don't yet know which. I'll find it."

She pocketed the shard and looked to Killian.

"But as of right now, she's gone."

"Damn it. Thank you, Rowena." Killian pursed his lips. "I won't be comfortable until she's locked up with the other two."

Shadow bled out from beneath his boots, restless and agitated, responding to mood. Yvane would surface again. She didn't abandon a power play once it was in motion.

Divina moved to the food table. She didn't often imbibe in mortal ways, but she'd always found the ritual grounding. She selected a few slices of fruit and arranged herself on the mat in front of the fireplace.

"It seems to me that getting Zinnia through her awakening and back home was just the tip of the iceberg when it comes to shitshows."

Samthrax crossed his legs, slippered foot swinging in an idle rhythm.

"Careful, sunshine. You're talking like you plan on sticking around for the sequel."

Divina flicked her eyes to the demon. Debonair, smug, and far too bloody demony to trust. "My conscience doesn't permit leaving good people with the likes of you."

Samthrax's grin widened, delighted rather than offended.

"See? Banter. I knew you were into me."

Pauline reached for another pastry, shaking her head.

"Ha. You be delusional, chèr."

Seraphina didn't need this turning into sport. This was so Samthrax—poke, prod, circle until someone bit back. There were plans to make. And selfishly? She wanted a shower, Killian, and a bed.

"Alright. Enough."

Samthrax leaned back, palms lifted in surrender. The smile stayed.

His eyes remained on Divina.

Angel, but with more regulations than grace.

That combination lodged under his skin and refused to dislodge.

Oh yeah.

There was a story there.

One he fully intended to dig up like he was fossil hunting.

Seraphina took the room in without moving—twins, Killian, the rest. The mundanni life she'd tried to keep intact was well and truly behind her now.

"So," she continued, "we've got a Council licking its wounds, two locked up, one missing, and at least one unknown ally capable of resurrecting old infrastructure."

Rowena interlaced her fingers in her lap. Stripped down like that, it sounded bad. "That's the size of it, yes."

Matthew spoke before he could stop himself. "Europe is riddled with old networks."

Killian angled toward him, measuring. "You've knowledge of these?"

"Aye," Matthew replied. "I could be of assistance."

"Any help would be appreciated."

Thought tugged at Saffron in a way that hadn't dulled with death.

What good was having no physical shell if she couldn't *use* it? There were currents beyond this place, voices in the ether that surely had answers. She'd find them once the house slept.

"Yvane won't let this go," she cut in. "She's too hungry. My guess is she's already looking for another angle."

Killian pushed to his feet. The shadows followed, obediently.

"That's exactly what she'll be doing. Which means we need to find her before she finds one." His jaw tightened. "And we don't forget Brinnan. He's still out there, and he won't miss an opportunity to circle back to Seraphina or Zinnia. Vigilance is the new black."

"Yeah," Zinnia added. "The scumbag popped up during my unplanned vacay. It was weird. He let us feel him, but he didn't make a move. Not that I noticed anyway."

Matthew's brow furrowed. "Actually, lass, I've a notion he let the hunters into the cave. They'd no business finding that place without help."

Well, that made sense.

"So, he's playing cat and mouse?"

Saffron snorted. "Without a doubt." Frost touched the air. "My brother favours patience."

"How is this family so f'd up?" Sebastian blurted out.

Not long ago, he'd had been worrying about school and stupid teenage problems. Now he was dropped square in the middle of a goddamn Brothers Grimm nightmare.

Sage didn't argue. The magic was incredible. The constant threat that came packaged with it? Less so.

"Things will settle, son."

Seraphina heard the words leave her mouth not fully believing them herself, but at this point reassurance was all she had to give.

Killian walked over to the bar.

"We all need to reset. Tomorrow we strategise. If anyone leaves this house, it's with an escort."

Samthrax lifted his mug. "Look at you. Domestic dictatorship. I'm weirdly turned on."

Divina resisted the urge to throw a ball of light straight at his head. The demon moved through this world like he belonged in it, like these people were his people—and they let him. This had to be the freak'n twilight zone.

Zinnia leaned back into the couch, eyes sliding shut, shoulders sinking as her body finally relaxed. She was home and by God it felt good.

Conversation crept back in. Plates shifted. Whiskey and wine found glasses. The deliberate pivot from danger to normal did its job, coaxing everyone's nerves into something survivable.

Across the room, Sebastian tightened his grip on his coffee mug, wishing it held something stronger. The whisper hadn't stopped—it never did—but it pulled back when he snapped at it, sulking into silence.

He knew better than to trust that.

It was a game the dark liked to play with him.

And he wasn't sure he knew how to win.

***

Brinnan watched.

The house itself didn't matter. Stone and glass were props. Wards to him were simply etiquette.

What mattered were the bodies inside—how they clustered, where fear relaxed its grasp, where devotion pooled too thick to drain quickly.

Maison Bellarose burned bright tonight.

He tested the boundary from the Between and met resistance.

Angelic law at work.

So, the angel was here.

Irritation swamped him. Divina had thought ahead. She had chosen the one force that didn't bargain, didn't erode, didn't bend to shadow at all.

He pushed again to confirm it.

It was sealed to him—above and below, root to roof.

For now, at least.

He could do nothing more than observe.

Inside, the hybrid sat.

Her signature still carried the Veil's bite. That unfinished seam she'd torn open had *marked* her. The Veil didn't let go of keys easily.

Seraphina stood at the axis of it all. Shadowkeep clung to her the way blood congealed on a battlefield.

Killian hovered close, predictable in his vigilance.

Saffron lingered, proof that even the best laid plans went awry.

The Veilwalker was there too.

That was… inconvenient.

Matthew wore age the way some men wore armour. Old paths recognised him. Old doors listened. He would complicate things if left unattended.

The Gateborn mother's magic was waking to thresholds she'd refused for years. That development bore watching.

Pauline remained exactly what she had always been—rooted, watchful, impossible to hurry. Hoodoo witches didn't rush endings. They outlasted them. Brinnan marked her and moved on.

The demon postured and played at restraint, tethered yet indulged.

The twins registered—

The boy still piqued his interest.

The dark in him sat coiled, aware of itself. Not shadow borrowed or learned, but something seeded. Something that listened back when spoken to.

That kind of dark didn't belong to this age.

Prophecy loved children. Loved unfinished things. Loved to see what pressure would do before choice hardened into will.

Brinnan smiled.

Did they think return meant safety? That there was strength in numbers?

Ah, the fallacy of it all.

He withdrew into the Between, irritation cooling into calculation, already mapping his next move.

The angelic seal would hold—for a while.

Let them eat. Let them sleep.

Nothing inside that house was finished yet and neither was he.

***

Zinnia couldn't sleep.

She lay on her back, staring at the ceiling, half-expecting the patterns to rearrange themselves into something useful if she looked long enough. Every time she closed her eyes, her mind betrayed her—hunters torn apart because of her actions. The Veil reaching, clawing, insisting she belonged to it.

The past week alone had been enough to earn her a padded jacket and a daily relationship with brightly coloured pills.

She rolled onto her side and punched the pillow into a more cooperative shape. This was ridiculous. She needed to think about literally anything else.

Matthew appeared immediately.

That helped.

He was midway through tugging off his breeches when a soft knock dragged her clean out of the fantasy.

If that was Samthrax, she was going to strangle the turd.

She swung her legs out of bed, crossed the room, and flung the door open with every intention of letting it rip.

It wasn't the demon.

It was Matthew.

Shirt half undone. Hair damp from a recent shower. His eyes darker than they had any right to be—like he'd spent the last hour arguing with himself and losing.

"Lass. If this isn't—"

Zinnia grabbed his collar and yanked him inside.

The door shut behind him. Decision made.

His hands came up instantly—he spun her around and braced them on either side of her, trapping her against the wood without touching her. Close enough that his heat sank into her skin and her body went *thank fuck* while her brain muttered *you're an idiot*.

"You were gonna do the noble thing," her breath already uneven. "Weren't you."

"Aye."

"Don't."

His eyes flicked over her face, searching carefully. "Zin... I need to know ye want this."

Her laugh came out low and sinful. "Matthew, I'm standing here in a halter top and underwear that has seen more combat than most soldiers. What do you think?"

His mouth twitched, but he still didn't move.

Zinnia took his wrist and guided his hand to her waist. His fingers flexed there, barely restrained, control hanging by a thread.

"You did promise to woo me once we got back," she murmured. "Consider me wooed."

Matthew came in hard, claiming her mouth. It had been taunting him for days—soft and wicked and made for sin. He needed to know if it tasted as good as it looked.

It did.

Zinnia made a sound she would absolutely deny under oath and fisted his shirt to keep him close.

Sweet mercy, the man could kiss.

His mouth moved down her jaw, over the racing pulse in her neck, and her magic—quiet all day—flared awake. Hot. Hungry. Very interested.

Her toes curled. One hand slid into his hair, gripping, angling him where she wanted him. Tongues tangled. Breath turned ragged. There was nothing graceful about it—no choreography, no careful pacing. Just want.

No way in hell was she stopping this now.

His hands slipped beneath her top. Callused palms found her breasts and closed around them, firm and possessive. His thumbs rolled over her hardened nipples, testing, learning. When he tugged one gently, her back arched off the door.

Oh.

Yes.

She made a very important mental note that his talented mouth would be replacing those fingers soon.

Matthew lifted his head, eyes locked on hers. His control was disappearing—visible in the tight set of his jaw, the way his breath hitched.

"Tell me to stop."

"Not a snowball's chance in hell."

"That was ye last exit point, Lass."

There was no humour in it this time. Only promise.

He lifted her effortlessly and carried her across the room to the bed.

Zinnia hooked her legs around his hips and dragged him closer. "You're thinking too much."

"Maybe," he murmured against her mouth.

She bit his lower lip—he inhaled sharply. "Less talk, more action."

Matthew laughed, low and wicked.

And then he finally stopped pretending this wasn't inevitable.

Clothes hit the floor in reckless abandon. Hands took and answered in the same motion. Zinnia dragged her nails down his spine, and he answered by hauling her flush against him, firm and unyielding.

"Christ," she groaned.

"I'm no' him," he breathed back.

Heat detonated between her legs and spread outward, swift and merciless. Thought vanished in a rush of need that left no room for wit or strategy. Her body surged ahead of everything else, hungry, insistent, done pretending patience was a virtue.

Her magic reached, and she didn't even try to leash it.

The connection snapped into place—bright, hot, alive. Every place he touched flared in answer, sensation magnified until it felt almost unbearable. She could feel him through more than skin; the restraint he'd been gripping by the throat, the desire he'd fought to contain.

It poured into her.

Her pulse spiralled out of control. Thought disintegrated. She wasn't strategist, witch, or reluctant heir in that moment.

She was want.

Heat.

Raw, primal instinct.

Nothing in her life had prepared her for this—for the way pleasure hit not just between her thighs but through her magic, through every nerve ending she possessed. It was more than bodies colliding. It was power meeting power and refusing to retreat. It was her soul flinging itself wide open and finding his already there.

Her hands clutched tight as sensation climbed too fast, too fierce. "Don't you dare hold back," she warned, voice roughened beyond recognition.

The fire roared higher.

When he thrust into her, the stretch was deep and demanding, a fullness that forced a startled sound from her throat. He filled her completely, and for a heartbeat she could do nothing but take it, muscles tightening instinctively around him as her body adjusted to the sheer breadth of him.

"Ye right, lass?"

She answered by arching up into him, nails biting hard into the curve of his arse, dragging him deeper. "Move," she managed.

And he did.

The force of it jolted through her, knocking every coherent thought from her skull. It wasn't gentle. It wasn't reverent.

It was hard. Unrestrained. Exactly what she needed.

Each thrust sent shockwaves through her core and out into her magic. The bond between them flared white-hot, amplifying everything—the stretch, the friction, the brutal rhythm building fast. Her body answered greedily, meeting him stroke for stroke, hips lifting, demanding more.

He was claiming her.

And she wanted him too.

He bent to her ear, teeth grazing the sensitive curve before his voice dropped low and wrecked. "Ye ready, baby? I'm about to lose myself in ye."

That was all it took.

Pleasure detonated, ripping through her in blinding waves. Her body seized around him, every muscle tightening, dragging him with her over the edge. She cried out—and the sound undid him completely.

He followed with a hoarse groan, rhythm breaking, hips driving hard as control deserted him. He held her through it—through the tremors, through the slow ebb of heat, through the quiet that followed when their world was all about skin and shared warmth.

They shifted without speaking. Matthew drew her back against him, fitting himself along her spine, arm sliding around her waist and locking there because letting go wasn't an option.

His mouth brushed her shoulder. "Ye alright?"

Zinnia stared at the dark wall ahead of her, body pleasantly sore, magic humming low and content beneath her skin. "I mean… I'm still deeply traumatised," she muttered. "But that was a bloody excellent distraction."

His chuckle rolled through her back.

Her hand found his where it rested at her stomach. She laced their fingers together before she could overthink it.

"Stay."

Matthew's grip tightened instantly, his forehead pressing between her shoulders. "Aye," his voice was all gravel. "I'm goin' nowhere."

For once, the ghosts of the week didn't haunt them.

Wrapped around each other, spent, they drifted under.

Twenty Eight

Saffron waited.

The house relaxed in layers. Floorboards sighed. Pipes cooled. One by one the minds she loved slipped into sleep—Seraphina first, stubborn even in rest. The twins last. Sebastian's thoughts were swirls of shadow mixed with his light; he worried her the most. Sage sank quickly, her dreams already bright with colour.

Saffron watched the embers pop in the fireplace, sparks collapsing inward before flaring once more. Night had always been her favourite part of the day. In darkness, the world stopped performing. Truth crept closer. Reflection replaced the hustle.

She preferred honesty.

The pull returned.

It had been there since dawn, refusing to be drowned out by the loud comfort of everyone being safe and under one roof again. It lingered beneath laughter, full stomachs and relief.

Ignoring it had required effort.

She did not appreciate being summoned.

Especially by something that did not introduce itself.

She had chosen to remain near her family, and that choice came with limits. Leaving carried cost. The farther she went, the less she sensed. The less she sensed, the slower she reacted. In a family like hers, slow was fatal.

Whoever was calling her understood that.

That alone annoyed her.

Brinnan was hunting. Yvane was missing. The twins had begun to draw attention simply by existing. Power gathered around them whether they invited it or not.

But if this summons was tied to that prophecy—

Her irritation cooled into focus.

Saffron rose from the armchair without disturbing a molecule.

Her form gathered itself, silver and effervescent, light drawing close instead of spilling wide.

The wall in front of her lost its solidity. Depth replaced surface.

The Ethers opened before her.

It was time to see what and who this was.

"Alright, hold onto your panties, I'm coming."

She passed through.

Stars arced above and below her in solemn procession, constellations unmaking themselves and reforming elsewhere as though guided by unseen hands. Entire clusters reoriented while she watched, sliding into new alignments that hinted at language she had no clue how to read.

A vast sweep of white curved before her—so blinding *I wear my sunglasses at night,* started playing in Saffron's mind. She squinted against the glare and the tune.

At the centre of that immense arc, figures had gathered.

They were concentrations of brilliance, each distinct, each placed at a precise point along the curve.

They oozed command.

Behind them, structures towered—if towered was the word. Vast constructions of light and substance stood suspended in the distance. Columns? Vaults? Entire cities? She could not tell. The brightness swallowed detail. Whatever they were, they were not meant for mortal comprehension.

The stars continued their migration around the arc.

Saffron did not speak.

This was a realm so far beyond witchcraft and bloodlines that she was somewhat lost for words.

"You are Saffron Bellarose."

A chill worked through her silver glow. The name entered her as sensation, not sound.

That was all kinds of unsettling.

"I am," she answered, her voice smaller than she intended. "And I would know who speaks my name… and where you have brought me."

Of the twelve arranged along the crescent, one brightened at the centre. Its glow shifted toward a deep, living green.

"You stand within the architecture that underlies your world."

Another flared—rose-gold this time, its hue magnificent against the dark.

"We are the record before it is written. The judgment before it is rendered. The memory of what has been… and the calculation of what may yet be."

A third brightened—blue, sovereign and firm.

"You stand within the Astral Mandate."

Well, that explained absolutely nothing.

It did, however, sound terrifyingly official.

"I don't understand why I'm here."

The green light answered again.

"We have observed the convergence."

Above them, two constellations moved closer together.

"The twin prophecy resolves through your grandchildren. Instability accelerates. Intervention opportunities are diminishing."

The rose-gold spoke next.

"You bound yourself to earth. You relinquished ascent. You chose love over power."

Yes, she had. And she would choose it again. Every time.

"We require one who understands cost. Please observe."

The starlight above them dimmed by degrees until only a narrow band remained between Saffron and the crescent.

Within that band, movement began.

Sebastian stood in the courtyard.

Sage faced him mid-argument, hands lifted.

Saffron felt the imbalance immediately. It tugged at her the way a miscast spell tugs at its caster.

Sebastian's breathing altered.

Each inhale drawn to the same depth. Each exhale released to the same count. The rhythm was not accidental.

Sage reached for him.

"Stop," Saffron whispered, useless and desperate all at once.

The green at the centre spoke.

"This is the convergence already in motion."

Sebastian did not look at his sister in the way he always had—with annoyance first, affection close behind. His attention travelled over her, assessing height, distance, advantage. He looked at her the way he would a problem to be solved.

That look did not belong on her grandson's face.

His hands hung loose at his sides.

Then his fingers flexed.

Sage stepped closer.

"Seb, stop, please."

Sebastian tilted his head, maintaining eye contact. Dark strands slipped free at his shoulders and wrists, moving with a contained intelligence, tethered to him yet restless.

The green of his eyes darkened at the rim until the colour appeared almost inked in. A second awareness surfaced behind them.

His mouth curved, but the expression reached no further than his teeth.

Seb had always carried storm in him—temper, humour, defiance. He was messy with feeling. Loud with it.

That was not her grandson.

"You see the dual inheritance," the rose-gold observed. "The twin binding and the Graves line."

"I do." Saffron did not look away. If she still possessed a pulse, it would have been hammering at the base of her throat.

Sage seized Sebastian by both arms, fingers digging in. She was speaking now—urgent, relentless—begging him to fight, to stay with her.

Magic tore free of her the moment she touched him. It surged from her hands without restraint, slamming into him with more force than finesse.

Sebastian's body jumped as if he'd been plugged into an electric socket.

He gripped her arms now too, locking eyes onto his sister. She tried to pull free when she realised what was happening. But he held firm.

He was sucking her power into him.

Her shoulders sagged first. Then her hands let go.

Her knees struck stone.

The tightness drained from his frame. His stance reset—balanced, centred, composed.

Sage remained on the ground.

The green spoke again.

"In the twin prophecy, strength consolidates. The weaker is consumed."

Saffron's voice was steel.

"She is not weaker."

"In equilibrium, no," the rose-gold answered. "In volatility, yes."

Sebastian looked down at his sister.

For a heartbeat, his face opened.

Recognition. Shock.

And then calculation returned.

"The Graves ancestor seeks embodiment," the blue stated. "The twin bond provides a vessel reinforced by shared origin."

Saffron's hands curled into fists.

"You're telling me my grandson is being invaded, and the solution is to let him devour his sister?"

"We are showing you the cost of inaction. We are showing you the different paths."

The vision changed.

The courtyard dissolved.

Stone gave way to the foundations of Maison Bellarose.

The sealed staircase beneath the Scriptorium stood exposed.

The Shadowkeep door hung from one hinge.

Chains lay slack across the floor. The portal stood available and waiting. Wards carved by generations of Bellarose witches had split down the centre, releasing all the horrors it had contained.

Oh, sweet baby Jesus.

Sebastian stood on the top balcony of the manor.

Shadow pooled at his boots and drifted outward across the stone, slipping down stairwells, across rooftops, into alleyways. It moved through the enclave with quiet familiarity, touching doors, sliding beneath thresholds.

When someone in the square lifted their head too quickly, the shadow tightened.

They lowered it again.

The world had been imprisoned by evil.

The vision rolled forward.

Sage stood in the council chamber, sleeves rolled back, ink staining her fingers.

The room was loud. Arguments overlapped. Someone laughed inappropriately. She let them.

Power moved through the hall in orchestrated currents, not crushing, not consuming, but reinforcing. Wards along the ceiling glowed with patient strength.

Outside, the river ran clear. Boats crossed freely. Markets overflowed. Music rose from the lower quarter at dusk and did not falter when the hour grew late.

The vision shifted once more.

Now they stood together.

Sebastian leaned against the rail, speaking low to Sage as she studied a map spread between them. Shadow lingered along his sleeves, but it did not wander. It answered when he called it and withdrew when he did not.

Sage's magic wove through the Keep's foundations, reinforcing what he restrained.

Disputes flared and resolved within the Enclave. Coven banners changed as leadership changed.

The realm did not calcify.

It evolved.

The vision faded without flourish.

What she had seen could not be permitted.

"And you think I can prevent this."

It was not a question.

The green dimmed slightly before answering.

"Yes. With assistance."

"The boy reveres you," the blue continued. "His power is vast, and the inheritance within him must be severed."

The magnitude of it bore down on her. Failure would not only cost her a family. It would plunge the era into darkness.

"We are offering you the role of Wisdom Keeper."

That caught her off guard.

She had read of them once—buried in old texts, half-dismissed as myth.

But if this was the only way she could stop shit from hitting the fan.

She would take it.

"As you wish."

A circlet of obsidian and star-metal formed around a crystal so deeply purple it fractured light into shifting prisms appeared in her palm.

When Saffron focused, futures emerged within it. Each choice branched into consequence. Each hesitation carved a scar. Each sacrifice redirected catastrophe.

The amulet showed paths.

"With this," green intoned, "you will see the turning before it breaks. You will guide without coercion. You will preserve balance."

"No pressure."

"However, your own restoration is required first."

Before she could ask for clarification, power surged through her.

What she had relinquished at death returned—wards she had once commanded, fire she had once bent, sight she had surrendered. It did not stop there. Something vaster wove itself into her being—authority braided with restraint, knowledge tempered by consequence.

Wisdom took root.

And it was heavy.

"Welcome, Saffron Bellarose. Wisdom Keeper of the Astral Mandate."

The title and responsibility laid its mantle upon her shoulders.

"Remember, the amulet reveals outcome. It does not decide."

"Oh, I will be providing avid encouragement." Saffron replied.

"Call on us if you require."

Without further ado, Saffron found herself in Sebastian's room at the foot of his bed.

She slipped the amulet over her head. Feeling the warmth against her sternum.

Sebastian stirred in his sleep, brow furrowing faintly.

"I've got you my boy," she murmured.

His breathing smoothed into rhythm.

Across the hall, Sage slept peacefully.

Saffron moved between their rooms, newly whole, newly burdened.

No one knew she had gone.

By morning, nothing would appear different.

But the luxury of pretending the twins were fine had expired.

Sneak Peek: Witchblood

Book Three of The Bellarose Legacy

The story continues…

***

One

"Power divided seeks reunion.
Reunion rarely leaves both halves intact."
— *Astral Mandate Commentary on Convergence Events*

The city had not burned quickly.

That was the detail Valric Graves remembered most clearly.

Fire had taken its time.

It meandered street by street, almost thoughtful. Windows burst outward one at a time. Roof beams sagged in slow surrender. The air thickened before it blackened.

People always imagined chaos.

There had been none.

His brother had understood what was happening before anyone else did.

That was the trouble with twins.

Recognition travelled faster than sound.

The bond between them strained—luminous, furious, indivisible.

Shared blood. Shared structure. Shared inheritance.

Shared limitation.

Valric had leaned into it with precision.

His brother reached for him.

Valric reached back.

One second there were two heartbeats in his head.

The next there was only one.

He dragged the bond inward and consumed it whole. The rush hit hard and fast, running through him in a hot line that climbed straight into his head and lit him up from the inside.

His brother's knees hit the ground.

Valric remained standing.

Across the square, the bell tower listed to one side. It held for a moment. Then the top third slid off and hit the cobblestones.

He remembered thinking how small the world felt once he no longer had to share it.

They called it catastrophe later.

Mass casualty.

Rupture event.

They never called it what it was.

Correction.

The veil had thinned beautifully that night.

Drawn tight enough that he could see the framework beneath it. The grid. The joining points. The subtle misalignments where everything didn't quite sit as it should.

He pushed further.

That was when they interfered.

He sensed the magic gathering. Three covens moving as one, hands cutting symbols into the packed earth with more urgency than grace. Their chant locked into rhythm as sparks drifted upward through the smoke.

They weren't trying to kill him.

They were trying to evict him.

The circle took hold mid-step.

Colour erupted from the ground—violet laced with black, spiralling upward in violent coils that wrapped his legs before he could counter. Their voices climbed in pitch and the sigils flared.

Magic didn't lift him gently.

It seized.

Bands of light lashed across his chest and shoulders, pinning his arms to his sides. The square warped behind the rising glare—flame stretching into smears, buildings bending at impossible angles—until the entire scene tore loose from him in a single, wrenching pull.

For one sickening instant he felt himself split between where he stood and where the spell intended to send him.

Then the city ripped away.

When his senses caught up, he was standing in a place that did not behave the way it should.

The horizon shifted if he studied it too long. Land stretched, then retracted. Sound arrived without origin and left without trace. There was no weather. No decay. No cycle to measure against.

It suited him.

Time did not matter here.

Blood remained the only constant.

The Graves line had continued exactly as it always did. Sons born carrying more than they understood. Some tried to master it. Some tried to bury it. A few let it slip and paid for the indulgence.

Case in point.

He had almost succeeded in opening one.

Killian.

Older when it surfaced in him. Disciplined to the point of severity. Anger refined rather than squandered. Valric had approached. Instead of capitulating, Killian had shut him out.

It should have gone differently.

But the twin bond had never rooted properly. The brother's death during infancy had sealed it before it could stabilise. What should have been a doorway calcified into a wall.

Killian wielded it well.

Valric withdrew.

Years passed without measure. Until now.

He turned toward the weak point where the boundary softened and slid through it.

Sebastian.

This one had potential.

The twin bond held him in place. His sister was the counterweight. Counterweights could be shifted.

Valric had been inside his thoughts for some time now. A whisper here. A nudge there.

The boy resisted.

Resistance meant engagement.

And temper—temper was an opening.

So Valric watched.

Tested.

Waited.

The tether had grown easier to follow with use. What had once required effort now traced without friction. Tonight, it shone more clearly than before. Something had altered.

He allowed his awareness to widen.

The Bellarose witch.

There was a distinct change in her. She was still of the ethers, but her soul carried a new imprint. He pressed closer—then recoiled as if struck.

She bore the mark of the Astral Mandate. Limitation stripped away.

Authority settling around her like a second skin.

Unpleasant development—but manageable.

His attention drifted over Maison Bellarose, brushing its perimeter. The stone layered with protections. Intention sunk deep into foundation. Generations of magic embedded in mortar and timber. Defensive. Proud.

But it couldn't keep him out.

He followed Sage's thread.

Her magic was balanced even in sleep.

That balance would have to be broken.

He turned to the second thread.

Sebastian lay on his back, breath deep and even. Shadows gathered in the corners of the room as though they preferred his proximity, pooling quietly along skirting boards and beneath furniture.

Valric did not force entry. He simply aligned.

The connection responded at once, familiar to the point of intimacy.

Sebastian's breathing altered by degrees. Each inhale drawing slightly deeper, each exhale steadier than the last.

The shadows edged closer to the bed, dark lengthening along the floorboards, drawn not by command but by invitation.

Across the hall, Sage stirred. Her magic reacted while she slept on, sweeping outward before curving instinctively toward her brother. It spilled through the bond without her conscious knowledge.

Sebastian absorbed it.

Valric felt the transfer move along the tether unimpeded, settling into the boy, completing the circuit between them.

Sebastian's fingers flexed against the sheets. His body moving restlessly. The shadows drew closer still.

His lips parted.

One word emerged, softened by sleep yet cast in certainty.

"Mine."

Within the realm that held him outside their reach, Valric drew in the borrowed breath as though it were his own.

The key to his prison was already turning.

And soon, he would step through.

About the Author

C.M.N Rogers is a New Zealander living under Australia's dazzling skies, where she writes dark, deliciously magical fiction for readers who like their fantasy tangled with trauma, blood oaths, and just a hint of redemption. Her books aren't just stories—they're wild, witty adventures into bloodlines, ancient magic, and the divine chaos of alchemising adversity into power.

When she's not conjuring epic tales, she's a tarot-reading, dog-obsessed sass-master who loves probing the mysteries of the soul. Whether she's trekking foreign lands with a grin, dishing advice on finding your inner light, or debating whether coffee should be considered a food group, she's always knee-deep in life's quirks and questions.

As founder of **House of Nine Press**, she's all about helping others navigate life's labyrinth with a wink and a nudge. Keep your eyes peeled—she'll soon be unleashing her BookTok energy as **@cmnrogers.author**, where shadowy spoilers and witchy wisdom await.

Also by C.M.N. Rogers

C.M.N. Rogers writes dark, emotionally rich urban fantasy grounded in legacy, power, and the fierce bonds of family. Her stories blend supernatural suspense, generational secrets, razor-edged humour, and deeply human characters navigating impossible choices. Her work explores what it means to inherit both trauma and strength—and what we're willing to burn to protect the people we love.

Witchborn: The Bellarose Legacy - Book I
https://books2read.com/cmnrogers
Some bloodlines are cursed. Some legacies bite back.

Seraphina Bellarose wants nothing more than a quiet life far from the magic she abandoned—until her mother is murdered and her dormant powers surge awake. Returning to the Crescent Enclave with her teenage twins, she's forced into a world of haunted estates, unruly magic, and a sarcastic demon she never meant to bind. As old enemies rise and long-buried secrets claw free, Seraphina must face the man she once loved, the monsters hunting her family, and the terrifying truth running in their blood.

Unbroken: What Domestic Violence taught me.

https://books2read.com/cmnrogers

For years, I lived inside the grip of domestic violence —hiding bruises, rewriting the truth, and surviving battles no one else could see.

I lost my voice.

I lost my confidence.

I lost myself.

Unbroken is part memoir, part survival guide, and part blueprint for reclaiming your life. Inside, I reveal my story—and the psychological traps that keep women stuck, the invisible damage no one talks about, and the reality that begins after you leave.

This is not a story about being a victim.

It's a story about becoming whole again.

If you have ever felt trapped, silenced, or shattered —this book is proof that you can rise, rebuild, and become unbroken.

www.ingramcontent.com/pod-product-compliance
Lightning Source LLC
Chambersburg PA
CBHW011931050726
47590CB00011B/3232